CHANGE OF LIFE

CHANGE OF LIFE

MENOPAUSAL SUPERHEROES - BOOK 2

SAMANTHA BRYANT

To my mother, who nurtured my morbid heart with lots of Vincent Price and Gothic romance.

LINDA MAKES A FIRST IMPRESSION

Linda Alvarez strode across the gymnasium floor, trying to remember to keep her shoulders back, her hips straight, and to take long steps, as her husband had coached her. She still found the feeling of the jockstrap strange, even after practicing with it for a week, and fought the urge to tug the straps and readjust it. She nearly stumbled and hoped she passed it off as style instead of clumsiness. The gym had been abuzz with activity when she walked in, but it went silent in a wave as she made her way to the desk at the far wall. She could feel the eyes of the other agents on her and knew the Director had been right about the attention her case had garnered in-house. Even at the Department, where they specialized in the unusual, where their cases weren't just classified but often unclassifiable, a man with such incredible strength was a person of interest. Linda was grateful the Director had agreed to keep the rest of her story quiet. It would be far worse if they all knew she had only recently become a man.

Her cheeks were burning by the time she presented her badge to the young woman behind the desk. The woman beamed at Linda and winked.

"Just a second, Mr. Alvarez."

Mister. That still took some getting used to, even after all these months. Inside, she still felt like Linda Alvarez, wife to David, mother, and grandmother. Like she had spent all these months trying to convince her daughter, this change was not a choice she made, it was something she was learning to adjust to. It was like that old joke about immigration: I didn't cross the border; the border crossed me. Luckily for her, David had stayed. Linda was both jealous of and grateful for the man in her husband's past, the one that had loved him when he'd been a youth. If not for him, she might well have found herself alone, learning how to live as a man.

Straightening out the mess that a sudden gender change made with all Linda's official records was something else the Director was taking care of for her. This ID card and the driver's license the Department had arranged for made her new life as Leonel Alvarez very official and somehow more real. The woman handed back the ID and announced that Agent Lester would be right out.

Linda turned and scanned the facility. The giant room seemed equipped to handle almost any kind of physical training an agent might need. There were climbing walls, obstacle courses, weapons displays, gym mats, rappelling gear, and other things Linda didn't even recognize. She was watching a pair of men practicing knife fighting when she spotted a tall, muscular man crossing the gym, obviously heading in her direction. He was very handsome and walked with a swagger that suggested he was well aware of his appearance and accustomed to the attention it attracted. He also looked familiar, though she wasn't sure where she might have seen him.

"Alvarez!" His voice was loud and confident, his tone warm and welcoming. "So glad you decided to take the Director up on his offer."

He extended a hand to shake Linda's, and she reminded herself to return the grip firmly, but not so firmly as to break his fingers. She must have done well, because the man seemed pleased.

"Mike Lester. I'll be your trainer." He clapped his hands together and rubbed the palms into each other in a gesture of enthusiasm. "Let's see what you can do."

He led her to a corner of the gym with a variety of free weights. "Your paperwork says you're quite strong. What do you bench?"

Linda was confused for a moment, then realized what he was asking. She framed her answer carefully, making sure she didn't sound disrespectful. "I don't know, sir. I've never lifted weights."

Mr. Lester snapped his head up to look at her. Disbelief was clear in his expression, and Linda shifted uncomfortably as his gaze slid across her biceps and across the rest of her body. He stood back up from where he had been looking at the weights on the ground, apparently selecting some to work with. He had a large disk in his hands.

"I bench five reps of three-fifteen, clean," he said.

Linda could tell by his tone that she was supposed to be impressed by this phrase, though it meant little to her. From tone-up sessions at Curves, she knew reps meant how many times you did something, but she did not quite understand the number or what made it clean.

In the long tradition of new students everywhere, she kept her ignorance to herself and nodded to the teacher.

He nodded back and said, "Let's start with finding out what you can comfortably hold."

He held the disk out to Linda. It looked big and heavy, so she widened her stance in preparation, then took it. It didn't feel like much, almost as if he had handed her a textbook.

"Hold it from beneath, like this." He moved her hands into the desired position, so she was holding it in front of her like a breakfast tray.

She schooled herself not to tug her hands away from what seemed like an intimate touch. She was sure he hadn't meant it that way.

"I'm going to stack additional weights atop this one. Let me know when you start having difficulty holding it."

Linda nodded again. Mr. Lester crossed the few steps to the weight pile several more times and returned.

When Linda was holding six disks, he paused. "Doing okay there, Alvarez?"

"Yes, sir." She wished she knew if it was correct to call him sir. The trainer was younger than Linda, but he was in a position of authority. She guessed she'd stick with formality unless he corrected her.

Mr. Lester did not look entirely pleased by her response. He went seeking more of the broad, black disks and stacked them into her arms. When she was holding ten, he stood looking around, and Linda saw she was now holding all the weights of that size available in the room.

When a camera flash went off, Linda realized they had attracted the attention of all the weight lifters in the room. The guy who took the picture, an attractive African-American man with mischievous eyes, grinned and gave Linda a thumbs-up signal. She smiled back at him, wishing she had tied back her hair. A strand tickled her nose. She shifted the weight onto her left arm so she could pull the hair back, then resettled it into both her arms.

Complete silence took over the room, followed by lots of whispering chatter.

"Did you see that?"

"With one arm?"

"One thousand pounds!"

"Who is this guy?"

Linda blushed scarlet, ducking her head forward so her hair would fall onto her cheeks and hide her embarrassment.

Mr. Lester made a note in a small device he was carrying, then gestured for Linda to follow him, without looking at her or the onlookers. "You can leave the stack here." He gestured at a metal rack.

Linda slid the disks onto the shelf. The stack wobbled and the top two weights fell. Lunging, she caught them, one in each hand, and placed them gently beside the larger stack. Dusting her now-sweaty hands on the back of her new blue workout pants, she hurried to follow Mr. Lester across the gym, blushing again at the sounds of conversation building behind her. She didn't linger to hear what judgments were being made.

Linda caught up with Mr. Lester in the opposite corner of the gymnasium, where a variety of fighting dummies were stored. She couldn't tell if the trainer was upset with her or just focused on the task at hand, but she wanted this training session to go well and, so far, she thought it wasn't.

Trying to break the ice, she asked him, "You look familiar to me, sir. Have we met?"

He looked pleased to have been recognized. "Not officially. But I was part of the retrieval and cleanup team at the college campus at Springfield."

Linda didn't remember that day very clearly, but she thought she remembered this man convincing her to let go of Jessica so they could address her wounds after she'd been burned in the fight. She pictured the man in one of the dark blue jumpsuits the retrieval team had been wearing. Yeah. That was him. "Thank you for your help with Jessica's care. She's healed well."

"So I've heard. The Department is excited to get someone with her skills." Mr. Lester turned and winked at Linda. "And it doesn't hurt that she's hot."

Linda was taken aback. For a moment she said nothing. She wasn't expecting to talk about Jessica's physical attractiveness. Then she realized this was Lester's way of asking if she and Jessica were a couple.

"I know, right?" she responded, trying to seem casual, though her protective nature had her hackles up already. "My girl has to beat them off with a stick." She found she didn't like the idea of this man eying Jessica while her friend was still vulnerable from divorce and the recovery from her burns. She decided there was the air of a wolf about him. It wouldn't hurt to let him believe Jessica was more than just her friend.

It also delayed the whole conversation about David. After spending so many years with her husband, it was so strange to suddenly have her relationship with him become a point of contention, with some people arguing they shouldn't have the right to be together. Linda had always supported the right of those who love each other to marry, regardless of gender. It was strange to become the center of that fight instead of just an ally, but for her, nothing had changed. She wasn't interested in testing Lester's politics today.

She was interested in seeing if he might tell her more about what happened after the cleanup in Springfield, though. The fight had torn up the campus and several people had seen Jessica fly. In the aftermath, Linda had been too worried about Jessica's recovery to worry about the public explanation for the strange happenings that day. Now that Jessica was healed and joining her at the Department, Linda found that she wanted to know what the public story was and what had happened to Helen Braeburn, the woman she'd thrown against a wall and broken.

She kept her question vague, as if she didn't know the names of the other people involved. "I hear that they took the fire-throwing lady someplace. Did they get anything out of her to help with the search for the crazy doctor?" Linda didn't say it aloud, but she had been plagued with bad dreams about that day. She was especially worried about the part she had played in Jessica's injuries and, even though it had been in defense, she regretted the force she had applied to Helen. She should have been able to solve that problem in some other way. Throwing a sixty-something-year-old woman into a brick wall was just wrong. She'd been praying the woman survived her injuries. She didn't want murder on her list of sins.

"Last I heard, she was still asleep," Lester said. He didn't sound especially concerned.

Linda guessed it wouldn't be that big a deal from his perspective. She had been hurt while trying to kill people, after all. Even if she had been manipulated by Dr. Liu, as they all had, she wasn't an innocent. Linda guessed this meant Helen was being cared for, and presumably studied by the medical team here at the Department. She'd have to be. She could set an ordinary hospital on fire if there was a spark in her dreams.

"A coma then?"

The man nodded. At least she wasn't dead. People came back from comas. One of her cousins had come back after nearly a year. He was as normal now as he had ever been. Linda tried to scrub at some of the guilt on her soul with that brush. It helped a little.

"So, what's next?" she asked, returning her focus to training.

"Heavy bag. This one is fitted with a sensor to detect the level of force you bring to bear in a punch. Here. Put these on." He handed Linda a set of fingerless gloves with leather padding over the knuckles.

She slid her hands in and flexed them. *I might enjoy this part.* It would feel good to work out some of her bad feelings in an honest sweat.

"You ready?"

"Yes, sir."

"Mike, please. No need to be so formal."

His smile was certainly winning. Linda felt a tingle of response in her pants and told herself to focus. She'd be working with a lot of handsome men here at the Department. She couldn't go all weak-kneed every time one of them smiled at her. She guessed her brothers hadn't just been pulling her leg when they talked about the lower head having a mind of its own. She was still adjusting to the way her body responded when she felt attraction to someone, especially when it wasn't her husband.

"I'm ready, Mike."

For the next few minutes, she followed Mike's directions and jabbed at the punching bag gently from several different angles and with several different kinds of thrusts.

When she seemed to have the motions down, he said, "Alrighty then, let's see what you can do, killer."

The word jarred her. Killer? *It's just a word*, she told herself. Just something guys say to pump each other up. *Focus.* So, focus she did.

Her next punch threw the heavy bag through the cinder-block gymnasium wall and out the other side, wedging it in a soda machine in an alcove across from the gym. Sparks flew out of the crumpled machine, now visible through the gaping hole in the gymnasium wall. People ran to see what had happened, and Linda cringed.

"I'm so sorry. I know a guy who can fix this."

MARY'S MOTHER IS MISSING

Mary Braeburn was smoking too much. She knew it was bad for her, but that was part of what made it feel so right. Her mother would understand the heart's truth in that illogical argument. But Helen Braeburn had been missing for months.

Mary knew it had something to do with her mother's newfound ability to produce fire and that crazy Chinese doctor she had taken up with. Cindy Liu was missing, too. It was like they had both just dropped off the face of the planet. No threatening phone calls demanding anything, no Jane Does in the hospital, or, God forbid, the morgue. Just here one day and gone the next. And the police had no significant leads, even after all these months. Until today. Mary had gotten a call, and now it was time to find out what kind of news awaited her.

After stomping the cigarette butt out and pushing it in with a turn of her heel, Mary stopped stalling and went into the police station.

"Hi, Steve," she said to the front desk clerk. He glared at her; Mary knew he didn't like it when she used his first name.

"Can you tell Officer Workman I'm here?" Calling the lead officer on her particular case by her honorific was just plain fun, for the way it made the clerk's face turn gray and pruney. Especially since Officer

Workman was a woman, even worse, a black woman. He'd never say it aloud, but that rankled him—being subordinate to a black woman. It was mean to poke at the grumpy bear, but this whole experience had been so frustrating, Mary found a petty joy in picking on the bureaucrats in her way.

Her teasing had not endeared her to the man, anymore than her lifestyle and appearance had, so that was probably why he took his own sweet time about letting the officer know she was there, even though she had an appointment and a deadline for getting to work. Mary affected nonchalance, refusing to give the man the pleasure of seeing her irritation at being kept waiting. Waiting would make her late to work, but she'd cross that bridge when she came to it. Until then, she'd just toy with her blonde dreadlocks and snap big blue bubbles with the gum she'd popped in her mouth to disguise her smoker's breath. The sound would annoy Steve.

She was in the middle of blowing an especially large bubble when Officer Workman appeared at the door.

"Mary," she said, her tone completely neutral. Only the subtle smile lines around her dark chocolate eyes revealed that she found Mary's exploits amusing.

Mary hopped right up and gave a bouncing little bow to the now-somewhat-red-faced clerk before following the officer into one of the meeting rooms.

"You really shouldn't tease him like that," Officer Workman said. "It won't help you or your mother to get on his bad side."

Mary leaned forward. "You said the rental car was found?" She tried not to sound excited.

She knew all too well this lead might go nowhere, too, just like the video of her mother at the Urgent Care Center had. They had verified her mother's presence at the medical center and her treatment for an injured foot by a doctor who said she threatened him with fire. None of that had led to information about where she had gone from there.

Mary knew getting her hopes up was just a recipe for pain, and she'd eaten more than her share of pain pie here lately. She and her mother had only begun to get to know each other again after a few years of estrangement surrounding her parents' divorce. Helen always seemed to be nagging Mary to find a career or a husband, or to get an adult haircut and cover her tattoos. She didn't seem to understand that her daughter was happy as she was. Mary didn't need to buy a home or be owned by a man to feel like her life mattered. She liked the freedom of living above the poverty line, but below middle-class morality. She could do as she liked.

Mary had just been starting to find her peace with her mother and then, poof! She was missing, along with their opportunity for reconciliation and understanding. She turned to the officer.

"Where was it?"

Officer Workman tilted her head to one side before she answered. After all these months of working together, trying to find clues in this missing person's case, Mary knew the gesture meant there was something Officer Workman didn't want to have to say. Her stomach dropped out beneath her, and she gripped the edge of the table. *Is the news that bad?* She held her breath.

"It was in the impound lot at the college," the officer said.

Mary slumped back into her chair. So, the bad news was just that the local investigation had shown a new level of incompetence. "What?" She desperately wanted to ask what had taken the police so fucking long if the car had just been in an impound lot all this time, but she held her tongue. Belligerence wouldn't help, no matter how justified. She stared at the police officer, waiting for her to go on.

"There's not a lot of oversight there for cars that go unclaimed." The officer shrugged, frowning. She was probably embarrassed to have to admit that in six months of investigation, no one had thought to check all the local impound lots.

Mary knew she wasn't dealing with the FBI here, but that seemed like pretty elementary sleuthing to her.

She bit her cheek to hold in the accusations that rose in her throat. All she wanted to know was what they had found. "So, are there any clues in it?"

The officer shook her head. "The only prints in the car are her own, Cindy Liu's, and some associated with the rental agency personnel. There were some real estate listings in the front seat. We think she was showing houses in the new complex behind the campus."

"Was the car damaged?"

She shook her head again. "No. It was towed on April 17 and has apparently been sitting in the impound lot ever since."

April 17. Mary thought about that. April 17 was four days after she'd last communicated with her mother. Their last exchange had been a text conversation. Mary regretted that now. If she had called her mother instead of just texting, she would have heard her voice. That would have told her more about how her mother was doing than words on a screen. Maybe if she had called, she would have heard something that would help her now. Some clue.

Maybe her mother would have said something in conversation she didn't think to type in a text. April 17 was two days after the fire at Cindy Liu's house—the one she was pretty sure her mother had caused, one way or another.

Mary jumped up and paced the few steps allowed by the limits of the small room. A thought occurred to her, and she whirled back to the table. "Wasn't that the same day as the flamethrower attack on campus?"

The officer shuffled some papers around. "I don't know. Let me check." She left the office, tucking the file folder under her arm.

Mary got back up and paced while Officer Workman was out. Something felt really fishy about this whole story to her. She thought about the things she knew the police were not prepared to deal with.

One: Helen Braeburn could throw fire. Mary had seen it with her own eyes. It had been a frightening and fascinating scene. Mary had awakened to a sound she couldn't explain. When she'd gotten up to investigate, she'd seen sparks flying by the window. When she'd opened the sliding door, she'd found her mother standing in the yard in the middle of the night, wearing one of her father's old T-shirts and juggling fire. It was beautiful to behold and the happiest Mary had seen her mother in more than a year. It also scared the hell out of her. And she couldn't tell anyone about it.

Two: Cindy Liu's hot flash treatment was why Helen Braeburn

could throw fire. Her mother had told her as much. She said Cindy was a genius. Now Mary worried Cindy was a dangerous genius who had done something to her mother. Without the willingness to believe the impossible was happening, there was no way for the police investigators to follow this particular trail. It would be up to her.

Three: Cindy Liu's house had burned down two days before the last known sighting of Mary's mother. If the officers believed Helen could throw fire, they might have better luck connecting the dots. Cindy Liu's house had burned down under mysterious circumstances, and a small explosion had destroyed one of the support walls. To the police, this was a separate incident, mere coincidence. It was being investigated as arson. Mary was sure her mother was responsible for it, whether by accident or on purpose.

Four: The doctor at the urgent care, the last witness who could place Helen Braeburn anywhere, said she had threatened him with fire. Unfortunately, the video from the surveillance system was so grainy as to be useless to back up his story, and the police had assumed he was just under stress and misinterpreted what he had seen. Mary knew he was telling the truth, but she wasn't about to say so and let them write her off as crazy, too.

Five: The rental car Mary's mother had taken for her girls' night out with Cindy Liu had been at the college since April 17, and that was the day of the flamethrower terrorist on campus.

Mary felt like an idiot. Up until now, she had never connected the fires on campus with her mother. She'd believed what she'd seen on the news about a disgruntled student with a flamethrower, swallowed that fishy story hook, line, and sinker. It seemed so obvious now. The student flamethrower was a cover-up, a believable story for the public. The truth was a much harder sell: Mary's mother was there. That begged the question: Who else was there? Who was covering this up?

Officer Workman came back into the room. "You're right," she said, settling back into her chair. "It was the same day." She looked at Mary expectantly.

Mary smiled tightly. There wasn't anything she could say that wouldn't sound absolutely insane. She tried to shrug as if she didn't care, though she was sure it came off as more like a twitch. "Weird, huh?" She picked up her messenger bag and slung it over her shoulder. "You'll call me if you find anything?" Mary turned and hurried out the door, already lighting her next cigarette before the door had finished closing behind her.

JESSICA TAKES WING

Jessica Roark was in the corner of the Department's secondary gym, stretching and trying to calm her nerves. Even after all these months of recovery, she still felt protective of her arm. She knew she had to get over that. She couldn't be an effective fighter if she was always trying to keep one part of her body out of the fray. She stretched both arms in front of her and grabbed her toes. The left arm had a series of scars interlacing around the elbow and shoulder. It had healed wonderfully, considering. She had good mobility, flexibility and strength, and nearly perfect sensation. She was amazed by what the doctors had been able to do, but the skin didn't really quite match her other arm.

She didn't like to think about the donor skin that now was inter-mixed with some of her own skin taken from her back. She felt like a science experiment. Hadn't she had enough of that already? She called it her Franken-arm, trying to play it lightly for her mother and the boys. But she wasn't really joking. Part of her felt like some kind of patched together monster.

When her trainer and mentor walked in, removing a set of light-weight training gloves, Jessica pushed away her morbid self-pity.

She'd need all her focus for this session. Sally Ann Rogers didn't look intimidating, but Jessica had learned to respect her skills. Like Jessica, Sally Ann was small, probably about five-foot-two and no more than one hundred ten pounds. Unlike Jessica, she was a sculpted mass of muscle wrapped in lovely brown skin the color of milky coffee. Next to her, Jessica felt pasty and soft. Even Sally Ann's face seemed somehow toned and strong, though Jessica couldn't imagine the exercise routine that would yield that result. Maybe it was just her inner toughness shining through.

Sally Ann's area of expertise on the training floor was hand-to-hand combat in a variety of forms. So far, she'd worked on conditioning and various martial arts forms with Jessica, testing her and planning a battle strategy. Sally Ann's North Carolina accent might be soft, but there was nothing soft about her attitude. At first, Jessica hadn't been sure about the training, finding it hard to believe she could be of use in a battle situation, but she quickly came to respect the position that she needed to be able to take care of herself. She would be a liability to the other agents on her team if they had to protect her. Smallness of size did not mean she couldn't kick some serious ass—if she were well trained.

She liked being pushed again. Sally Ann didn't look at Jessica and see someone who needed protecting or coddling. She saw a fellow warrior who needed to hone her skills. Jessica liked the version of herself she saw in her trainer's eyes: a dangerous weapon, all the more unexpected for her nonthreatening appearance. Jessica looked forward to the day when she could truly hold her own.

Today was the next step in that direction—they would try out the air pack. The tech team said the prototype was ready to audition, so today she would find out if she could use it to control her movement.

Sally Ann had taken Jessica as far as she could with lessons in using momentum and her gymnastics background to control her direction. Jessica had even learned to control the height of her float and rate of descent by belching, more and less discreetly, depending on the goals. It wasn't powerful like the synergy of her body and the

Chinese emeralds she'd taken from Dr. Liu, but it wasn't helpless floating. She missed those emeralds, but at least she was no longer afraid to walk under an open sky.

When she'd told her mother about belching lessons, Eva had laughed until she cried.

"All those years!" she said. "All those years teaching you to be a lady, and the skill you need most now is belching."

Eva was once again her daughter's staunchest supporter. Now that Nathan was out of the picture, she was going to need her mother more than ever. Single motherhood was not something she had ever imagined for herself. But it was definitely better than living with a man she didn't love and pretending nothing had changed. Nathan was no David Alvarez. Jessica wondered if she'd ever find the kind of love her best friend had, the kind of love that could remain strong in the face of change and trouble.

Sally Ann walked up. A few feet farther behind Sally was a short, thick man who walked with his head bent down, examining the tablet in his hands. A wagon followed him, rolling of its own accord. When Sally Ann stopped, the scientist almost walked right into her, but the wagon stopped immediately. Sally Ann gave him a stern look, but smiled at Jessica.

"Roark, this is Dr. Peeples, from our sciences department. I think you've met? He's the lead on the team that developed the air pack you'll be trying out today."

Dr. Peeples held out a hand and Jessica took it. He had a firm grip and a direct and curious gaze that made her feel important. He was obviously pleased to have been invited to the test. She hoped she wouldn't let him down. Sally Ann checked the wall clock.

"It's time, Roark. Should we wait for Alvarez? Or do you want to go ahead and get started?" Sally Ann was openly curious about Leonel, as were many of the staff at the Department, but she never pressed or wheedled for information. While Jessica had slipped into the training program without much notice, Leonel had caught everyone's eye from day one, when he accidentally knocked a wall out of the training room.

At the far end of the gymnasium, the double doors swung open and Leonel came rushing in, waving a hand over his head. "I'm here! I'm so sorry I'm late."

All three of them turned to watch him jog across the gym. His hair had grown out to a single length now, no more layers curling into his face like he'd worn when he'd been a woman, and he wore it loosely down to his shoulders. It looked good, to say the least. Sally Ann must have thought so, too, because she winked at Jessica and let out a low whistle.

"The good ones are always taken, aren't they?"

"Neither of us is really his type, anyway," Jessica said.

"He likes them bigger?" Sally Ann guessed.

"He has a husband."

"Oh. Damn." Sally Ann sounded genuinely disappointed, and Jessica smiled to herself.

They let the subject drop as Leonel came into earshot. He smiled pleasantly and shook hands as Jessica introduced him to Sally Ann. He greeted Dr. Peeples warmly, and Jessica remembered that Dr. Peeples had been the point of contact for Leonel with the medical team. Maybe he was in charge of all the cases like theirs. Sally Ann had told her they called people like her and Leonel "freak cases." It wasn't a put-down, though. People who lasted in the Department any length of time found freaks fascinating. It was what the whole organization was about: cases that fell outside the ordinary into a realm most people thought impossible.

Sally Ann herself was a freak. "Nothing bold and exciting like you," she said. "I'm sort of psychic when it comes to papers." She hadn't explained any further, but Jessica looked forward to seeing this particular skill in action someday. Today, though, it was the Jessica show. She stretched her already limber body again. *It's about time to get my freak on.*

Finished talking with Dr. Peeples, Leonel turned and gave Jessica a big hug, swinging her off the ground. "Can you have lunch after?"

Jessica nodded. "I think so, assuming it all goes okay."

"Don't worry," Leonel said. "I'll climb up there with a soda if you get stuck." He grinned to show he was joking, but Jessica knew she could rely on Leonel's help anytime. Though, with this new device, she was hoping not to need it.

Sally Ann turned to Dr. Peeples. "So, shall we get this party started?"

Dr. Peeples slipped his tablet into his pocket and unzipped the black bag in the wagon, revealing a sleek silver pack. "We designed it to be light and comfortable. Let's see if we succeeded!"

Jessica turned as directed and let the doctor slip the thin harness straps over her shoulders and clip the two halves together across her chest with a clip that didn't look that different from the one on her youngest son's car seat. They avoided each other's gaze as he fastened the device between her breasts. It had been a long time since she'd been touched by a man in a way that didn't involve medical treatment. Though this was, she supposed, still training, the touch had felt intimate. She hoped the doctor couldn't feel her pulse reacting. Jessica felt the two Thermos-sized bottles settle into the area between her shoulder blades. Dr. Peeples was right. They weighed almost nothing.

"So how does this work?" she asked.

Dr. Peeples reached around Jessica in an awkward sort of hug, then smiled apologetically when he stood back up. He was holding two small white sticks with buttons on top. He affixed one to each of her wrists with a Velcro band so that the knob was in the middle of each palm. "Do you play videogames?" he asked.

Jessica shook her head. "Not really. The boys have a Wii, and I had an Atari or something when I was a kid."

"It's okay. I can explain." Dr. Peeples pulled another similar stick out of one of his pockets and affixed it to his own wrist. "The idea is that you can use your thumb to manipulate the knob." He demonstrated the full circle range of motion of the button. "Different motions will release a gust of air and push you in the direction you select when you're weightless."

Jessica watched carefully. "So will I move in the direction I push the little lever thingy? Or is it sort of backward, where the direction I push is the direction the air will go?"

Dr. Peeples grinned broadly. "I'm so pleased you thought of that. Right now I have them calibrated to correspond to your desired direction of movement. So, if you push to the right, you will move to the right. But if you find that the other setup works better for you, we can recalibrate to accommodate you."

Jessica laid a thumb gently on each knob. "Do I have to do anything to turn the device on or off?"

"Push down until you feel it click."

"Okay." Jessica turned to Sally Ann and Leonel. "Wish me luck, guys!"

They both clasped her on opposite shoulders.

"You can do it!" Leonel said.

"You got this one, Roark," said Sally Ann.

Dr. Peeples sent the observers to the sidelines and gestured for Jessica to follow him to a padded area of the gym. "You probably won't be a very good driver at first, so let's try this out where there's some softness to run into, huh?"

Jessica gulped. "Good idea, Doc."

"Walter." The doctor held out a helmet to her.

"Thanks, Walter." Jessica tilted her head thoughtfully at the man, then put on the helmet and stepped into the center of the padded training area.

Even after all this time, it felt like a moment of truth each time she removed her weights and let herself float. She'd learned so much about how to use her environment and her gymnastic talents to control her movement, but she had also ended up being towed down from the rafters by a team of black-suits with rappelling gear. That was more than embarrassing, but Jessica knew this was about the safest environment possible to try this in. *Go ahead,* she thought to herself. *You can do it.*

"Hey, Leonel," she yelled. "Watch this!"

Jessica dropped to the ground and unclipped her weights. From the crouch, she sprang into a run across the padded floor, waiting until the moment she hit her top speed to twist into a handspring. When her feet hit the floor, she pushed off with all her might. With the combination of her force and momentum with her weightlessness, she bounced a good thirty feet into the air and grabbed the handholds affixed to the wall mats. She quickly pulled her body into the wall and pushed off again, backward, somersaulting in midair and grabbing the steady rings dangling from the ceiling. She knew they were forty feet above the gym floor. She pulled herself into a tight tuck and spun around three times. She felt strong and sure.

Leonel put his hands around his mouth to form a megaphone and yelled, "Amazing! Ten-point-oh from the *Mexicana* judge!"

Jessica let herself drop so she was hanging from her hands. Then, taking one last wistful look at the steady rings and the comparative security they represented, she closed her eyes and let go. When she opened her eyes again, she had risen another seven to ten feet into the air. There was nothing at all within reach. She was floating helplessly. She fought down the sense of panic and pulled herself into a ball. Once she felt she had stopped spinning, she tried to flatten out her body horizontal to the floor, like a skydiver. The position made her feel more secure.

"Okay!" Walter's voice came through her helmet. "Try the right trigger. Keep your movements small and slow at first."

Jessica rubbed her thumb across the toggle button without applying pressure. She had the strangest urge to cross herself, as she'd seen Leonel do on several occasions. It must be nice, she thought, having faith in a God that protects you. But right now, it was faith in herself she needed. She pushed the button very gently to the right, bracing herself for impact.

At first, she thought nothing had happened. But then she realized she was a few feet closer to the wall. Another push like that and she'd be able to reach the gym mats. She pushed the button again. Suddenly she bounced off the wall and spun back into the middle of the room.

"Are you all right?" Walter sounded really worried.

"I'm okay. A little nauseous from the spinning is all!"

"You don't have to shout, Ms. Roark. It's a good microphone," he said.

"Jessica," she said, modulating her tone.

"Jessica," he acknowledged. "Do you want to try again?"

"Just try and stop me," she said.

PATRICIA PUTS THE "TIRED" IN RETIRED

Patricia O'Neill rolled over. Six o'clock. Her body just couldn't seem to accept that it was okay to still be asleep at six o'clock in the morning after so many years of early morning meetings. She was retired now, and had been for months. She'd made her own schedule, and didn't want it to start before the sun rose, damn it. If her day started that early, it was too hard to stay busy. She'd run out of things to do by three, with the long stretch of afternoon into evening still looming ahead like some kind of endless tide.

Retirement had seemed like such a good idea at first. It was going to be difficult to keep her condition a secret at work if she burst out in scales and spikes every time she lost her temper. Her intern, Suzie, had gone back to school to finish her degree. There was no one at work she felt connected to, and after the events of the last year, she just couldn't build up excitement over issues of HR and PR anymore. It just wasn't interesting. She talked it through with her accountant and couldn't see a reason not to take advantage of the provisions of her contract and go ahead and retire. She'd skipped the proposed ceremony and formal announcement, letting her replacement inform the underlings. There was no love lost between them, anyway. Yes, it was time to leave work.

Besides, if she retired, she could devote all her energies to finding Dr. Cindy Liu, her best friend turned enemy and criminal. She'd envisioned herself tracking down leads and hunting down informants. She'd imagined Jessica and Leonel joining her in the search, fighting by her side like they had when they'd gone to save Jessica's mother. Instead, they had sold out and become government toadies. In her imagination, it had been very exciting, and she'd been successful. But the reality had proven quite different.

The truth was she had no idea how to go about finding a sixty-eight-year-old Chinese-American woman who appeared to be a thirteen or fourteen-year-old girl. That is, if Cindy had succeeded in stalling the process that was making her younger. If she had failed, she might well be an infant now. All Patricia knew was that she had seen Cindy getting on a bus on the day of the fight with Helen. Where she'd gone from there was anybody's guess. And the trail was getting colder by the day.

Giving up on getting any more sleep, Patricia rolled her body up and out of bed in one fluid movement, landing on her feet and stretching her arms above her head until her back cracked satisfyingly. After peeling off her pajamas, Patricia stepped into the spacious bathroom and turned on the shower. While she waited for the water to come to temperature, she ran through a series of stretches, touching her toes and rolling her neck, then bringing out her scales and spikes in various combinations: just the talons, just the facial armor, the spikes at varying lengths, and, finally, fully armored. She admired her shape in the mirror, nodding her head sharply to make her spiky red hair bounce. Returning to fully human form, she ran her hands over the armored plates on her upper chest affectionately. They were the one part of her change that was always with her. She found it comforting to know she was always at least partially bulletproof.

After her shower and breakfast, Patricia pulled up her e-mail on her computer. It was full of disappointment again. Bounced messages, dead ends, and cold trails. She was getting damned sick of messages that started with, "I'm sorry, but…"

Patricia pulled up the chart she had made to assist in her research and catalogued the latest responses in an annotated timeline she used to track leads. On the last day she'd seen Cindy, she'd been on a city bus, looking like a young teenager. That bus had been headed back to the main station, unfortunately, so Cindy could have gotten a ticket to anywhere from there. She hadn't bought a ticket with her credit or debit cards, but she had taken out the maximum daily limits on all her cards from the ATM at the bus station. There had been no further activity on the accounts after that. Even today, the remainder of the balance sat untouched. She could have covered a lot of ground by bus, and there was no telling even what direction she had gone. Patricia didn't doubt her old friend's ability to find a way to get additional funds as well, by theft, trickery, or simple ingenuity.

Unfortunately, at least for her search, Cindy Liu was not the only young Asian girl traveling alone by bus that day. Three different ticket agents and seven bus drivers recalled young Asian passengers that roughly fit Cindy's description. Patricia had tracked down each of those travelers. She had found several protective parents suspicious of her motives and one loudly abusive nanny, but not a trace of her old friend. Cindy must not have been one of the Asian girls that had stuck in anyone's memory that day.

Another chart was a history of Cindy's life, with annotations of people who had been important to her, people she might have gone to for help. It was a wider network than Patricia might have suspected at first. Cindy wasn't a friendly person. But when you took into account her varied career and her several degrees and study programs, it turned out she know a lot of people. Apparently Cindy was just as bad as Patricia about keeping up with people from her past. In phone call after phone call, she found people who remembered Cindy but hadn't heard from her in years. As the only child of a deceased refugee immigrant mother and a long-deceased reclusive scientist father, the family connections ran out quickly as well. The list of leads left to follow was short, and Patricia did not feel hopeful about finding Cindy after so much time. She could be anywhere.

As angry as she was with her old friend, Patricia also really missed her. A forty-year friendship was nothing to let go casually. Friendships had never come easily for her, and it seemed cruel that the only women she knew how to talk to were gone from her life at the same time. Patricia wasn't a talker, particularly. Too much touchy-feely stuff made her want to take a shower. But that wasn't to say she didn't want someone to talk to, someone to listen when she wanted to vent, someone to make her laugh. Luckily, she wasn't one to give in to self-pity.

She picked up the phone to call Leonel—he was an early riser, too. She hung up without letting it connect. They seemed to fight every time they talked lately, and Patricia was already feeling discouraged. For all they'd been through together, she wasn't sure she actually liked Leonel or that he liked her. They just weren't the same kind of woman. In spite of his appearance of a handsome and virile man, Leonel was still very much the little homebody he'd always been. He'd rather be baking cookies with his grandchildren than running with the movers and shakers of the world. Patricia had never had much respect for the *Better Homes and Gardens* lot. She thought they were missing the big picture.

Leonel wasn't home as much as he used to be, these days. Not since he had joined the Department. She wondered how his family was taking that. He'd spent a lot of the past few months in training. He was annoyingly tight-lipped about it all when she tried to get him to talk. She half expected him to put on mirrored sunglasses and tell her it was "classified." Department, indeed. Department of Fools.

Now that Jessica was recovered from her burns, she had signed on, too. They'd promised to help with her rehabilitation and to train her to use her power rather than being victimized by it. She'd probably signed the contract without even reading it. It was good enough for her that Leonel was going. His little sidekick would follow him anywhere.

They had invited her, too, but Patricia told them to take a walk. She wasn't interested in working for the government, even a subcontracted corner of the system like the Department. She didn't have any faith in their ability to do anything right. What made the government qualified to organize truly astonishing and powerful people like

Leonel and Jessica, if they couldn't even write a fair and equitable tax code? The most recent elections had only confirmed her belief that the government was just like religion: a distraction to keep you from doing anything about the shit hole the world was becoming. Everything was so entrenched, Patricia was beginning to think the country should be called the United States of Inertia.

Patricia laced up her workout shoes and headed out the door for another workout over at the CrossFit place they'd put in at the mall just down the road. Maybe she could work through some of her frustration in sweat. What kind of friends were Leonel and Jessica, anyway? Leaving her to clean up the mess alone, to spend long hours searching fruitlessly for the woman who had done this to all of them. Neither of them even seemed to care what happened to Cindy or if she was ever heard from again. They were both so infuriating.

She missed them.

SALLY ANN TAMES A PAPER TIGER

"You were right about Roark." Sally Ann tossed a folder down as she joined the group at the conference table and flopped back into the large chair, letting her feet swing into the air, which gained her an acidic look from one of the suits. She hadn't said who she was talking to, but all eyes turned to the Director all the same.

"I told you there was more to her than you can see." His expression was on the verge of gloating. Only someone who knew him well could have seen the "I told you so" that hung in the corners of his eyes.

Sally Ann nodded. "Her gymnastics training is going to be an asset, and the new jet pack Wally made is pretty freaking awesome." She elbowed Dr. Peeples in the biceps. He smiled, even though she had called him Wally. "I'll be able to make a very useful operative out of her yet."

Sally Ann poked Agent Lester in the stomach, harder than was necessary. "How's your newb doing?"

"He's a knockout!"

It was a poor joke, but the group laughed gamely. Mike Lester had received a fair amount of ribbing about his first session with Leonel Alvarez ending with a catastrophic injury to the gymnasium wall.

"Think he'll have any more breakthroughs?" she asked.

Mike groaned and rubbed the back of his head.

The Director stood then, and everyone fell silent. Even after working with him for a few years, Sally Ann still didn't know how he did that. It was freaky. The man never had to raise his voice.

"You've all seen the report?" A murmur of agreement went round the circle, and he continued, his voice grim. "Then you already know that our progress is not acceptable. We've gotten nowhere fast on this case, and Dr. Cindy Liu is still loose."

A picture came up on the screen behind the Director's head, a still from the video feed at the ATM where Liu had fallen off the grid. In the picture, a young Chinese-American girl, maybe thirteen or fourteen years old, leaned into the machine, an intent expression on her face. Her gaze was directed downward, at the keypad, but it was still a good frame, giving clear detail of the lines of her face and the details of her clothing. But knowing what she looked like hadn't helped the team locate her, even though the search had started immediately. After the withdrawal of funds at the ATM, she had simply evaporated.

The group was quiet for a long moment, each member of the team waiting to hear what the Director was going to say. These were some of the most talented and skilled operatives the Department had, and, if they hadn't found a good lead yet, Sally Ann wondered what the chances were that they ever would.

She spoke up. "Have we considered that there may be another player? Someone who took her in and is sheltering her?"

The Director grinned, a smarmy look that meant he had a plan but wasn't going to share it just yet. He put a sheaf of papers in front of Sally Ann. He winked at her and she grimaced. It was her cue, she knew, but she hated doing this. She especially hated doing this in front of others. As a minor act of rebellion, she didn't start right away, but turned her attention to the analyst who reported on his team's efforts to track Liu through lab material orders. Some small lab in BFE Indiana had ordered some of the same sort of emeralds Liu had used in so many of her experiments. That caused a bit of excitement among the eggheads around the table, and the talk quickly escalated over Sally Ann's head. She tuned out, deciding to wait for the summary at the end to try and work it out.

Once her colleagues were distracted, she spread the documents from Liu's lab out in front of her. The Director had her working through them a few at a time. Sally Ann was pretty sure she would eventually touch every scrap of paper that had been removed from that woman's lab. And there were *a lot*. Even after the explosion, reams of paper were still being found and processed. Apparently Liu liked the old-fashioned approach for her lab records. Some were singed and only half pieces, but Sally Ann was examining them all in turn.

She picked up the documents, one after another, holding each one in her hand for a second or two, then placing it into a separate stack if she didn't feel anything. She didn't feel anything on most of these. Then, the next one she picked up seemed to vibrate in her hand and Sally Ann was filled with manic euphoria. She saw Roark, seemingly unconscious, floating in a weird-looking tube.

"She's the key!" The phrase was almost aural, an intense exclamation that echoed in her head. There was anger and an especially ugly kind of desperation underlying the words. Sally Ann dropped the paper to the table and hurried to the nearest ladies' room.

Inside, she stood with her head over the sink basin, waiting to see if the remains of her lunch were going to make a reappearance. When they didn't, Sally Ann filled the sink with cool water and splashed her face, then dabbed the water away with paper towels, carefully smoothing her hair back down. It wouldn't do to go back looking all frizzed out. She'd worked hard with the flat iron this morning.

That was probably the most intense vision she had ever experienced. She'd been working on strengthening her skill, at the Director's request, and guessed this was evidence her mental workouts were working. She wasn't sure that was a good thing. She felt weak in the knees and angry with the Director for putting her in the path of such a train wreck of emotions.

Sally Ann pulled herself up onto the counter next to the sink and sat down, letting her legs dangle. She'd need a minute to collect herself before she went back in there and faced the team.

When Sally Ann had signed on, the entire organization consisted of a dozen or so operatives. The Director had recruited each one personally. Over the years, she'd heard some of the tales of how the other agents were approached, and they all echoed her own. The Director had an uncanny ability to know just when to make his offer. He'd approached her right after she'd been shelved for doing her job too well, when her resentment at being trapped behind a desk was fresh and painful. He'd offered her something better.

Sally Ann had chalked it up to good instincts at the time. Now, she was pretty sure he had known about her paper-reading skill and had recruited her for that in particular. She had worked with the man for three years before she began to suspect he might have a touch of something special about him, too. She couldn't define it, and he certainly didn't talk about it, but the man knew things he shouldn't be able to know and could be almost magically persuasive. Most of the time, she was glad she had made the move both from police work and from North Carolina. She loved the work she did here. She made a difference. Petty bureaucracy didn't build unnecessary walls in her path. The means may have been a little shady, but she couldn't argue with the rightness of the ends.

She trusted the Director, even though she didn't know his real name. Normally, that kind of thing would drive her crazy, but somehow it was all right in the case of her boss. She felt it as a gut instinct. She believed he had the right of things, that he would make good decisions that kept the balance to the good. She'd trust him with her life, and, indeed, had done so on many occasions. So far, she'd had no reason to regret that.

Sally stood, readied a quip about the bullshit in the room having risen to such a level that she'd had to hit the can, and stalked back to the conference room, swinging the door open wide.

The room was empty, except for the Director who sat opposite of her seat, holding the paper that had sent her from the room.

"So, I take it this lab report on our Ms. Roark was of special interest?" he said, pushing the paper back across the table toward her.

Sally Ann didn't pick it back up. She nodded.

"Excellent," he said. His eyes blazed with an intense fervor. "Tell me what you saw."

LINDA'S LIFE IS STILL A SOAP OPERA

"We've been over and over the soap, Leonel. There's nothing in it that can explain your transformation." Dr. Walter Peeples put the charts and graphs he'd been showing Linda back into a folder and snapped the rubber band closure.

Linda felt his frustration in the abruptness of the gestures.

"I mean, sure, it's packing a pretty full punch of testosterone and other male hormones, but in three months of laboratory trials, we've yet to duplicate your results in any test subject."

Duplicate the results? Linda was stunned. *Were they trying to do this to someone else?* She rubbed a hand over her face, scratching at the stubble already returning from her morning shave, then left her hand resting on the back of her neck. She had really hoped there might be news this time. Ever since she'd joined the Department, she'd submitted to test after test, given samples of blood, urine, and bodily fluids she never even used to produce. All she wanted was an explanation. A little reassurance of some kind. How in the world could a change like hers be brought on by simply using soap?

Peeples was her liaison to the medical division. He didn't run the tests himself, just collated the results and translated them into terms a non-scientist like her could understand. He was good at his job, and

Linda usually appreciated his positive outlook and gentle demeanor, but her frustration was growing.

"There must be something you're missing," Linda said. "Maybe something about the water at my house? In my diet or the air?"

"We've tested your water. It's a little hard, but there's nothing that should be able to cause a chemical reaction like this. There's nothing unusual in the data from your husband and family, which suggests it's something about you and not something about the environment. And if it's something about your DNA or your molecular make-up—well, there are thousands and thousands of factors to examine. Narrowing down the exact cause is not simple or fast." He laid a hand on Linda's arm. "The truth is, we may never know the exact cause of your transformation."

He closed some tabs on his computer screen and spun back around in his chair to face Linda. "I am excited about the new data on your strength. You might be the strongest person on the planet. That's going to be a real asset to the Department. The Director had a good feeling about you, and it looks like he was right yet again. That man always just knows."

Linda tried to summon sympathy for the hardworking scientists who were trying to unravel the mystery of what had caused her transformation, but was instead overwhelmed with feelings of self-pity. The self-pity made her feel angry with herself. She lashed out. "So, all these months of giving samples, taking tests, and answering questions, and still you can't tell me anything?"

Walter sighed and Linda immediately felt bad for abusing him. "A team is still working on it, Leonel, but understanding what happened to you could take a long time. I wish we could interview your Dr. Liu. Maybe she could connect the dots for us."

Linda sighed. Finding Dr. Liu was no easy proposition. Patricia had put all her energy into it all these many months, and every lead had proved a dead end. Linda wasn't convinced that finding her would help, anyway. The woman was hardly altruistic in her motivations. She had kidnapped Jessica and held her captive and used Helen to try and burn both Linda and Patricia. It was Cindy, not Helen, that

Linda held responsible for Jessica's burns. If it didn't serve her own ends, there was no way the woman would cooperate. If Walter imagined two scientists calmly discussing a new discovery and sharing ideas, he had another think coming.

"I can answer one question for you, though," he said, a brightness returning to his tone. Linda perked up. "We feel certain your transformation is permanent. We've been watching your samples in a variety of studies, and there's no sign of reversal or additional change."

Linda wasn't sure if that was good news or not. She had come to feel comfortable in her new body and was managing her new strength, but there were still costs in her relationship with David and the rest of the family. Part of her wondered if her husband mourned the loss of the woman she had been. Did he miss her female body, the way she sometimes did? When they made love, was he only going through the motions for her sake? Every time his gaze followed another woman's form as she walked by, Linda fought down a whole new kind of jealousy. She hadn't found a way to talk with him about any of that.

She'd been months rebuilding relationships with her daughters as well. While she felt like she was the same person inside, the external changes were a lot to adjust to. She had yet to begin to try and reintroduce herself in the neighborhood, and she knew the gossip was fierce. The isolation from their friends wasn't helping tensions with David, either. In some ways, it would be easier if she could just be cured and go back to being Linda on the outside again.

Then again, she didn't feel as though being Leonel was an illness that needed curing. In fact, once she knew David would still be hers, she had come to enjoy a lot of things about life as a man. There were the physical things that came with six inches of additional height and strength, but more than that, she liked the feeling of freedom. Thanks to her training at the Department, she was better prepared to defend herself than she had ever been before, but, at least in a daily life situation, she also felt she was less likely to be attacked. The world was a different place when you walked through it as tall, strong man instead of a short, pretty woman. People looked to her automatically and asked her opinion. Her new, deep voice carried in a crowd, and she could cow a group of rowdy grandchildren with a single barked command. Then there was the new world of the bedroom to consider.

If she could go back, part of her would hesitate to do so. She might never feel completely like a man, but she doubted she could ever live life completely as a woman again.

There was a creaking sound, and Linda realized Walter was shifting on his feet, still waiting for her to respond to the news. She clasped the man on the shoulder and smiled. Whether she was entirely pleased or not was irrelevant. There was no reason not to be gracious to the man who had worked so hard on her behalf.

"Thank you, Walter. It is good to know that much, at least." Linda changed the subject, pushing her complicated emotions aside for the time being. "What about Jessica? Have you been able to figure out what kind of gems those were?"

Walter sighed again. Obviously, he didn't have any news. Linda felt bad for him, always having to be the one to tell her they still didn't know anything. "We've tried samples of hundreds of stones with no success. We're starting to wonder if the gems had been acted on in some way. The documents the three of you acquired from Dr. Liu's laboratory point to an array of experiments involving those gems, including chemical interactions and radioactivity. We're beginning to suspect the gems were altered by those procedures. I'm not convinced we'll ever be able to reproduce them."

Linda grunted. She was so tired of maybe and theories. All she wanted was some answers.

"I do have some good news for Jessica, though."

Linda looked up, examining the man's face more carefully. There was something in the way Walter said Jessica's name that tickled her ear. There was something soft in the tone, something warm.

Walter continued, "Did she tell you about the improvements to the air pack?"

Linda laughed. "Tell me? She's talked of nothing else."

Jessica was undeniably excited about the freedom of movement the new device gave her. It had been exciting watching the first learning session. Even in the first lesson, it had been obvious this device could help her overcome the limitations of her weightless condition.

"You must be proud of the work you've done on it," Linda said.

Walter grinned. "Not that it's ever dull around here, but the lab has been a very exciting place since you and Jessica joined the Department."

Linda considered that. "Surely you've seen other amazing things?"

"Oh yes. I could tell you stories…" Walter got a dreamy look on his face and Linda found herself wishing he could indeed tell her those stories. It was exciting to think about the work she could be a part of here at the Department.

"Are there other agents like me and Jessica?"

"No, actually. At least not as powerful as you. Some of our field ops have some skills that suggest a touch of the uncanny—the Director has a way of finding and collecting people with special talents. But you and Jessica are the first real freaks we've recruited into our organization."

Linda was surprised. "The Director seemed so comfortable with the idea of us. I guess I thought stuff like this was mundane around here."

A shadow crossed Walter's face. "Oh, we've seen a lot. It just hasn't always ended well."

"Oh!" Linda was taken aback.

It should have occurred to her that someone in a situation like hers could be dangerous. Helen was an excellent example. She'd been handed incredible power, and she had willingly used it to harm others. It only made sense that the Department would be the ones to deal with those kinds of situations, to protect the public from the types of destruction someone with unusual abilities could cause.

A desire to protect others was part of what had drawn Linda to the work. It was just startling to realize that once, agents had been sent out to protect others from *her*.

MARY HAS A (CONSPIRACY) THEORY

Mary walked into The Market with minutes to spare before her shift was scheduled to start. She placed her wallet and keys in her locker, picked up one of the work aprons, slid it over her head, and smoothed it over her hips. Then, she checked her hair in the mirror and pulled the scarf free that had held her long dreads in a sort of ponytail behind over her shoulders—her attempt to look more mainstream for the visit to the police station. Her dreads spread out over her back like ash-blonde snakes made of rope. Their touch on her bare skin comforted her. As she was reopening her locker to put the scarf inside, Jorge came in.

Jorge was new. He was working the breakfast counter, which meant he always smelled of turkey bacon and hash browns. Smelling him now, Mary felt her stomach growl. As usual, she hadn't eaten anything. Food before noon was always unappealing. Now, she'd have to wait until her first break to get something to eat. There wasn't time before her shift started.

Jorge squeezed her shoulder as he walked by, and she smiled at him. His hand had been pleasantly warm against her skin, and the skin of his fingertips was a little rough from too much time in dishwashing solution. As he let his hand fall away from her arm, a finger traced one of the swirls of the tribal markings that made up her arm-length tattoo. She'd already noticed Jorge was a toucher, and wondered if that was going to be a problem. She let it go for now. There wasn't time to take on a confrontation.

"You doing okay, Miss Mary?"

Jorge always called her Miss Mary. Mary wasn't sure how to take it —flirtation or condescension?—so she decided to let that slide, too. She was letting a lot of things slide that she might have taken on another day.

"You look beat. Rough night?"

Mary shook her head. "No, rough morning. Talking to the police about my mother again."

"No news?"

Mary shook her head again, fighting the tears of disappointment that pricked the corners of her eyes.

"I feel you. The police were useless when my brother went missing, too."

Mary hadn't known that Jorge had a missing brother. "Did you find him?"

Jorge nodded. "No thanks to the police."

Mary wanted to stay and ask him more, but she had to get on the clock or the manager would have her ass on a platter. The Market was a casual place to work and a lot of rules didn't apply, but punctuality was still required. On the way out, she turned and looked back at Jorge. He was unpacking a small lunch box, spreading a variety of containers across the work table. He had just laid a book on the table, *Terrorism and the Illuminati*.

"Could you meet me after my shift?" she asked. "I'd love to talk with you some more."

Jorge smiled broadly. He had wonderfully straight, white teeth. "Definitely. Eight o'clock, right?"

Her shift went quickly. One of the things she loved about working at The Market was the variety of her days. None of the work was very difficult, so, to keep from becoming bored, the workers traded tasks all the time. Mary had helped restock the bakery cases, made coffee drinks for a while, worked the cash register during the dinner rush, and culled the old produce over the course of her workday. The other thing she liked about this kind of work was that it wasn't particularly brain-absorbing. She'd spent the time thinking over the news about her mother's car and had decided her night would involve some research into the flamethrower incident at the college. It was a good place to start.

She had nearly forgotten her appointment with Jorge, but he was there in the break room when she walked in. He had gone home and slept and showered in between. He wore a pale blue Cuban-style shirt over some aged-to-perfection blue jeans. His hair was sculpted into a wave atop his head. It made Mary take note of his sexy cheekbones. When he smiled and stood to greet her, Mary knew she was in for a very pleasant evening.

"You hungry?" he asked.

"Famished," she said.

"Come on. Let's go to *Ixtapa*. My aunt is working. I can get us a deal on whatever they have left at closing."

"That sounds perfect," she said.

A half hour or so later, they were at Mary's place, sitting on the floor, surrounded by small containers of nearly everything the *Ixtapa* served. Jorge had removed his beautiful blue shirt and hung it neatly on the back of one of the kitchen chairs, and sat bare armed, in a white tank top. He had nice arms, muscled but not bulky, neither hairy nor hairless.

When Mary had eaten her fill, she sprawled out on the floor, leaning up on one elbow to watch her dinner companion finish off the last of the *carnitas* in a homemade flour tortilla. He reached across her to grab another beer from the six-pack behind her, then leaned back against the edge of the futon and gazed at her for a long moment.

He sat up straighter, his shoulders settling in a way that showed he had decided something. "My brother was taken for medical experiments."

Mary had been admiring the line of Jorge's shoulders and was puzzled for a moment as to what he was talking about. "Your brother that went missing?"

He nodded. "They had him for four months."

"How did you find him?" Finding him mattered a lot more to Mary than who exactly had taken Jorge's brother to begin with.

Jorge gestured at his bare feet. "Footwork, plain and simple. I followed every tiny lead, no matter how ridiculous. The ones the police wouldn't waste manpower on."

Mary moved closer, so her knees bumped against Jorge's. "Where was he?"

"He doesn't remember. We found him almost right where he disappeared, outside a club downtown. A girl he used to date texted me a photo of this homeless kid. She didn't even know Miguel was missing. She just thought it was weird how much that homeless guy looked like my kid brother. I got in my car and was there half an hour later."

"So, what makes you think it was some kind of medical experiment?"

"He had all these weird cuts and marks on his skin, like those suction marks that hospital monitors leave, you know?"

Mary nodded. She wondered why Jorge had jumped to the conspiracy angle. Couldn't the kid just have actually been in the hospital and they didn't know it? Drugs or alcohol poisoning or a coma after a car accident seemed much more likely to her than mad scientists roaming the streets looking for boys to experiment on.

"You got a computer?" he asked.

Mary did. A nice one, too. A MacBook her dad had bought for her when she enrolled in college. She later dropped out, but her dad never said anything about wanting the computer back. She figured it was his guilty conscience gift for having left her mother and moved out west. She went and got it.

The pair spent the next hour or so looking at websites and online bulletin boards about missing persons. Jorge showed her the wiki he'd built for tracking information about his brother, including pictures of the markings on his skin. She had to admit that some of the marks were hard to explain, and the stitches looked professional. It was definitely strange that the police had never even talked to potential witnesses. It almost seemed like they didn't want to find the missing young man. "I still think they're out there—these medical guys. But we've got him back, so it'll be someone else's problem now," he said.

The next morning, when Jorge left her bed, hurrying to make the breakfast shift, Mary got up. Talking with Jorge had given her a lot to think about. She was thinking the lack of leads on her mother's disappearance wasn't just shoddy police work. She wondered if the car had been there all along or had just been brought back and planted there for the police to find. Suddenly, it all seemed much more sinister, like a cover-up, a conspiracy. She went to her computer. It was time for some research. She'd start with the flamethrower incident on campus last spring.

TROUBLE KNOCKS ON PATRICIA'S DOOR

Patricia had just settled down with her supper when there was a knock at the door. She was excited that someone was there, but realizing that made her angry. It was so pathetic. What was next, getting some cats? It was probably just a Jehovah's Witness or something. She dropped her napkin over her food to keep it warm and went to answer.

She peeked out the side curtain. The stoop was fully illuminated by the security light, but Patricia didn't see anyone. She almost turned and went back to her dinner, but something tugged at her curiosity. She opened the door, chain still in place.

There was an envelope sitting on the welcome mat. It was turned so she could read the writing on the front without opening the door. *Please*, it read. In Cindy's handwriting. Her hands shaking, Patricia closed the door and pulled back the bolt and chain. She flung the door open and stepped to the edge of the railing.

"Cindy?" she called out into the night. There was no answer. Whatever Cindy had to say was going to be in that letter. Patricia wasn't sure if she wanted to know what she had to say or not.

She picked up the envelope, pausing to peer into the darkness in both directions before going back into her apartment. She didn't see anyone. Not that she expected to. She wondered if Cindy had delivered the letter herself or found someone else to deliver it for her. Part of her hoped Cindy had done it herself. That would mean she was alive and well. Well enough to pay the consequences for her actions.

Patricia went back and sat the envelope on the table, propped up so she could look at it and consider it while she ate. Ignoring it for the moment, she uncovered her spinach and chicken pasta, which was, happily, still warm. She scooped a bite into her mouth, sucking in the noodles the way a person can when no one is watching her eat.

Wiping her chin, Patricia thought about what she wanted from this letter, what she hoped for. Was it an apology? Had Cindy come to her senses and realized the destruction she had brought to the lives of others? Once upon a time, Patricia would have expected that. She would have assumed Cindy and she shared a sense of the value of life. The Cindy she thought she knew was working for the greater good, inventing things that would help make the lives of women better and longer.

But, obviously, she had crossed several lines along the way. Not little lines, either. Big double yellow highway ones, like kidnapping and threatening people's mothers. She had put products out on the market and into the bodies of unsuspecting people. Had she known what could happen? Or was she as surprised as her customers when unusual things began to happen? Had she stopped being able to view people as people? Were they all just lab rats to her now? Even Patricia herself?

But all these months spent looking for Cindy had not been solely about revenge. No, if she were honest with herself, she'd have to admit that part of her hoped for some kind of reconnection, atonement, and forgiveness. So, yes, evil or not, crazy or not, dangerous or not, Patricia missed Cindy. She had worried about her. Had Cindy been taken into the system? She would look like a teenage runaway or an abandoned child. Some well-meaning person might have turned her to the authorities. Was she living in some horrible state orphanage? Was she living on the streets? What if she hadn't been able to stop the process and was now a baby?

There was only one way to find out. Patricia picked up the letter.

It was in a big envelope made of heavy paper. She looked again at the outside. No address information anywhere. Just the word "Please" written across the front. Patricia recognized the handwriting, but she was sure that, had she dusted the envelope for fingerprints, she'd have found nothing. She weighed the envelope in her hand. It was a little heavy. Heavier, for example, than a bill or a statement from the pension people. That could have just been the paper, Patricia supposed. The envelope felt flat. That was probably good. No key to a train station locker or mysterious object to track down. It was probably just a letter.

Enough procrastinating, she thought, and tore open the envelope. A pinkish powder spilled out onto the table, releasing a sweet smell into the air. Had Cindy sent her some potpourri? Maybe she had really turned into a child again, attracted to glitter and sparkling sand. Patricia felt suddenly very sleepy. She tried to force herself awake, but it was like she had sunk into a pool of amber. The world was thick around her. She fell into her plate of pasta, breaking the dish with her cheek.

LINDA GOES SLEUTHING

Linda pulled her battered blue pickup truck into her favorite parking place on the end, backed in, with three possible exits. Her time at the Department already had her strategizing her everyday life. She wanted a clear exit plan with alternatives. Just in case. Not that she expected trouble at Patricia's condo. Other than Patricia herself, that is.

Patricia wasn't returning her calls. Things had been strained between them, but that didn't mean they didn't still care about each other. It wasn't like Patricia to let more than a few hours lapse without returning a missed call. After all they had faced together, Linda didn't believe her friend would leave her hanging without good cause.

She was surprised to find Patricia's Mercedes parked in its usual spot. Did that mean she was home? Why wasn't she answering the phone then? Linda's concern amped up to worry. She took the stairs to Patricia's stoop in two strides. Nothing looked amiss. The welcome mat was slightly askew, but there were any number of perfectly innocent explanations for that. The night security light was still on, but maybe Patricia had just forgotten to turn it off. Nothing looked broken or scratched or forced. There was no reason for alarm.

So, why, Linda wondered, *do I feel so alarmed?* She walked up to the door and peered through the glassed-in side panel. Patricia had hung some sort of gauzy curtain over it, and it was hard to see much of anything. There were no lights on inside, but Linda knocked, anyway. Maybe Patricia was ill, or had a headache and was keeping the lights dim. There was no response.

Shielding her eyes with one hand, Linda tried again to peer through the glass. She couldn't make out anything beyond the small hallway right behind the door. She pulled out her cell phone and dialed Patricia's number again, but it went straight to voicemail. Patricia must have either turned off her phone or it had died. That was unlike her, too. Linda was really becoming concerned.

Taking a quick look around to make sure no one was watching, she gripped the lever-style doorknob and bent it all the way down, breaking the entire mechanism. She'd get David to repair or replace it and apologize to Patricia later. The wooden crunch didn't attract any undue attention, so she pushed the door open, surprised to find that the deadbolt had not been thrown. She stepped inside, and closed the door behind her.

Now that she was inside, she could hear a radio playing somewhere.

"Patricia?" she called out, her voice echoing harshly in the small tiled hallway. In moments like this, her own voice still took her by surprise. She still expected to hear her woman's voice, even after all this time. No response.

Linda poked her head into the living room. The television was on one of the streaming music channels, soft jazz. She picked up the remote and turned it off. Nothing seemed amiss. Just the ordinary amount of disarray anyone's living room might have when no company was expected.

There was a small pile of newspaper clippings and webpage print-outs on the coffee table. A quick glance was enough to tell Linda that Patricia had not given up on finding Cindy Liu. All the articles were about young Asian girls who had made the news. All of them were about the age Cindy was when they had last seen her. Something about the stack of clippings made Linda sad. She could imagine Patricia poring over them, looking for some sign of her old friend. Patricia might seem tough on the surface, but Linda knew pain when she saw it and Patricia was hurting in the wake of what Linda privately called *Huracán* Liu.

Linda dropped the stack of articles and walked around the corner into the dining room, no longer bothering to call out to announce her presence. The dining room table was set up for a meal, but the food was long past edible, the sauce congealed into an unappetizing lump on the plate. Linda wrinkled her nose at the smell, but stepped up closer to look all the same. The chair was pushed out like Patricia had just stepped out and planned to come right back to her dinner. A crumpled napkin lay on the floor next to the chair.

The dinner plate in front of the chair was full of some kind of pasta dish with tomato sauce. When Linda stepped closer, she saw that the plate was actually cracked into three pieces, laying on the table like something heavy had fallen on top of the plate and no one had bothered to clean up the shards. Linda sucked her teeth thoughtfully. A broken plate by itself didn't mean anything, really, but she had a bad feeling in general. It was hard to imagine that anyone could have taken Patricia against her will, but that was exactly what she was starting to believe had happened. Sure, there weren't a lot of signs of struggle, but that actually made her feel more suspicious. If Patricia had left willingly, she wouldn't have left food to rot on the table.

Looking more closely, hand over her mouth and nose, Linda saw some kind of pink, shiny grains on the tablecloth. Patricia didn't have any children in her life, and was certainly not a pink, sparkly sort of woman. She was more the navy blue power suit sort. Or yoga pants and tank top if she expected to transform.

She ducked her head into each bedroom, just in case, but she found what she already suspected. Patricia wasn't there. Her car was out front, the door had been locked, her broken dinner plate was on the table, but her friend was nowhere to be found. Linda pulled her phone out of her pocket and dialed in a number and then her access code. It was time to call in the experts.

MARY FALLS DOWN A RESEARCH RABBIT HOLE

Mary was restocking the dairy case at The Market, trying to move slowly so she wouldn't clank the glass bottles from the local dairy farm too loudly as she worked. She hadn't been to bed yet and felt hungover, despite the substance-free nature of the night. The strongest thing in her system was only coffee. She was regretting the lack of rest now, as the long hours of her shift stretched out ahead of her. She was thankful, at least, that the store wasn't very busy on Sunday mornings before church let out. There would be the usual large and boisterous brunch crowd that afternoon. That wasn't going to be fun.

Jorge suddenly appeared at her side, and Mary dropped one of the bottles. She gasped, fumbling for it. Luckily Jorge's reflexes were faster. He caught the bottle by the plastic loop around its neck and lowered it gently to the floor, then handed her the cup of coffee he'd brought for her.

"Careful Miss Mary," he said, smiling as he watched her take grateful sips from the recycled-paper cup. She gave him a wan smile in return. "You don't look so well," he said, concern wrinkling his forehead in a way that Mary found surprisingly endearing.

"I didn't sleep."

"At all?"

Mary shook her head. "I guess I fell down a research rabbit hole."

Jorge nodded. "That's easy to do. Did you learn anything useful?"

After handing him the cup, Mary returned to placing the bottles on the shelves. "I'm not sure," she said, shrugging. "There are a lot of conflicting reports."

Jorge handed her the coffee back and nudged her to move so he could take over placing the bottles. Mary watched him work. Even with a headache and sandbags under her eyes, she could appreciate the grace of his movements as he deftly completed the task. Finished, he picked up the plastic trays and gestured with his head that she should follow him to the back room.

After he placed the trays on the flat where the empties waited for pick up, he signed them both out on the staff whiteboard as "on break," took her hand, and pulled her through the back door.

There was a nice little alcove behind The Market. A long time ago, someone had planted a small Japanese maple that still thrived despite the cramped quarters and limited light. If you could ignore the less pleasant odors emanating from the dumpster farther down the alley, it was nice to sit under the tree and look up at the patch of sky visible through its dark red leaves. When Jorge patted the ground beside him, Mary settled in and let her head fall back against his shoulder.

"You want to tell me what you found out?" he asked.

She felt the rumble of his voice through his chest and shifted her body more snugly against his side.

She recounted for him the more interesting videos and reports she had found as she tried to find out what really happened on the day her mother disappeared. The official story of Springfield College was that a disgruntled student had brought a flamethrower to campus on April 17 and destroyed some of the plants in the main quad, but that he had been quickly subdued and arrested and no one had been injured. There was a very convincing video of a young man being placed in a police car and still photos of the flamethrower he had supposedly used. The college had put out a press release expressing sympathy for the young man and his family and assuring the public that reasonable precautions were in place to ensure the safety of all their students and staff. That was the story Mary herself had believed.

But the Internet at large told another story altogether. Mary tugged her phone out of her pocket to show Jorge the video someone had posted of what seemed to be a woman flying through the air. The woman had blonde hair pulled back into a ponytail and was dressed in a white blouse and jeans. In the video, she flew into the frame, then levitated in midair for a moment before flying back out of the frame in the opposite direction. Even when they froze the frame and looked more closely, Jorge and Mary couldn't get a good look at the woman's face. Nor did they find any sign of the trickery that might have been used to make her appear to fly.

Mary thought it was to Jorge's credit that he didn't freak out or accuse her of pranking him.

"There's some strange shit out there," he said, handing her back the phone.

Mary flipped through her saved pictures and found a photo of a creature crouching in the bushes. "This one is even stranger."

She had saved seven shots of the bizarre creature, pulled from Twitter feeds and public Facebook posts. It looked like some kind of humanoid lizard or maybe a dinosaur. But it was wearing a half-destroyed white tank top and had flaming red hair. In one of the shots, it was turned toward the camera and the eyes glowed a yellowish shade.

"This one has been seen in other places, too. At the mall and at a house fire."

Jorge looked perplexed. "I don't understand, Mary. This is strange stuff, but what does it have to do with your mother?"

Mary took a deep breath. She knew what she had to say was going to sound crazy. She looked at Jorge, trying to read his face. He believed his brother had been taken by some mysterious group for medical experiments, so obviously he was open to the idea of conspiracies. But just how open was his mind? Could he accept the seemingly impossible?

"It's a long story."

He took her hand in his. "What time does your shift end?"

She sighed, letting her achy head fall into her hands. "Not till three."

"Go home, Mary. Tell the boss you're sick and go rest. I'll bring you some lunch when I get off work at noon and you can tell me the whole thing."

Just then, with the sunlight putting leaf shadows on his soft, brown grease-stained shirt and his warm hand cupping her shoulder, Mary thought Jorge might be the most beautiful man she'd ever seen.

PINK SAND IN JESSICA'S SANDBOX

"So, her car was there, and her purse?" Jessica said, reaching for the bowl of chips in the center of the table.

Leonel nodded. "Dinner was still on the table, like she'd just gotten up to answer the phone. But other than a broken dinner plate, there was no sign of a struggle." Leonel's worry was evident in his voice.

Jessica's stomach fluttered and she had to burp to keep from floating above the table. Patricia was a woman to be reckoned with, even when she was in human form. When she took on her reptilian armor, no one could take her against her will. What on Earth had allowed someone to take her and not leave a wreckage behind?

"Did the team find anything?" she asked.

"A few grains of this weird pink sand. One of the techs raised it to his nose to see if he could identify it and passed out on the spot."

"Pink sand?" Jessica felt her heart rate rise. This was just the kind of weird she had been worried about. The kind of weird that came with intimations of Dr. Liu.

"Yeah. The lab guys have it now. Being lab guys, they are very excited about it. I wouldn't be surprised if we start seeing the Department using something similar a few months down the road, once they figure out what it is and how to make it."

"It's got to be Cindy, don't you think?" Jessica fought down a feeling of panic and burped delicately into a napkin to bring her rear end back into contact with the molded plastic chair. "She's back, isn't she?"

Leonel reached for Jessica's fingers and squeezed them. "It sure sounds like her. And now she has Patricia."

Jessica grabbed Leonel's hand with both of hers and leaned close to look into his eyes. She spoke with an assurance she didn't truly feel. "We'll save her, Leonel."

"Excuse me, Roark. You busy?"

Jessica looked up in surprise to find her trainer, Sally Ann, and a very embarrassed-looking Dr. Walter Peeples standing by their table. Sally's eyebrows were raised, and Jessica knew there would be some questions later. For now, though, she wanted to know what news they had brought.

"Walter! Sally Ann! Sit down. You remember Leonel?"

Once all four of them were arranged at the table, Jessica turned and smiled brightly at Sally Ann, still assiduously ignoring the open curiosity on her face. "Do you have information for us?"

Sally Ann laid a photograph on the table. It showed a fortyish man with dark hair and small round glasses. Jessica passed it to Leonel. They both turned back to Sally Ann and Walter. "Who is it?" Jessica asked.

"So, you don't recognize him?" Walter asked.

"I don't," she said. Leonel shook his head.

Sally Ann sighed. "Damn. I was hoping you had some history that could help us out here. Because this case is strange even by Department standards." She pulled a file folder out of a messenger bag and spread the contents on the table. "The man in the picture is Daniel Price. He was a scientist of some renown, in the area of repairing nervous system disorders. He died ten years ago in some kind of laboratory incident. Details are sketchy."

"Okay?" Jessica was confused. *What does a dead scientist have to do with anything?*

Walter pulled out a grainy printout affixed with a sticker indicating it was from the security cameras at Patricia's condo. He pointed at a man standing next to a plain black SUV. He was leaning on a black cane and gesturing toward Patricia's condo. Two men in suits and dark glasses were beside him. "This is Daniel Price."

Leonel grabbed the photograph. It was dated the day before, eight o'clock p.m. "This is the dead man? How can that be?"

"That's the question of the day, isn't it?" Sally Ann slid the photographs back into the folder. "The only recent fingerprints found at the scene besides those of Patricia O'Neill and our friend Leonel here were from Daniel Price, deceased."

Leonel crossed himself. Jessica felt the hairs on the back of her neck rise. "Are you saying Patricia was kidnapped by a dead man?"

"That's how it looks," Sally Ann said. "Unfortunately the surveillance team doesn't have anything helpful. They were asleep at the time."

Leonel thumped the table, rattling the whole structure dangerously. "They should have been watching out for her!"

"Calm down, Leonel." Sally Ann's tone grew defensive. "They failed a tox screen. It looks like the kidnapper knew where our team was and drugged them. No one failed in their duty here."

Looking at Leonel and Jessica in turn, Sally Ann's face softened and became more sympathetic. "I know how worried you must be and, given what we know about your friend, the Department definitely has an interest in this case. We're diverting resources. The lab guys are examining the pink sand. We're tracking the car Price arrived in. We'll find her."

"And when they do? We really want to be there for this one," Leonel said.

Sally Ann bit her lip. The gesture was uncharacteristic for the woman Jessica had come to see as made of iron. She realized her trainer must really have a soft spot for Leonel.

"I can't promise you that, but I'll put in a good word with my superiors. You've both done very well in your training. This might be a good mission to include you in. You do have inside knowledge about some of the players."

"Thank you." Leonel's voice was teary. He must have been more shaken up than Jessica had realized. "Please excuse me."

Jessica, Sally Ann, and Walter watched him walk away.

When he turned the corner into the hall where the bathrooms were, only Jessica saw his hesitation before he entered the men's room. She turned back to her companions. "Leonel feels things strongly," she offered by way of apology.

"I guess he's a passionate person," Walter said, shrugging. There was a strange edge to his voice. "You are fortunate to have him."

Jessica's jaw dropped. Did Walter really think she and Leonel were a couple? Sally Ann kicked her under the table and Jessica closed her mouth. "I am fortunate to have a friend like Leonel, but his husband is the one who really 'has' him," she said.

She and Leonel had agreed to start letting the information that he was gay and in a committed relationship get around. Leonel hoped it would stop the desk clerk from flirting with him.

"Oh?" Walter looked confused, then relieved. "Oh!" Suddenly, he seemed embarrassed. He picked up his coffee cup, still half full, and walked over to the coffee urn on the other side of the room.

Sally Ann leaned across the table. "I think you have a conquest there, Roark."

Jessica watched as Walter filled his cup and turned and talked to another man in a lab coat standing near the coffee urn. Was it too soon to be thinking that way? He had been a great coach, teaching her to use the air pack, but there was more to it than that. There was definitely a spark between them. She watched Walter smooth an unruly blond curl back down. His lab coat didn't hide his solid athletic build. Jessica turned back to Sally Ann. "What's the Department's position on inter-office relationships?" she asked.

SALLY ANN AND THE WIDOW PRICE

Sally Ann stepped from the sedan and smoothed her blue pencil skirt over her hips. Checking her reflection in the car door, she decided the skirt had survived the journey mostly unscathed. The pantyhose, however, had not. There was a huge snag running down the back of one of her calves. Sitting back down, she wriggled out of the hose, revealing her muscular brown legs beneath. She tossed them into the backseat. She didn't really like wearing them, anyway. Luckily, she had shaved her legs that morning. So long as she still wore the pumps, she should pass for a pencil pusher, if one who spent a fair amount of time doing leg work at the gym.

She reached into the back of the car and grabbed the suit jacket from its hanger before pulling it on over her white silk blouse. She checked her teeth and hair in the side view mirror. She had styled her short dark hair with a curling iron this morning to look more corporate and less kick-ass. She winked at the polished looking woman in the mirror.

"My, my Agent Rogers, you do clean up nicely." She stuck her tongue out at her reflection. *Hoity-toity bitch.*

The Director had selected her in particular for this mission, though she had difficulty understanding why. She was a woman of action, rather than talk. Interviewing the widow of the dead man who had recently kidnapped Patricia O'Neill sounded like a wild goose chase to her. But, inscrutable or not, the Director knew what he was doing. He'd proven it again and again and she would trust in that and do her best to find out what he wanted to know. There must be something here she was well suited to discover. She was guessing her recent success with the lab papers had him hoping there would be some paper to handle here as well.

Vivian Price answered the door immediately after Sally Ann knocked, so she must have been watching her approach through the window. Either she was anxious about this visit, or lonely. Maybe both.

"Mrs. Price?" Sally Ann put on a winning smile and extended a hand, which the woman accepted in a limp grip. It was like shaking hands with celery that had gone soft in the refrigerator. "I'm Agent Rogers. We spoke on the phone?"

"Yes, of course. Please, come in." The woman gripped her sweater closed at the neck in a self-protective gesture, and Sally Ann wondered if she just had a nervous demeanor or if there were something in particular that had her worried.

She reminded Sally Ann of one of her aunts, a woman the rest of the family had felt sorry for, a woman who seemed to attract tragedy and projected an air of eternal suffering. "Poor Auntie" had been used to describe her so often that Sally Ann used to think that was her name.

Once the door was closed, Mrs. Price became warmer. "Won't you sit down?" She indicated a large, soft blue chair.

Sally Ann perched at the front of it so her feet could touch the ground. Mrs. Price seemed tall to Sally Ann, but so did most people. A quick comparison to the furnishings had her at an estimated five-foot-eight. Tall, but hardly an Amazon. She moved like an ex-athlete. If Sally Ann had to guess, she'd say tennis. Mrs. Price sat on the sofa opposite and picked up a glass from the coffee table between them. Sally Ann knew from the smell that there was whiskey in the glass. A little Irish courage for this interview? That was interesting as well.

Or just sad. Maybe she needed whiskey just to get through a normal day.

As the woman set the glass down on the table, her hand shook and the ice cubes rattled. She cleared her throat nervously. "I was surprised to hear from the authorities after all this time. Daniel's been gone for ten years."

"We're trying to close some of the older cases on the books." Sally Ann pulled a notebook from her bag and flipped to the page with the relevant data and questions on it, taking the cue to get down to business. She had chosen the paper and pencil approach, figuring it made her more approachable. "Daniel was declared legally dead after seven years. Is that correct?"

Mrs. Price nodded.

"But no corpse was ever found?"

Mrs. Price shook her head, looking down at her hands in her lap. "They said his body must have been destroyed in the lab explosion. But I never understood that—the explosion, I mean. It wasn't like he worked with dangerous chemicals or anything. He studied the nervous system. He was working on an experimental surgery that would restore lost nervous system connections in paraplegics. Why would anything explode?"

Lack of a body was indeed suspicious. Sally Ann knew well that this was tantamount to no death, especially in her line of work, and, in this case, there was the added evidence on film that Daniel Price was still kicking. Of course, she didn't tell Mrs. Price she had seen her husband recently, walking and talking and kidnapping lizard women. Instead, Sally Ann pressed a pen against her lips thoughtfully. It was an artful gesture, suggesting she shared Mrs. Price's doubts about that official story. Just as she hoped, it got Mrs. Price to keep talking.

"And wouldn't you think that some trace of him would have survived? Can't they identify a person by their teeth or hair these days?"

Sally Ann scribbled in the margin of her notebook as if she were taking notes. She wanted Mrs. Price to feel that every word she said was vitally important to her, but really she was only half listening while she discreetly surveyed the room and the woman herself, trying to find something to guide her investigation.

Mrs. Price looked about fifty years old, just beginning to be soft around the throat in that way that sent women running for the plastic surgeon. She had narrow shoulders but wide hips. Even though it was a warm day, she was dressed in a long, dark skirt and wore a sweater over her blouse. The room was kept dim, though from the size of the windows, Sally Ann could see it would be easy enough to make the room feel light and airy instead of dusty and dismal. Perhaps the woman suffered from migraines or something else that gave her light sensitivity. Perhaps she was paranoid about being watched.

The room they sat in was nicely decorated, if old-fashioned for Sally Ann's tastes. There was an array of family photographs on a table display, mostly featuring a boy at a variety of ages, and some nice framed prints of landscapes on the walls. The chair Sally Ann was seated in had that rough upholstery favored in academia, probably for its longevity. Sally Ann could easily imagine a group of academics sitting around in this room talking about their pet theories and office politics. Vivian Price had probably been very good in her role of professor's wife, but now that her professor husband was gone, there was the distinct scent of loneliness clinging to the walls.

Sally Ann already knew from the bank records that Mrs. Price had not received a settlement from the insurance company until Daniel was declared legally dead. What wasn't clear was where her income came from in the seven years leading up to that declaration. The finance guys hadn't yet gotten back to Sally Ann about where that particular trail had led. Her income had been substantial and regular —enough to cover the mortgage and household needs as well as her son's tuition at Cornell. She didn't earn much herself, doing mostly medical transcriptionist or office clerical work over the years. She hadn't worked outside the home at all when her husband was living or in the first year or so after his death.

"It must have been hard to manage all these years."

Sally Ann stood up and crossed to an array of photographs on a small bookshelf. They were all framed in matching gilt-edged frames, just this side of tacky and just the other side of classy. The widow Price must not have been born into money, but she'd been in the game long enough to have learned to avoid the showiest displays. Sally Ann picked up a photograph of the son in his graduation gear.

"How did you ever manage to pay for college?"

Mrs. Price drew in a sharp breath. If Sally Ann had not been listening carefully, she might not even have heard the sound. But she had heard it and knew it meant she had hit on a sore spot. She sat the picture back down and bent to look at the others, affecting an air of only partial interest in the answer to the question she had just asked. She let the silence grow and felt Mrs. Price shifting uncomfortably in her seat behind her. Good. Discomforted and off-kilter was just right for getting her to let something slip, if there was anything to let slip.

"I…" she began, then went silent again.

Sally Ann turned.

Mrs. Price tilted her head up, her entire posture becoming defiant. "I had some help. One of Daniel's colleagues arranged for a sort of fund to provide for me and for Danny. Jr."

So, she had pride, but not so much pride that she turned away money when she needed it.

Sally Ann turned back to the photographs and picked up one that featured Daniel Price standing with a few other men and women in front of a podium. They were gathered around a trophy Daniel held outstretched in front of him. Sally Ann carried the photograph back over to the couch and sat beside Mrs. Price.

"How generous! Was it one of these people?"

Mrs. Price looked at the photograph, then shook her head. Sally Ann noticed the wetness of the woman's eyes and looked away delicately as she wiped the tears on the cuff of her sweater sleeve.

"No. That's the rest of the team he was working with—that's the award they had just won, from the Lasker Foundation. Daniel was so excited by having their work funded longer term. He had such hopes. We all did." Her voice cracked. "They were all killed in the accident. It was Vic—Dr. Chaney who helped us out. I think I have his photograph somewhere."

She stood and wandered into the hallway, and Sally Ann let her pretend she hadn't known exactly where the photograph was. "Here it is."

Sally Ann followed to where the woman called from. The photograph she indicated was a posed photograph of two smiling men leaning across a desk toward each other, their hands grasped in the middle as if arm wrestling. Daniel Price was mugging a look of pain and fear. The other man stared intently at Daniel. Mrs. Price pointed.

"That's Victor. He and Daniel became friends when they were both at Michigan. That's just a little while before our son was born. Victor was Danny's godfather."

There was a softness in the woman's voice when she said, "Victor." Sally suspected her feelings for Mr. Chaney were not solely comprised of gratitude and friendship.

"Was?" Sally Ann asked, thinking about how she might get a copy of the photograph without alarming Mrs. Price, or better yet, just get her hands on the original for a few minutes to see what impressions she could pick up. "May I?" She lifted the frame from its hooks on the wall, acting as if she wanted to view it in better light, and took it with her into the living room before holding it under a lamp.

Mrs. Price leaned against the doorframe, her arms crossed over her chest. "Victor died not long after Daniel did. He'd suffered for a long time with a degenerative problem in his nervous system. That was part of why he and Daniel became friends. Victor was always hoping for a cure." There was that tone again. Mrs. Price had definite feelings for Mr. Chaney.

"He didn't have children?"

"No. Victor never married. He said he was married to his work. But he doted on Danny. He came to all Danny's events. So devoted. At the funeral, he said he was so sorry it had to be Daniel."

Had to be Daniel? That was interesting phrasing. It was interesting that he came to Danny's school events, too. Most godfathers were content to send a card and some money. Sally Ann let the picture frame fall from her hands, angling it so it would bounce off the table's edge on the way to the floor. As she planned, it landed with an audible crack, spreading shards of glass across the hardwood floor.

"Oh! I'm so sorry." Moving quickly, Sally Ann retrieved the frame and finished cracking it in her grip so that the picture drifted out and fluttered to the floor. While Mrs. Price scurried away to get a broom and dustpan, Sally Ann picked up the photo and sat on the couch to concentrate. She'd only have a few seconds to form an impression before the woman came back.

Closing her eyes and taking a deep breath, she laid the photograph across her knees and ran her fingers lightly over the surface. She heard laughter, two men and a woman. She got a rush of mixed emotions: longing, pain, anger, regret. Then, just like in the conference room, one clear thought: *"He knows too much. It'll have to be Daniel."* It had all taken only a moment. When Mrs. Price returned, Sally Ann seemed to be merely sitting and holding the photograph. She'd been able to fight off the nausea more easily this time. She laid the photograph on the couch, glad to let go of it and, with it, the maelstrom of emotions contained in its paper.

"I'm so sorry, Mrs. Price. That was inexcusably careless. At least let me clean it up for you." She took the whisk broom and dustpan from the other woman's hands before she could protest, and knelt to pick up the larger shards of glass and pieces of frame and put them in the dustpan.

Wordlessly, Mrs. Price stepped across the room and returned with a small wicker wastebasket. Sally Ann could feel disapproval radiating from the woman, but she knew she hadn't left Mrs. Price room to complain. It seemed to have been an accident, and she was cleaning it up herself. Sally Ann dumped the refuse inside and quickly swept the area.

She stood, dusting off her knees. "I wouldn't walk barefoot here for a few days just in case, but I think I got the worst of it."

When Mrs. Price had replaced the wastebasket, she sat down on the couch again. Sally Ann joined her and reached to pick up the photograph from where she had set it on the coffee table, consciously trying not to pick up any vibrations this time. Her ability to dampen the power was improving with practice, too.

"Did you take this photograph?" she asked.

Mrs. Price smiled, breaking the grumpy expression that had taken over her face into something much more open and appealing. "Yes. It was the day Daniel learned he had been approved for tenure. Victor still hadn't heard about his own review, so he told Daniel he'd arm wrestle him for it. There was a camera on Daniel's desk, so I snapped this picture. Victor had it printed and used to keep it sitting on his desk. When he died, I laid claim to it, as a memento."

She took the photo from Sally Ann and looked down at the two men. Sally Ann couldn't have said which of them held her gaze longer.

"You know, when Victor died, so soon after Daniel's accident, I felt like I'd been widowed twice." She squeezed the bridge of her nose with her fingers, stopping the tears. "They found him at home. He had fallen and bashed his head on the bathtub. His cane was missing—he must have left it somewhere. His balance had gotten so poor."

Sally Ann made a sympathetic noise. "Mr. Chaney provided for you and Danny in his will then?"

Mrs. Price nodded, obviously emotional. "He was very good to us. I don't know what we would have done without his help." paused, considering. "He seemed to think it was all his fault somehow. Of course, it wasn't. But he talked as if he could have saved Daniel. Isn't that strange?"

Very. Sally Ann didn't say it out loud, though. Instead, she gathered her things and drew the interview to a close. She'd already gotten what she came for: a lead.

PATRICIA UNVEILS THE DRAGON

Patricia awoke strapped to a hospital gurney. A bright light burned above her. There was a whooshing sound off to the right. She arched her back trying to see behind her, but couldn't make out anything other than more bright lights. The room smelled sweet, and Patricia remembered the pink powder. *That bitch!* To think she'd been feeling all sentimental, worrying about what had ever happened to her good friend, worrying she was lost to the system or dead somewhere.

She was going to wish she was dead when Patricia was done with her. Apparently the Cindy she knew was gone, if she had ever existed. She was taking all her plays straight from the crazy handbook. And she was crazy if she thought bright lights and gurney straps were going to keep Patricia O'Neill in a place she didn't want to be in.

Patricia closed her eyes to channel her anger and upset and trigger her transformation into what she'd come to think of as the Dragon Lady. It wasn't like she had to dig for it. This was fresh hurt, new betrayal. It was right there, barely beneath the surface. In a matter of seconds she felt the gurney beginning to collapse beneath the weight of her fully armored self. The Hyde to her Jekyll. The metal supports squealed as they bent and Patricia stood, shaking off the remnants of the restraint straps like ribbons.

She took a strong stance, arms at the ready and weight balanced on her toes to facilitate quick movement, and waited for the attack. But none was forthcoming. The bright lights were painful. Patricia shielded her eyes with one taloned hand, but couldn't make out any details of the room. She stalked to the nearest light and pushed it over, knocking it into the neighboring light. That one hit its neighbor in turn and before long Patricia was standing in a pile of broken glass and steaming light poles, grinning. The destruction had been satisfying.

The lights extinguished, Patricia made out the details of the room. She seemed to be in a medical training room. Above the operating floor where she stood she could see a glassed-in observation area where the students would watch the demonstrations. If there was anyone up there, she couldn't see them from the floor. In the now dimly-lit room, the large glassed-in window seemed almost mirrored. The whooshing sound she had heard when she first regained consciousness was coming from a machine against the far wall. It glowed a pale yellow. Patricia walked toward it, still fuming. Each step shook the shattered glass on the floor.

The machine had a glass top. Something about it seemed familiar. In spite of herself, she felt curious. There was something to be said for looking for answers before smashing the place up. She'd need to know where she was and if Cindy had anyone else helping her. As she moved closer to the machine, she could hear another sound inter-mixed with the whooshing, a metallic tapping. It seemed to follow a pattern, but she couldn't parse it. She stood still, listening. Was it Morse code? Who the hell would be trying to communicate with her in Morse code? She only barely knew what Morse code was and certainly couldn't translate it into words.

Patricia stopped and examined the machine from where she stood in the middle of the room. It was a long rectangular box, maybe six or six and a half feet long. She thought it was silver, though it was hard to tell in the diffuse light. The only room illumination came from was the observation area above her, now that Patricia had broken all the other lights. There were industrial handles on the top of the case that somehow reminded Patricia of outer space. Or maybe it was just the other-worldly yellow light that emitted from the glassed-in portion of the top. Whatever the device was, the tapping was definitely coming from within.

Patricia looked around again. She felt apprehensive, though she couldn't have said why. Nothing about the sounds or the lights had changed. She saw and heard no one. Other than the tapping, and the whooshing noise the functioning of the machine seemed to make, it was deadly quiet.

Shaking off her foreboding, Patricia moved toward the machine. The spikes that sprouted from her upper back and arms seemed to grow longer. She was aware of them in a way that she usually wasn't, but she made no effort to calm herself and pull them in. She still felt some kind of attack was imminent, and she wanted to be ready for it when it came.

Alongside the machine, she wiped a layer of moisture from the glass with a torn section of the tank top she had been wearing and peered through it. Inside was an Asian girl, approximately age twelve, her face tense with concentration. She was tapping against the metal tubing that ran over her head. Her movements corresponded with the sounds Patricia was hearing. Patricia felt her heart begin to race. The girl turned and met Patricia's gaze. She stopped tapping and spread her palm against the glass, tears filling her eyes. It was Cindy Liu.

"So you must be Patricia."

The voice was something out of an old scary movie, something played by Boris Karloff. Patricia was sure that when she turned she would see a mummy or some other horror. She flexed, pushing her spikes out to their full length and turned, ready for action.

A man was standing in the shadows. He stepped forward into the pool of yellowish light created by the tank that housed Cindy Liu. He was a short, brown-haired man with freckles, wearing a round pair of gold-wire-rimmed glasses. He seemed to be around forty. Dressed in khaki pants and a blue plaid button-up shirt, a white lab coat open overtop, he leaned on a black walking stick with a shiny metal handle. He looked surprisingly normal.

Patricia glared. Whether this man was normal or not, there was nothing about this situation that garnered her trust. She had been knocked unconscious and brought here. Even now, she didn't know where here was, other than a medical theater. Her former best friend was crying in a tank behind her, in the body of the girl she had become. The man reached out a hand toward one of her spikes. Patricia pulled back roughly, almost growling.

"I'm sorry. It's just so fascinating. Cindy never said how... majestic you are." The voice didn't match the man at all. It sounded somehow dusty, as if it had been a long time since he had spoken or as if the act of speaking itself was painful in some way.

Patricia stomped one foot, shaking the entire laboratory floor. The man grabbed at the empty air, shock shaking the look of wonder from his face and replacing it with fear. He managed not to fall by spreading his legs wide and stooping into a kind of bow.

"Who are you?" Patricia demanded, for once glad for the tone of her lizard-voice. It sounded more threatening.

The man looked cowed. If he thought he could win her trust that easily, he had seriously underestimated her.

"I'm Daniel, or Anton, depending on how you think about it." He stood looking at Patricia, like he thought the names would mean something to her. They didn't. "This"—he gestured to his body—"is Daniel Price. This"—he tapped the side of his own head—"is Anton Lorre. I'm Cindy's father." He extended his hand, as though he thought she would shake it. When she didn't, he pulled it back and rubbed the back of his head. His face was troubled. "I think we need to talk, Patricia." He turned and walked to the door, then stood holding it open expectantly.

Patricia looked back down at Cindy in the tank-like device. Her hand was still against the glass. Patricia spread her taloned hand over it and nodded once.

"Cindy doesn't have a father," she said.

The man's face tightened. "We haven't been close."

"He's been dead for most of Cindy's life. I don't know who you are, but—"

"I am Anton Lorre!" The man's voice echoed in the rafters of the open room.

Patricia narrowed her eyes, flicking her nictitating membranes and letting the scales fill in fully on her cheeks. She stepped toward the man, prepared to slice him open with her talons if that was what was required to gain answers. "If you're Cindy's father, then why are you keeping her in a tank?"

"It's for her own good."

Patricia snorted. "You do know she only *looks* like a child, right? She's sixty-eight years old."

His face took on a haughty demeanor that was mirrored in his tone. "The tank provides a controlled environment."

Patricia chilled at the way the man said "controlled." She wondered what kind of control he meant. "She came to you for help, then?"

"Not exactly. I had her brought to me. I still have a few contacts out there." He gestured at the ceiling. The point was perhaps muted by the fact that all Patricia could see were the rafters. "My daughter is brilliant, in her way. If we can stabilize her condition and perfect her formula, we might yet be of use to each other." There was a note of pride in his voice, and of something more sinister, along the lines of ownership.

What's in it for you? Patricia left her real question unasked, instead asking, "Where are we?"

"This is my research compound."

"Which is where?"

The man smiled. A horrible expression that pulled only one side of his mouth above the teeth, like a stroke victim. "In due time, my dear."

Patricia was no one's "dear." She was starting to believe the man might be in his nineties after all. He at least had some antiquated ideas about how it was appropriate to address a woman.

"Okay, then. What do you want from me?"

"It's complicated and will take some time to explain. In the meantime, I'll ask you to be our guest." He pulled a small device from his pocket and clicked a button.

A heavily-armed man entered the room a moment or two later.

"Please see Ms. O'Neill to her quarters," he said.

Patricia turned, flexing impressively. Price or Lorre or whoever he was flinched and she was pleased. "I'm not going anywhere without answers."

Mr. Price leaned forward with both hands on the head of the walking stick he had planted like a third limb between his feet. "You won't be going anywhere either way."

Patricia knew she could break the man as easily as a wineglass. He seemed frail. She could also feel the stubbornness beneath that frail exterior. Her thoughts pin-balled around in her head. She didn't have enough information to make a good decision. If she killed him now, would she simply be killed herself? She glanced at the man who had entered the room to take her to her quarters. She felt sure she could take him in a fight, but she had no idea what other kinds of forces were marshaled here, what their capabilities might be. She didn't even know where she was.

"Let me talk to Cindy."

"She's taking a treatment right now. She'll be asleep for the next twelve hours."

She hated his smug face just then, but restrained herself from knocking his head from his shoulders.

"I'll wait."

A barely disguised tremor of rage shook the man's frame. He turned to the armed man. "Bring in some chairs," he ordered.

The man stepped into the hall and whistled harshly. A second or two later he called, "Two chairs."

Patricia crossed her arms across her chest, a gesture she knew made the spikes on her biceps stand out especially threateningly and stared at the man who claimed he was Cindy Liu's father. When Patricia and Cindy first met, back in college, Cindy said her father was dead. She'd said very little about him in the intervening forty years. Patricia had the impression Cindy didn't really know that much about him herself, since she'd still been so young when he died. What she did know about her father had come filtered through her embittered mother, whom Cindy characterized as a bit of a drama queen, prone to self-serving exaggeration. From her own research, Patricia knew he had been a scientist, the first American-born child in a Hungarian family, and that Cindy's mother didn't approve of his work and had accused him of a lack of morality. She also knew he had died in some kind of lab accident, burned to death. There had been no body left to bury. Patricia remembered that macabre detail well.

Two more men dressed for combat entered the room, each carrying a plush-looking chair, like the kind you might find in a waiting room. Another one entered carrying a tray and a small table. The three placed the furniture in a neat arrangement, in some sort of bizarre parody of the set crew setting up for an interview on a talk show.

"Won't you sit down?" Price gestured at the chair, then swept his long lab coat to the side dramatically and took a seat himself, crossing his legs at the knee like an old European gentleman in a film.

Patricia closed her eyes and concentrated for a moment, bringing her spikes back in. No need to destroy good furniture. In the past few months, she had practiced a great deal and had learned a lot about controlling her changes. As long as she stayed focused, she could decide how far to let her armor extend and bring it up and down quickly. It wasn't that different from learning to play a sport. Muscle memory from practice. Spikes retracted, she sat down, crossing one leg atop the other, so her great taloned foot hung in the space between their chairs. She tucked her hands behind her head with an air of nonchalance and waited for the man to speak.

"Fascinating. Someday you must tell me how you control that," he said.

Patricia huffed harshly through her nose. That hardly seemed likely. The man must have realized she wasn't interested in satisfying his curiosity, because he let the subject drop immediately. He picked up one of the two glass bottles of Dr. Pepper on the tray.

"Cindy told me you favor Dr. Pepper," he said, holding one out to her. When she didn't take it, he shrugged and placed it back on the side table. "It's no chocolate phosphate, but it's growing on me." He downed half the bottle in a big swig, then dabbed at his mouth with a napkin from the same tray.

Patricia stared at the man. What was his angle? What did he want from her? She wished he would just get to the point already. "So, you're Cindy's father, huh? Care to explain how that's possible?" She tapped her talons on the arm of the chair, making sure they scratched against the upholstery.

The man wiped his mouth again with the back of his hand. "Her mother was my lab assistant. In another era, she'd have been a scientist in her own right, but this was the forties. Late nights and crisis moments, no time to meet other girls. That sort of thing. She might even have loved me. We didn't marry, though I always made sure they had sufficient funds."

Patricia rolled her eyes. "I wasn't asking for the story of your love life. Obviously, there's more to this story than that. Let's start with your apparent age."

"Oh, this?" Daniel gestured at his body. "This isn't my body. At least not originally. Let's see. I think this makes my fifth body since the lab accident. They tend to wear out rather quickly. The electricity necessary for the transition makes neuromuscular connection breakdown over time. I'm due for another new one soon, unless our Cindy can make this one last longer."

A year ago, she would never have considered that the man's words might be true, but a lot had changed in her fifty-eighth year on planet Earth. She'd had ample reason to reconsider what the limits of truth might be. For now, she would accept his version of events, even if it meant she was talking to a ninety-eight-year-old man who had purportedly died in a fire before Patricia herself was born and was now inhabiting the body of a forty-something man. It wasn't the strangest thing she had experienced this year. Looking down at her claw-like hand resting on her armored knee, Patricia thought Price's story sounded entirely plausible. No stranger than a floating woman or a very strong man who used to be woman.

"I'm sure your history is fascinating, Mr. Price."

"Daniel," he interrupted.

"Mr. Price," she continued. "If you are who you say you are, you are old enough to be my father, appearances notwithstanding."

The man made a strange wheezing noise. Patricia looked at him, perplexed, and then realized he was laughing.

"I always thought I would like you, Patricia O'Neill. I wish we had met years ago. But even Cindy didn't know I was still alive until I brought her here."

"Why am I here, Mr. Price?"

"To the point, as always. Cindy said you were a no-nonsense sort of girl. Coming from her, that's really saying something." He grinned. The effect was off-putting. The way his skin stretched across his teeth repelled her. "Cindy asked me to bring you here, Patricia. We need your help." Patricia looked over at the tank that held the woman in question. The tapping continued.

"You have an interesting method of asking for help," said Patricia, still bristling at having been called a girl. "Trickery? Kidnapping? Subterfuge? What makes you think I would help either one of you under these circumstances?"

"We're desperate. Maybe that made me act rashly." He didn't sound as though he doubted the wisdom of his approach.

Patricia was finding it harder to keep her temper and wondered if there was any reason that she should. She leaped to her feet and went back over to the tank. She stood over it, looking in. The tapping had stopped, and Cindy looked like an ordinary child, sleeping inside. She raised a fist, raising her scales and armor plating to cover her lower arm more fully. "What's to stop me from simply breaking this glass right now and ending this?"

Price raised an eyebrow. The rest of his cheek didn't seem to move, stretching out his eye socket grotesquely. "It will kill her." His voice was cold.

"I don't believe you."

"I could be lying. But are you willing to take that risk?"

Patricia found she wasn't. She sat down and pulled back her scales and armor so she could pick up the Dr. Pepper. It was perfectly chilled, the condensation making a sheen on the glass.

"So, start talking," she said.

MARY, QUITE CONTRARY

The burned-out remains of the house that belonged to Cindy Liu were surrounded by a low fence now, labeled with signs warning against trespassing. Mary stood at the edge of the wooded area behind the house, watching. She'd been by the house several times. She wasn't sure what she was looking for exactly, but she felt sure that if she were going to find her mother, the home of the mysterious Dr. Liu was the best place to begin her hunt. There had to be a clue there about where they would have gone. Mary still thought her mother might have gone willingly with Dr. Liu in search of answers. But there was no reason for her not to make contact and let her daughter know she was safe. Unless she wasn't.

From her vantage point, Mary sketched the back of the house. The fire damage was pretty extensive. Not at all like the little scorch marks left on the lawn by her mother's practice sessions. This fire had gotten out of control. The finished sketch looked like a scene for a gothic novel, the ruined manse on the moors. In reality, it was more a bungalow in the burbs. But context was everything.

She closed the sketchbook and put it back inside her messenger bag. Her notebook was in there and she pulled it out and flipped through the pages. Jorge had offered to help her build a wiki to collect her information, but she wasn't ready for that yet. She thought better on paper. Plus, if someone was covering up her mother's disappearance, calling attention to her search with a website was not the best of ideas. It was better to fly under the radar on this one. Strange things were happening, and she wanted the chance to find out what they were before someone found her and shut her down.

Mary wanted to go inside and explore, but she was cautious. The structure was badly damaged by the fire and explosion. Chances were it would all fall down around her ears. She wouldn't be able to do her mother any good from a hospital bed.

Mary had watched the video footage on YouTube again and again. There was something really strange going on here. Because the fire and explosion had happened mostly behind the house, there wasn't much footage of the actual fire in the videos. What there was, though, was footage of some kind of lizard woman screaming and chasing bystanders away. In spite of all the comments that the footage had to be faked, Mary didn't think so.

She had printed the best of the still pictures of the creature she had found and added them to the growing file she carried in her messenger bag. Between those and the video of the flying soccer mom on campus, Mary was starting to feel there was way more to this story than she had first suspected. She was growing more certain that Dr. Liu had experimented on other women, too. Maybe Jorge's theory of roaming mad scientists experimenting on the populous wasn't that far-fetched. She wanted to know who these other women were. They had been in the same places as her mother, and strange things were happening to them, too. Were they also missing?

So she stood in the edge of the little wooded area, watching the house. She'd come three mornings in a row, and each morning, she had seen the same thing. At ten o'clock, right after the neighbor lady left for the gym, the men appeared. Two of them, wearing white suits and face masks. They disappeared into the house and came out again an hour later. Their timing was perfect. They were always gone by the time the stay-at-home mother returned from the gym with her toddler and baby. Mary wished she had a way to find out what they were doing in there.

A plan was developing. She could sneak in at night. She had her father's old camera with an infrared filter. It was a remnant of his former career, studying bats. He'd given it to her when he retired, saying he was done with late nights. She could call him for a tutorial, saying she wanted to do some late night nature shooting with a friend. Then, she could sneak in and photograph the area. If she had the film printed at the art lab, she could study the pictures at her leisure. There had to be answers in there.

In the meantime, she would continue to try and nail down her mother's whereabouts on the day of her disappearance. She thought about the timeline she'd developed so far. Mary backed into the trees and cut through the neighbor's yard to return to her car, left two streets over. She never heard the man following her.

~

"She's awake."

Mary heard the voice, but when she tried to open her eyes, she plummeted back into darkness. Waking felt like a steep climb up a slimy-walled pit. It took several more tries before she was able to convince her eyelids to lift. When she finally succeeded, she immediately doubted what she saw. She had to still be asleep.

Trying to shake the vision and come to reality, she sat up in bed, ducking her head and rubbing at her eyes with the heels of her hands. She opened her eyes again. She was in a child's room. The walls were painted pink and decorated with a border featuring fluffy white bunny rabbits. The bed she was in had a canopy made of white lace, and the bed sheets were a shade of pink that matched the walls. It looked like someone had painted the room in Pepto-Bismol.

"Where the fuck am I?" she asked the walls.

After sliding her feet out of the bed, she sat up. She felt a little dizzy and her mouth was dry, cottony, and tasted terrible. She stood, gripping one of the posts of the bed to support herself as she found her balance. She was wearing a hospital gown, she realized. One that was too short for her, and printed with pink checks and white daisies.

She could see a bathroom a few steps away and pushed off toward it. Her knees wobbled, but she was able to stumble to the doorframe and into the bathroom. She made it just in time to relieve her suddenly painfully full bladder into a too-small toilet. She was washing her hands at a sink that only came up to her thighs when she heard the door open.

"Ah! I'm glad to see you're out of bed. Here." The woman handed her a pile of pink hospital scrubs. "These will fit you better."

When Mary just stood there, dumbstruck, the woman smiled. "It's all right. I'll wait." She picked up the shirt Mary had dropped, handed it to her again, and pushed her back into the bathroom and closed the door between them.

Mary stood behind the door listening. She heard the sound of bedsprings creaking and figured the woman must have taken a seat on the bed. Mary had no idea what was going on, but figured whatever it was would be better with pants that covered her ass, so she pulled on the scrubs as quickly as she could, gripping the towel rack for balance. She banged her elbow painfully, scrambling to open the door.

The woman was, indeed, seated on the bed. She was a short, slender woman with big squarish black glasses and brown hair pulled back from her face in a severe bun. She didn't look any older than Mary, though she wore a lab coat and a badge that announced she was Dr. Kimberly Suggs.

"That must feel better. Please sit down." The woman patted the bed beside her and pulled a small medical light out of a pocket. "Just follow the light, please." Mary cooperated with a series of small commands, similar to what the doctor had asked her to do when they'd thought she might have a concussion after that car wreck last year. Her mind tried to form questions, but it was like her thoughts were too spread out and she couldn't quite rein them in and form something coherent from them.

"I'm sorry for the confusion. We weren't expecting to bring you in today, and in the last minute run-around, someone listed you as thirteen instead of twenty-three, so they sent you to the pediatric wing. We thought it best to just let you recover here. I'll have you moved to another room soon."

Mary finally managed to speak. "Does that mean you have my mother?"

"Us? No. She's being held at another division. We're the pediatric division." The woman tapped her ear, apparently activating some kind of earpiece. "She's fine. Is transport ready?"

Turning back to Mary, the woman smiled. "I know you must be confused. They'll explain everything soon."

There was a tap at the door. Dr. Suggs stood and opened the door, admitting a tall, thin man who had to duck to get through the doorway. He was pushing a wheelchair.

"You probably don't need the chair, but we don't want to risk you falling. The drugs can affect your nervous system for a few hours after waking."

The man approached the bed and placed his arm under Mary's, presumably to help her stand. His grip was gentle but firm. She let him lead her to the wheelchair.

Dr. Suggs waggled her fingers at her as the man rolled her away. "Bye-bye now!"

LINDA AND DAVID ARE SHIPS
PASSING IN THE NIGHT

Linda was exhausted. She'd had morning PT and hand-to-hand practice, followed by afternoon coursework, and then finished with weapons training. It was much more intense than the days she had lived before the change. She hadn't been to a farmer's market or an estate sale in months. She was struggling to find time to keep the house stocked in groceries, and David was resisting picking up any of the slack.

She guessed she had spoiled him with so many years of managing all the household affairs without asking him for much support or help. After all these years of marriage, he was having trouble adjusting to the changes in their family dynamic. She found herself spending the weekends cooking ahead for the week like she had done when the kids were in school and her days had been about shuttling them around to their lessons and games. Part of her missed quiet afternoons with her grandchildren.

She wasn't sure she'd want to go back, though, given the opportunity. These days of training were tiring, but they were also exciting. Her studies promised an exciting future full of adventure and intrigue. She remembered well how bored she had sometimes been by her days. They'd slip by so quietly, especially after the children had all moved out and begun families of their own. She'd sit down for dinner with David and realize she couldn't think of a thing to say about her day. He wasn't going to be interested in the bargain she'd made, or her latest idea for home organization. Even the best of her days made for dull listening.

Now dinner conversation was a whole separate problem. She wasn't as interested in his stories about the men he worked with when she was full to bursting with stories that seemed much more exciting to her. She found herself just letting stories trail off mid-sentence when he didn't share her enthusiasm, and it broke her heart not to share her experiences with him. She thought, were their positions reversed, she would be excited for David and interested in his new opportunities. She was annoyed that he seemed less than thrilled about hers. It didn't seem fair.

The Director had said the training program would take at least six months, maybe longer depending on her aptitude and focus. She found it difficult to tell how she was doing. She had nothing to compare it to. She had no idea if she were on target, behind, or ahead. She just kept bringing her best effort and hoping it would be good enough. It was important to her, and becoming more important all the time.

The class that afternoon had been another strategy session. She and the other three agents in training were asked to analyze old cases and discuss the decisions the agents had made. Leading a team required some very complex thinking: balancing the safety of the team with the objectives of the mission. Agents had to make crucial decisions when the mission parameters changed, and they didn't always have the full set of information to make the best possible choice. Linda suspected it came down to an instinct, a gut feeling. She only hoped she had the instincts the Director seemed to think she did.

She found that she thought about things differently than her fellow students. The other three agents in training were young men in their later twenties. Two of them had a history of military service and the third was some kind of computer genius. The major difference she noticed was that they seemed much more capable of separating their emotions from the situation than she was. She didn't know if that was age, culture, or gender, but it was disconcerting to hear them talking about acceptable losses when those losses were human lives. She wondered if they had ever had to face a situation where they were directly responsible for harming someone. It seemed rude to ask.

Linda's own experiences still haunted her. Sometimes, when she was fighting, she felt an aggressive energy rising in herself. She had to fight it down, or risk seriously injuring one of the other trainees. She'd felt that energy before, when she'd thrown Helen Braeburn against the wall of a building and broken her bones. She knew how dangerous it was, how hard it was to stop and make a rational decision in the heat of the moment. She could still see the woman lying against the wall where she'd fallen like a discarded doll. A very realistic doll, bleeding from the mouth.

Worse was when her friends were endangered. Two of those young men had military experience. Had they been in combat? Had they seen someone on their team hurt or killed? Had they been too late to help, like Linda had? Her strength had proven useless to protect Jessica from the fiery onslaught. She wasn't quite ready to ask them yet. They were unfailingly professional in their dealings with her, but only that and nothing more. She'd overheard two of them joking about the new recruit being a "little old for this."

She'd been wounded by the remark and had shown off a bit during the PT session that afternoon. After that, the younger men had just kept a quiet, watchful distance. When they went out for a beer after class ended for the day, they didn't invite her. It was going to be hard building friendships with these men. So much of their communication seemed to happen beneath the surface, expressed by body language or posture instead of words. She was learning how to be a man on the surface, but inside, she still felt very much like a woman, a woman in a man's world who wasn't sure how to find her place.

These were the things she longed to talk to David about, if she could ever figure out how to get the conversation started. For now, though, she needed to rest. Rolling onto her side, she pulled a throw pillow against her chest and closed her eyes. There should be time to nap for a while before David came home for dinner.

It was pitch dark outside when Linda woke, still on the couch, an afghan pulled up over her shoulders. Her feet were sticking out the other end and had gotten cold. Sitting up, she rubbed her eyes, then wandered to the bathroom. She had been practicing standing to urinate, especially since she often had to do so in locker room situations where it would look odd if she sat, but, in her home, she reverted to comfort and sat down, remembering to tuck her penis downward to control the direction of the stream. She dabbed at the tip with toilet paper afterward. She still wasn't able to get used to the idea of simply shaking off the remaining drips of urine when finished. It seemed unsanitary to her.

After she washed her hands, she splashed her face with water to shake the drowsiness off. She suddenly realized that she must have slept right through David's return home. She walked into the kitchen and checked the clock on the microwave. Three o'clock in the morning. *Caray!* She hadn't prepared anything for dinner. She looked around the kitchen for signs of what David had managed for his supper and found the takeout box in the garbage. She frowned. He was eating too much pizza lately. It wasn't good for his cholesterol.

Moving quietly, she went upstairs to their bedroom. She opened the door and waited for her eyes to adjust to the darkness. David was sprawled across the bed diagonally on his stomach, one hand gripping her pillow. He looked troubled and murmured a bit in his sleep. Resisting the urge to crawl into bed and pull him against her chest for comfort, Linda pulled the door closed as gently as she could. It was only two hours until he had to get up for work. She'd let him rest. She could make something special for breakfast.

Back in the kitchen, she turned on the coffeepot and began pulling the ingredients to make *bolillos*. She hummed to herself as she kneaded the dough and set it to rise. She checked the refrigerator and saw why David had felt he needed to get takeout for dinner. The shelves were woefully empty. Apparently, David had not found the time to go to the grocery store, either, even though he wasn't on any big projects right now. There were eggs and some ham, so she could mix those up and serve them with the warm rolls. It wasn't as fancy as what she had hoped for, but maybe it would remind David of their penny-pinching days when their children were young and David was just beginning to work with Randy in the contracting business.

While she waited for the dough to rise, Linda sat down with a cup of coffee and stared out the back window at her poor, neglected garden. She wondered if she should try to set up a window garden of herbs so she would at least still have fresh cilantro and oregano. She just wasn't home enough lately to tend to the vegetable garden like she used to.

Trying not to clatter the dishes too much, Linda unloaded the dishwasher and put everything away in the cabinets. She selected the blue plates with white trim and set them on the table, along with the new coffee mugs. The coffee mugs were one of the things David appreciated about sharing his life with a man now. He had never liked the delicate teacups Linda had favored when her hands were smaller. He'd picked these up when she was still struggling to learn to operate her new body. They were heavy and sturdy. Only these two had survived from the original set of eight, but really they only needed two, one for each of them. There was another set for when the family came over.

When Linda heard the shower turn on, she put the rolls into the oven and prepared a fresh pot of coffee. She was frying the ham and eggs when she heard David come into the room. She turned to smile at him, the skillet in her hand. David didn't smile back, though his face softened when he saw the preparations she had made. He took his place at the breakfast table.

"You should have wakened me," Linda said, sliding half of the egg mixture onto each of their plates and turning to pull the rolls from the oven. She poured the coffee into the pretty red carafe one of their daughters had picked for her last Christmas and brought it to the table, then sat down to join him.

David was enjoying his meal, and, for a moment, Linda just sat and watched him eat, enjoying the quiet time with her husband. David was not a morning person, so she didn't press him to talk, though she felt there was much they needed to say to one another. This morning, she thought she'd just enjoy the peace.

SALLY ANN'S STUDENT SOARS

Sally Ann sat in the waiting area with Jessica. Her protégé was tightening her shoelaces for the fourth time. After that, she was going to re-do her ponytail and fiddle with her air tanks and all her clothes again. Sally Ann understood the other woman's nerves. She'd been there once herself.

"The rabbit goes into the hole," she said. "At least that's what Papa always told me."

Sally Ann had been trying to make her laugh, but Jessica actually jumped. She'd been that focused. The freaky thing was that when Jessica jumped, she didn't always come back down to the ground afterward. Sally Ann reached out a hand and pulled her hovering trainee to the floor.

Jessica wiped her hands down the front of her sweat suit and jogged in place. "What's taking so long?"

Sally Ann shrugged. There were a lot of things that could be delaying the start of this test. She hadn't been given the details, other than the objective. She wasn't supposed to know what her trainee was going to face, anymore than Jessica was. That part was realistic, anyway. Intel was never perfect. You went in with partial information and improvised from there. She just hoped Jessica was as flexible in her thinking as she was in her movement.

"You're going to be fine," she told Jessica. "No one ever looks up."

Agent Lester came in. "They're ready."

And just like that, Jessica's test began. The Director hadn't said so, but Sally Ann knew the test was for her, too. A test of her abilities as an instructor. Jessica was the first agent she had taken on in the training program.

The observation room was quiet, all the occupants focused on the monitors and communications devices. The Director was there, along with Lester and several other agents. Sally Ann ignored them all and stalked over to the wall of monitors to get her first good look at the task Jessica was to undertake. Sally Ann recognized the building. Warehouse C. She herself had taken out a team of trained operatives there during her job interview, a fight that still garnered her nods of respect when she walked onto the training floor.

Sally Ann glanced at the mission specs. Jessica was to drop down from a helicopter, enter the facility through a skylight, make her way to a specific room undetected by the guards, retrieve a small bundle, and escape to the roof.

"Do the other agents know who they're testing?"

The Director shook his head, and Sally Ann suppressed a whoop of delight. Jessica would have the full advantage of surprise. If the agents thought they were testing someone more ordinary, they'd be totally unprepared for the skills she brought to the table. She pulled up a chair and leaned back, affecting an air of unconcern.

The room went quiet as the helicopter flew over the building, a small, black-clad figuring suddenly falling from the underhanging skids. The figure plummeted for a few seconds, then changed trajectory, veering quickly back and forth. As she neared the rooftop, Jessica's face was visible. Sally Ann was pleased at the look of rapt concentration she saw there. Stopping inches from the rooftop, Jessica hovered for just a moment, then landed soundlessly in a crouch. She paused there, taking in her surroundings.

The Director started a timer.

As she had probably been directed, Jessica went over to the skylight and tugged on the handle to open it. It didn't budge. Sally Ann shot the Director a dirty look and he spread his hands in a helpless manner, as if he hadn't arranged for her planned entryway to be blocked. Sally Ann leaned forward, putting her feet on the floor, willing the woman to find another way. Jessica closed her eyes and stretched up on her toes, then let herself fall backward. In mid-fall, she twisted into a spin and flew across the rooftop. She made a quick circuit before taking up a position on the highest piece of the machinery.

Sally Ann spotted it at almost the same moment Jessica did. A secondary skylight. Much smaller, but standing open. Jessica flew to it, again landing soundlessly as a cat. She lowered her head into the opening. After a pause, she slithered the rest of her body in.

"Camera five," the Director said, marking something on the tablet he held in his hand.

The view on the monitors changed and a storage room was visible. The room was dark, but the camera had infrared. At first, Sally Ann couldn't see Jessica.

"Adjust the lens upward," said the Director.

There was a swoosh of movement, and then Jessica was visible, scooting across the ceiling like some kind of insect. When she arrived at the door, she lowered herself to the floor. She shook awkwardly, and Sally Ann knew she was using the cushion of air technique they'd been working on to hold herself off the floor. They watched as she tried the door handle and found it unlocked.

Sally Ann elbowed the Director when Jessica opened the door only a crack and waited, an eye to the narrow opening. "See? She's a natural at this."

They all watched with Jessica for long seconds. Twice she reached for the handle of the door, then stopped, though Sally Ann couldn't see the reason. She watched the time climbing up on the stopwatch and wondered what was considered a good completion time on this exercise. The Director's face was impassive and unreadable. Sally Ann fought the urge to bite her nails, instead stretching elaborately and cracking her neck.

Finally Jessica moved into the hall. The camera view changed again, and Sally Ann could see that there were agents just around the turn, agents Jessica wouldn't be able to see.

"What are they armed with?" she asked.

"Pink paint."

When she looked back at the monitor, she saw that Jessica had again taken up a position with height advantage. She peered around the corner and spotted the two guards. That was when Jessica took her own trainer by surprise. Sally Ann expected that her trainee would go for stealth, crawling across the ceiling silently. There was a center bar where the open double doors were meant to seal. Jessica had grabbed it and positioned herself sideways. Before Sally Ann could figure out what she had in mind, she had spun herself around it, building momentum, which she turned into a whole body kick into the head of the guard nearest her. He hit the wall with a solid smack and slid down. Jessica hadn't stopped moving. She had grabbed the weapon from the second guard and hit him on top the head with it. Both men down, she turned and ran through the room and into another hall.

The whole room gasped. "Damn," said the agent who was manning the cameras. "Jeez, Sally Ann, what are you teaching this one? That's gonna leave a mark."

Sally Ann stifled her laughter. "How long does she have?"

"Ten more minutes."

Sally Ann's laughter died. That wasn't long. Especially not if she encountered any more guards or resistance. "How much farther does she have to go?"

"She's already there."

Sally Ann stood up and starting pacing the room. She thought this whole thing might be less nerve-racking if she was the one on the inside. Watching and waiting was the worst. She covered her face with her hands, but immediately spread her fingers so she could peek through.

"She's doing great, Rogers," someone said.

Sally Ann nodded, holding her breath.

Jessica dropped from the ceiling in an office. Sally Ann missed how she'd gotten into the room, but her clothes weren't streaked with paint, so she must have made it past any remaining guards, one way or another. From a crouching position behind the desk, Jessica reached up and snagged the package from the surface. Her hand darted back up to place something on the desk in its place. Sally Ann mentally congratulated her on thinking of that, a small detail that would leave her theft undetected a little longer, if someone were to open the door and only peek in.

"Three minutes left," the Director announced.

"She's going to make it," Sally Ann said, her grin growing wide.

As they watched, their newest agent crossed to the window, opened it, climbed through, and flew off into the air.

"Yes!" Sally Ann stood and did a victory dance across the observation room, including some gyrations that earned her a low whistle from someone. "That's my girl!" She high-fived the entire room before running out the door to go and greet her student.

PROUD MARY KEEPS ON TURNING

The man who pushed the wheelchair was mostly silent. Other than admonitions to be careful of edges or warnings that he was going to change direction, he offered no conversation. Mary huddled in a corner of the chair, feeling small and frail and trying not to give in to fear. What would come would come, and she would deal with it then. She shivered. Without saying anything, the man pulled up to a box on a wall and pulled out a blanket. He tucked it around her, and, in spite of her fears, Mary felt comforted by its softness and the concern for her comfort.

"Where are we going?" she asked.

The man smiled with only his lips and shook his head. He stepped behind the chair again and resumed pushing her through the halls.

Mary watched for hints of what hospital they were in, but there was no signage anywhere. That struck her as exceedingly strange. So did some of the scenes she glimpsed as they scooted through the halls. At one point, she was sure she'd seen a person crawling up a wall. Through a doorway, she'd spotted a couple of orderlies holding down a thrashing young man who cried out in a language Mary didn't understand. When the orderly helping Mary paused to scan his ID card at a set of doors, Mary made eye contact with a woman who was sitting and watching TV. She smiled at Mary sweetly, then stuck out a forked tongue in a quick flicker.

The drugs must still be in my system, she thought, hoping it was the truth and knowing it probably wasn't. As much as she might like to pretend to the contrary, she was living in a world where mothers threw fire, soccer moms could fly, and dinosaur women saved people at the mall. That woman probably really did have a snake's tongue.

She remembered staking out Dr. Liu's house, but she had no memory at all of arriving at this hospital or of what had happened to her until she awoke in the child's room. She looked down at the pink scrub top she was wearing and wondered where her own clothes were. For that matter, her bag, her phone, and her car.

The doctor had known she was her mother's daughter and had admitted that her mother was also here. Mary coughed and grimaced at the taste in her mouth. She guessed that meant she had been knocked out chemically. Under the blanket she rubbed her arms and neck, trying to find the needle site, but couldn't feel anything. She had inherited her mother's sensitive skin, so she would probably be able to find the site later by the bruising, but for now, she had no idea where and how the drugs had entered her system. She supposed it could have been inhaled. Nitrous oxide had left her with an odd taste in her mouth when she'd had it at the dentist, but she remembered that as being more sickly sweet. Whatever this was had left her with a metallic taste in her mouth and a continued feeling of muddle-headedness.

The orderly took a corner especially swiftly, and suddenly, Mary was retching. There wasn't even time to try to communicate to the man before she had thrown up all over the blanket and onto the floor.

"I'm so sorry, miss. I must have taken the corner too fast." The man quickly removed the blanket and used it to wipe the worst of the mess in front of her on the floor, then tossed it into an orange bin alongside the wall. Another man showed up with cleaning materials, and Mary's orderly knelt and looked into her face, his expression analytical. "Did you get your shirt?"

Mary looked down and spots drifted across her vision. "I can't tell," she mumbled.

"We're nearly there," he said. Mary felt him release the brake on the chair and they were rolling again. With the dizziness affecting her vision and equilibrium, she found it difficult to hold on to any sort of landmarks or directional information. She eventually gave up and closed her eyes. She felt less nauseated if she didn't try to track where they were going.

She felt rather than saw it when they arrived in what was to be her room. The orderly called out for someone named Beth. Then Mary was asleep.

When she awoke again, she was lying in a hospital bed under a soft blue blanket. She had a feeling it had been several hours at least. She jolted awake and sat up, pulling the blanket up under her chin and swiveling her head quickly to take in her surroundings. She seemed to be in an ordinary hospital room, dimly lit by low lying fixtures near the floor that illuminated the path. There was overhead lighting, but thankfully, it wasn't turned on. Mary was grateful for it, as she began to realize she had one doozy of a headache.

The bed was rather high off the floor. The floor was covered in that white-with-colored-speckles flooring favored by so many institutions. It was ugly, so Mary guessed it must be the price that made it so popular with schools and hospitals and places like that. There was a pair of dark blue hospital slippers on the floor where her feet would go if she decided to leave the bed. Mary could tell the drugs were still somewhat active in her system from the way her stomach reacted when she looked down at the floor. She didn't think she'd try getting up just yet. What had they given her?

Or maybe it was more a matter of dosage. Mary was sensitive to medications and often needed a lesser dose that might be expected for someone her size. Ignoring her stomach's complaints, she felt around in the bed for a call button or remote or anything she might use to communicate with someone. She found nothing.

She considered calling out, but without knowing who might come, she hesitated. Instead, she stretched her body out in the bed, testing the feeling of strength in her limbs and the steadiness of her nerves. Neither was very good right now. Her hand trembled when she tried to hold it still out in front of her, and her knees and elbows felt watery. She knew that if she were to stand right now, she'd probably find herself sitting on the floor.

At least her head felt clear. Or maybe that was worse. With her brain less foggy, she could think about what was happening and imagine what might be yet to come. It was an ugly scenario every way her imagination played it. Possibility one: She'd been in an accident she couldn't remember and this was just a hospital. She didn't hold out much hope that was the truth, though. It was just wishful thinking to even give it the breath of hope. Possibility two: She'd been taken by the same people who had taken her mother. That one seemed like more than a possibility. The doctor had admitted as much, so the bigger question was: who were these people?

She didn't have much to go on to figure that one out. It wasn't like there was a seal painted on the floor giving the name of the organization. She didn't know if she was being held by the government, by terrorists, by some private group, by cultists, or by missionaries. It felt institutional to her, what with name tags and official looking scrubs, doors with key card access, and wheelchairs and hospital beds and all, but it's not like all these things weren't for sale to anyone with the money to buy them.

She thought more about the things she'd seen as she'd been wheeled through the hall. The images were the same sort she might make up for herself in a nightmare, but that didn't negate the possibility that they were real. She'd feel better if she knew what she'd been drugged with and what the possible effects on perception and memory were.

The last thing she remembered before waking in the child's room like some strange version of *Alice in Wonderland* was heading back to her car. She'd been planning to come back that night and snoop around in the ruin of Dr. Liu's home, looking for clues or leads as to what had happened to her mother. She didn't even remember being hit or captured. Whatever had happened to her must have caught her completely unaware, without even time to feel afraid.

Looking around the room again, she spotted her clothes, hung neatly on a hanger and displayed on the hook on the back of the door. They looked unsullied. Between that and her lack of bruises or other kinds of pain, Mary came to the conclusion that she had been taken without struggle or violence. She spotted her bag on a chair near the window. There was no way to tell if the contents were intact without getting up, so she decided it was time to give this whole vertical thing a go.

She pulled off the blanket, disentangling her legs. She didn't want to dump herself onto the floor because she'd gotten her limbs tangled. She felt cold as soon as she removed the blanket, so she pulled it free from the other bedding and draped it over her shoulders as a makeshift *serape*. Then she scooted forward on her butt until her hips were lined up with the gap in the bed rail. She turned and put her legs through. They dangled several inches from the floor, and Mary again doubted her ability to get down without getting hurt.

But Mary was known for her stubbornness, and she stubbornly wanted to know what was and wasn't in her bag before she had any further interactions with the staff. She pushed herself forward until she could touch the floor with her toes, then, grasping the railing on each side of her, she lowered herself onto her feet. Immediately, she felt dizzy and was glad she had kept hold of the bed. She waited and the dizziness subsided. She picked up first one foot, then the other, and slipped them into the blue slippers she'd spotted earlier. The softness and warmth of them was a comfort.

Feet ensconced in the slippers, she leaned against the bed again and contemplated the path between her and the chair by the window. There wasn't much to grab on to if she lost her balance. The few feet of floor between her and her goal seemed very long and devoid of anything she could use to aid her. Then she thought of the hospital table. Usually they were separate of the beds and on wheels. She turned to check and, sure enough, this one was of that familiar design. She tugged on it tentatively, and it rolled toward her. She transferred the grasp of her other hand to the rolling table and tried to steer it toward the window. It was hard to steer, like trying to direct the flange of a Ouija board while your girlfriends were all trying at the same time.

When she arrived at the other side of the room, she was drenched in sweat and shaking from the effort. She picked up the bag she'd gone to all the effort for and flopped into the chair, holding it against her chest. The bag felt appropriately heavy. After a beat or two of rest to try and catch her breath, Mary unfastened the old-fashioned buckle on the tan messenger bag she'd inherited from her father when he bought a nicer one. Her laptop wasn't inside, and she had a momentary panic before she remembered she hadn't been carrying it when she was taken. She had been carrying her phone, though, and was dismayed to see it was missing. All her papers were still in the folder. They appeared undisturbed, but she figured she shouldn't assume any level of privacy if her captors had her phone.

She turned her notebook to a blank page and added a new topic header: The Facility. There wasn't much to say, since she didn't know anything yet, but it made her feel better to make a place to record her thoughts. After recording how she physically felt and the one name she had learned so far, she flipped through the notebook again. She hadn't yet updated the timeline of her mom's disappearance, so she did that now, adding the information about when her car had been impounded and what the police said about it. She was sure her mother had been involved in the firefight at the college that day. What she didn't know was why her mother had gone to the college in the first place. She was sure it wasn't to sell houses. The other question was, what happened afterward? She knew she was in the right place to find out. If she could get anyone to tell her anything.

JESSICA GETS A LITTLE AIR

Jessica couldn't tell if she was being paranoid. She felt like she was being followed. Her time at the Department was making her hyper-aware of the people around her, but she could swear that the woman with the brown hair had been at the supermarket that morning and there she was again, outside the parking garage.

Perhaps the woman simply lived somewhere near Jessica and worked in the same part of downtown. Springfield was a pretty big place. She certainly didn't know all her neighbors or colleagues, let alone people in nearby neighborhoods and buildings. There was nothing particularly cagey or disturbing about this woman. She looked pretty ordinary. Forty-ish, slightly pudgy, wearing glasses that didn't really suit her face. Not exactly a portrait of a serial killer.

But she couldn't shake the feeling that this woman was watching her, paying attention to where she was going. So, when she arrived at the office building that housed the Department in downtown Springfield, she walked on past the front door. Just in case, she continued around the side of the building, then ducked into an alley and waited. When no one followed her in, she floated up to the rooftop to look down. She watched the corner where she had turned for a few minutes, but the dark-haired woman didn't show up.

She chided herself for thinking she was important enough to be followed. She was hardly an important agent yet. She was just the freaky trainee. Stepping to the edge of the roof, she peeked down into the alley. No one was there, so she tucked her T-shirt into the waistband of her yoga pants and stepped off the edge. For a moment, she just hung there like Wile E. Coyote, not yet having realized the ground had run out. Taking a deep breath, she burped into her hand several times, lowering herself to the ground. The process was jerky, but she landed softly on her feet and felt proud of herself for the smoothness of the maneuver. Her training with Sally Ann was really paying off in control and confidence. She'd done them proud in her recent test, too.

Smiling to herself, she walked back to the front of the building. She looked up and down the street, but didn't see her potential stalker anywhere. Deciding the woman had probably just been waiting for the bus, Jessica entered the building.

The front lobby of the Department seemed to be a bank. In fact, it actually was a bank. If someone came in off the street and wanted to take out a car loan or open an account, they could do that. Jessica walked to the left side of the lobby and ran her brand new ID card over the scanner next to the "Employees Only" sign. A small buzzing sound emitted from the box, and then she was able to turn the doorknob of the discreet black door and step through. From the lobby, it looked like this door led to the area behind the counter.

But instead, the doorway led to a stairwell going down. A few flights down was the real entrance to the Department. The real lobby wasn't as well lit and attractive as the bank lobby. It was a little dingy and sad-looking, but Jessica still felt excited every time she walked through it. She smiled at the man at the security desk who took her ID card and scanned it, then ushered her through.

Jessica had never considered anything like this line of work in her life. If you'd asked her what she was going to do when she was a child, she would have said she would be a competitive gymnast, then would teach gymnastics when she got too old. A knee injury when she was a teenager had taken that dream. She could still have taught gymnastics, but with no national titles to her name, she would have had an uphill climb to build a name and get any serious students. Besides, once she'd gotten married, she hadn't needed a career plan.

After she married Nathan, she turned her focus to the duties of a corporate wife. She held dinner parties, attended benefits, and networked with the people who could benefit her husband's career. She'd been pretty good at it, too. Even having children hadn't slowed her down much. She had plenty of daytime to spend with her boys before the evenings were given over to events. At least, she had until she got sick.

She had gone to her gynecologist mostly because she was concerned for her sex life. She'd been having mild pelvic pain for a few weeks, and Nathan was getting tired of getting the brush-off. She thought she might have an infection of some kind. She expected a round of antibiotics at worst. Certainly, she never even considered that it might be something serious.

At the checkup, after she admitted to also having bloating and appetite issues, the doctor had ordered screenings. She'd been fortunate that the cancer was identified quickly, but it had changed everything. It had changed her. It was those changes and not the changes of early menopause and superpowers that had ended her marriage. When her life was at risk, she looked around and saw it as a sad and shallow thing. Even when recovered, she could never recover her interest in and devotion to the surface of things. She wanted something deeper.

So, one door closed. Jessica was giddy over the doors that were opening. Working for the Department promised an interesting life, to say the least. The cases she had been studying as part of her training were half *Twilight Zone* and half *X-Files*. Even given her own history, she had trouble believing some of the things the Department had dealt with in its history. It was fascinating stuff. And now, she was going to be a part of it.

At first, she'd been convinced that the Department had only taken her because of Leonel, but the deeper she got into her training, the more possibilities she saw for her skill set. As Sally Ann said, "No one ever looks up." It was true, too. So long as she was quiet, Jessica could move across ceilings over the heads of people unseen. In a recent practice session, she'd managed to defeat a security system based on pressure in the floor. She just never touched down.

With the new air pack Walter and his team had developed for her, the world seemed full of new possibilities. Not the least of which was Walter himself. He had asked her to lunch today. Just her. No group of coworkers this time. She didn't want to let her hopes soar too high, but it was wonderful to flirt with someone again. And, even better, she didn't have to try and hide her work or her special talents from Walter. He already knew! He even already knew about her cancer survival and her burn surgeries. If all of that hadn't scared him away, maybe they had a chance. She hoped so.

After her training session, Jessica spent a little extra time in the locker room. She'd brought a date outfit today, something new and bright. Something that didn't say "mom" or "athlete." At least she hoped it didn't. She turned around again in front of the mirror, glad the locker room was deserted and no one was watching her preen like a teenage girl. The simple turquoise dress flattered her. She thought the color was nice against her pink-pale skin tone. The neckline dipped just enough to be flirtatious without being overtly sexy, and gauzy sleeves covered her arms. She still felt self-conscious about her burn scars, even after all these months. It was easier to feel attractive when she knew no one would be staring at her arm and wondering what had happened to her.

For her training sessions, Jessica always pulled her hair back into a ponytail, so for her lunch date, she decided to wear her hair loose. She'd recently had it lightened to something more like what her color had been pre-cancer, and the honey-blonde locks were cooperating nicely, resting in even waves on her shoulders. She pulled her phone out of her purse and checked the time. Eleven forty-five. Would she look too eager if she went ahead to the lab now? She had promised to meet him there at noon. It was only a three minute walk from the gym, even if she dawdled.

She decided to go anyway. He'd probably still be working and wouldn't even notice her at first. She could watch him work. And, if he thought her desperate, well, then there would only be the one lunch. She'd order dessert.

As she worked her way to the lab where Walter had said he'd meet her, she fought down a new wave of nerves. Sally Ann had assured her that dating Walter would be allowed. They didn't work together, at least not directly, and neither of them was likely to ever be asked to supervise the other. Sally Ann had also advised that she just walk up and ask him out to lunch. In all her dating history, which she now realized was pretty limited, consisting of only Nathan and a steady high school boyfriend, she had never been the pursuer. Even flirtations that hadn't ended up in relationships had started with the men taking notice of her. She wouldn't have known how to start that conversation. Luckily, she hadn't had to. He'd asked her.

It'd been very sweet. She'd been stowing her air pack into its case after a test run of some improvements. His part of the training was finished, but he lingered there, kind of shifting from foot to foot while she gathered her things and zipped them into the case. When she'd stood up, she was standing too close to him. He had drifted into her personal space while he waited for her. She had backed up quickly, catching her foot in the pack's strap, and tripped.

He caught her by the forearms and said, "I was hoping you might fall for me, but that's not what I had in mind."

She'd laughed with him. The moment stretched and became awkward as their laughter died and neither of them said anything else. Walter seemed to realize he was still holding her arm and let go abruptly. Then he just sort of blurted out the lunch invitation.

"Come to lunch with me on Friday."

She'd said that sounded like a lovely idea, and they'd parted ways. She'd turned to watch him walk away and caught him turning to watch her walk away. They'd laughed again. She'd nearly floated back to the locker room—literally!

She liked him. It had been entirely too long since she'd felt like this. And that made her nervous. She didn't know how far to trust her own feelings.

Lost in her mental meanderings, she didn't realize she had walked right past Walter's lab. She was standing at the end of a darkened hallway facing an unlabeled door. She didn't remember ever seeing this part of the Department before. She'd paid really close attention on her tour, too, and carefully learned where all the essential parts of the complex were, not wanting to look like she didn't know what she was doing any more than was necessary.

She examined the alcove looking for a clue as to what these rooms might be used for. She leaned against the glass and used her hand to try to block out glare and look inside, but she couldn't see anything. She turned and retraced her steps to find Walter's lab. She had just turned the corner when she heard a door open. She turned around in time to see the Director moving down the hall, talking in low, but animated tones with a woman wearing scrubs. They didn't notice her, so she didn't say anything. She was sure she heard the woman say something about how keeping that woman sedated wasn't keeping her from setting fires.

She almost turned and followed them, wanting to ask if they were talking about Helen. Leonel had told her the Department had her in custody. It hadn't occurred to her that she might be right there in the same building where she and Leonel worked.

But just then, the tiny chime of the calendar reminder on her phone went off, and she realized she wasn't going to be early to meet Walter after all. She hurried back down the hall, pushing aside contemplation of the mysterious room and its possible contents for the more pleasing contemplation of a lunch date.

PATRICIA FINDS THE PRICE IS WRONG

Patricia still didn't know what to think. Talking to Daniel Price had left her just as confused and lost as she had been when she awoke strapped to the gurney a few hours earlier. Now she was alone with Cindy, but couldn't ask her anything. She had proven just as un-wakeable as Price had claimed. Despite all the tapping and banging Patricia had tried, Cindy hadn't as much as fluttered her eyelids. Instead she just lay there, bathed in that eerie yellow light.

Price hadn't been very forthcoming about what this treatment was that he was giving his daughter, but he had implied it was the only thing keeping her from regressing deeper into youth. Patricia leaned close again and peered into the glass at her friend's resting face. It was strange how she both did and didn't look like Patricia's friend of forty years. Even in sleep, there was a stubborn set to her jaw that Patricia knew well, but the cheeks were even smoother and more rounded than they had been when they met in college all those years ago. It was as if Cindy had somehow had a daughter she'd kept secret for the past decade or so and Patricia was watching her now. There wasn't much that could be gleaned in the way of hints by looking at her through the glass. She was dressed simply in a gray T-shirt. She was wearing a necklace—a black string holding a small bag. Could that be the emeralds she'd stolen back from Jessica all those months ago?

Frustrated, Patricia stood and paced the small room, thinking and fingering the frayed edge of her tank top. The bottom hem had torn when she had transformed, and Patricia pulled absently at the dangling thread fragments. She wished more than anything that she could talk to Leonel and Jessica. Those two got on her nerves sometimes, and she couldn't understand why they would sign their lives over to a government agency, but, still, there was no one she trusted more.

Jessica, for all her apparent weakness, might be the strongest of them all. She was fierce in her loyalties and decisive. Patricia could use some of that decisiveness just now. Talking with Daniel Price had left her feeling confused and conflicted, and uncharacteristically hesitant to act.

Leonel was such a good reader of people. Maybe he could have gotten a clear take on what kind of person Mr. Price really was. Patricia couldn't tell how much stock to put in his stories. If he could be believed, this metal box and the strange yellow radiation it bathed Cindy in were the only things keeping her stable. She had to stay inside, or she would revert further into childhood and eventually into infancy. He was saving her.

And maybe he really was. Maybe if she opened this box and exposed Cindy to the air in the medical theater, she would die, or turn into an infant. Or maybe, just as likely in Patricia's mind, that was a crock of shit and Cindy was being kept in this box against her will because it suited Price's ends. Whether or not he was really Cindy's father, somehow living in someone else's skin, Price was definitely after something. She wished she understood what. Clearly, he thought Cindy could help him with his neuro-muscular problem, but then why was she here? She was no scientist. Had Cindy really sent for her? Or was she here as some kind of hostage to keep Cindy cooperating?

He had promised her the opportunity to speak to Cindy, after the treatment. In the meantime, he had recommended that she rest, too. The gurney she'd broken had been rolled away and the glass cleaned up. A sort of sofa had been moved into the room. Patricia hesitated to sleep, knowing her body would revert to its natural, vulnerable form when she did, but she also knew depriving herself of rest was simply making her vulnerable in other ways. She wished she could just discuss the whole situation with Cindy. Then she would know what to think and what to do.

That probably wasn't true, either, though. Cindy had fooled her well enough last spring. She had done things Patricia would've sworn were beyond the scope of imagining. She could no longer be sure she and Cindy shared any kind of moral compass at all. For all she knew, Cindy really had sent Daniel Price to kidnap her. Though why Cindy would want her here was beyond her understanding. Maybe they were working together on more than just Cindy's cure.

At the end of hours of circuitous conversation with Daniel Price, Patricia still didn't have the answer to most of the basic questions she had set out to ask. She didn't know where she was. She didn't know how she'd been brought there or how long she'd been there. She didn't know what, precisely, the man—if you could call him that—wanted from her. It was all hints and veiled threats. He wanted her help somehow, but he hadn't been specific about what he wanted from her.

His tale had been bizarre, the stuff of cheesy science fiction movies on late night television. But she found she believed him. She did know that the man was either insane or something that couldn't quite be classified as human anymore. Were you still a man if your brain had been moved from body to body six times, while your own body rotted away in a grave somewhere? Or did that make him some kind of creature? Some kind of zombie, perhaps? What was the cost to a person's humanity, living like that?

Talking to the man was an exercise in futility. He was about as direct as an earthworm meandering through the compost. If he had a trajectory in mind, she couldn't see it. He didn't refuse to answer anything, but neither did he answer anything neatly or directly. He would be an excellent politician. Patricia had found him nearly impossible to pin down.

So now she sat looking down at her friend, who was apparently still sleeping. She looked so innocent, as if she were truly a child instead of a retiree housed in a youthful shell. What had Cindy been trying to convey with all that tapping just before Daniel Price had announced himself? Her teary face could've meant so many things. She might have been apologizing for getting Patricia mixed up in this. She might have been frightened and trying to beg for some kind of help. She could have been relieved to see her old friend and hopeful of help. She could have been simply manipulating Patricia's sympathies yet again.

Patricia examined the case, looking for the mechanism that opened it. There was a kind of dial just below the glassed-in part, but it didn't have any recognizable markings. Just shapes. Patricia had no idea what they were meant to indicate or even whether that was the lock or some kind of setting for the device itself. The case was connected to a wall unit through some large, silver tubing, lined with a kind of insulation, the same sort of poofy, foil-lined stuff you saw in pictures of NASA equipment on the moon. The whole thing hummed at a low, rattling pitch that made Patricia's eardrums ache faintly. It made her think of a fifties-era deep freeze.

At last the low, thrumming noise the machine had been making ceased. Patricia stood. The machine shuddered, like a car with a bad idle. Almost without thinking, Patricia raised a light layer of scales on her flesh. She eyed the door, which stayed closed. Moving quickly, she shoved the cot and two chairs in front of the door. The makeshift barrier wouldn't stop someone from entering, but it would slow them down and give her a moment to react.

The shuddering slowed, with a steady thud like a load of laundry gone out of balance. There was a *whoosh* and a *click*, and the eerie yellow light faded, leaving the machine dark and silent. Patricia approached it, still having no idea how to open the thing. She peered inside, but with the light gone, she couldn't even make out Cindy's face. The darkness reflected her own face back at her, green and alien, yellow eyes almost seeming to glow.

Patricia tried the handle again. This time, there was some give. The door was heavy. Patricia concentrated and felt her body grow dense and thick. She still didn't understand how that worked, but that didn't stop her from using it to her advantage. Leveraging her now extremely heavy body against the machine, she hooked her hands into the handle and leaned back to tug the lid open. She scrambled around the machine to see inside.

Cindy still appeared to be asleep. Watching carefully, Patricia could see her chest rise and fall. Just knowing she hadn't killed Cindy by opening the lid brought Patricia's heart back down out of her throat and into her chest, where it beat like a jackhammer. Eying the door one last time, and finding her furniture barrier undisturbed, Patricia reached into the tank, automatically retracting her talons and scales so she could grab Cindy's narrow shoulders with her hands.

She shook her gently at first, then less gently, hissing, "Wake up, damn it. Cindy! I need to talk to you!"

Cindy awoke with a gasp and sat up so quickly that she nearly bashed into Patricia's face. Patricia backed up, overbalanced, and landed on the floor.

"Patricia!" Cindy's voice sounded raspy and raw. "What are you doing here? You've got to get out!"

"You didn't bring me here? What about the note?"

"I didn't write any note."

Patricia stared into the face of her once-best friend for a long moment. Cindy was sweaty, and her lank hair was plastered to her forehead and cheek. Her face, which had always been heart-shaped, was positively elfin in her adolescent body. Patricia was oddly touched by the angry red pimple on her chin. She shook it off, remembering.

"What's going on here?"

"Patricia, there's no time to discuss this. He's using you to get to me, and to Jessica, and you've got to get out of here!"

Patricia nodded and sprang up, decision made. She wasn't going to sit here any longer waiting for something to happen. It was time she took things into her own claws. She stood, flexing her scales into full form. Her nails, which had been retracted, sprang into talons. Narrowing her eyes, she looked around the room, letting her powerful night vision focus on the shadowy regions of the room. It didn't take long to locate the three cameras. The movement of their lenses as they tracked her around gave them away. Patricia picked up one of the chairs and used it to smash them.

She half expected an alarm to go off or for soldiers to arrive, but the room remained dark and quiet. "Come with me," she said, extending a claw to Cindy.

Cindy shook her head, large silent tears rolling down her cheeks. "I have to stay. This is all that's keeping me stable."

Patricia shoved the furniture aside. She went to the control panel beside the door and traced the edge with the index talon of her right hand, opening it like a can of sardines. Then she grabbed the wires within and tugged them out. When she tried the handle again, it didn't resist. She peered out at the empty hallway.

"I'll be back for you," Patricia promised, and took off at a run.

She didn't really have any idea where to go from there, so she turned right. She peered in door after door as she zigzagged down the hall and saw lab after lab that she couldn't really make anything out. What kind of villain didn't even have some goons for her to beat up?

Eventually she made it to an unmarked door at the end of the hall-way. She pushed it open and found herself in an empty lobby. There were a few scattered pieces of beat up lounge furniture and a high counter that might once have served as an information desk, but there was no one there. Something about it made Patricia feel nostalgic. It reminded her of the lobby of the business building at her alma mater. Apparently, this college had failed in the seventies.

The silence thrummed against her ears. It was eerie. There wasn't even any Muzak to cover the sounds of her footsteps as she stalked across the dusty tile, down the three stairs, and out the front door.

There, outside the building, she found three men together smoking cigarettes. From their pseudo-military uniforms, she took them for the security force. Patricia recognized them as the same men who had brought in furniture for her talk with Price or Lorre or whoever he was. She wondered just how skeleton the crew really was here. Spotting her, one of the men dropped his cigarette and pulled his sidearm.

He held it out at her, his hand shaking. The other two men fell back behind him, peeking out from behind each of his shoulders. The shortest of the three whipped his head around like he thought he might spot some help.

Flexing to pull out her spikes to full intimidation length, Patricia moved toward the trio.

"Don't come any closer!" yelled the one with the handgun.

"Why shouldn't I?" Patricia growled.

"Because I have Cindy." The voice came from the stairs behind her. It was Mr. Price. "And there's no place for you to go."

"Why should I care that you have Cindy? She did this to me!" Patricia was surprised by the wave of rage that overtook her, but more surprised by the tears that sprang to her eyes. She whirled on her captor and host. "It's time for some answers, Mr. Price. I've had enough waiting."

"No! Don't shoot, you idiot!" Mr. Price, moving surprisingly quickly, jumped over the railing and into the comparative safety of the bushes next to the stairwell, out of the direct line of fire. Patricia barely had time to register what was going on behind her, when she felt the distinct impacts she now recognized all too well as handgun fire making contact with her bulletproof scales. The shooter, one of the guards, was of the school of thought that if one bullet doesn't do it, fire more, because Patricia felt several more impacts, then heard the hollow clicking sound as he pulled the trigger uselessly.

She turned around. The remaining security guard was staring in horror at the worthless gun in his hand. His two compatriots must have fled the scene. The man dropped to his knees either because he planned to beg for mercy or because his knees would no longer hold him. Had Price told these men nothing of her? Or was it that her captor hadn't known bullets were useless against her? What had Cindy told him, exactly?

"I need a car," Patricia growled at the guard who was now trying not to cry.

"You can take mine," he said, disconnecting a key ring from his hip and throwing it at her feet. "It's the Mazda in the garage. Just don't hurt me."

Patricia bent and hooked the keys over one of her talons. "Thank you," she said. She looked for the garage the man had indicated, and identified a likely structure to the left. She didn't know where she was, but she'd just pick a direction and start driving. All roads lead somewhere eventually.

When she turned, Daniel Price was suddenly standing in front of her again. He had his hands on his hips and was looking at her sternly. Patricia snorted derisively. "I'm afraid I can't just let you leave, Patricia," he said, his voice heavy with disappointment, like a father in a fifties sit-com.

"Just try and stop me," she said.

He opened one of his hands and spread it flat in front of his mouth, like he was about to blow her a kiss. Then, he blew a fistful of pink sand into her face. Patricia hit the ground like a stone gargoyle, cursing her own stupidity.

LINDA'S OBSTACLES

"Mami? Are you even listening?" Lupita sounded annoyed.

Linda shook her head. "I'm sorry, *m'ija.* What were you saying?"

Lupita began her story again, her tone exasperated. Linda really tried to focus, but it was hard. She was tired and frustrated after the briefing that afternoon proved there was nothing to reveal. Patricia had been gone several days now, and Linda was losing patience. The Department had so many resources, and still they had not figured out where Patricia had been taken, let alone developed a plan for her rescue. Linda felt helpless and feeling helpless made her feel angry. More than anything, she wanted to punch something.

She forced her attention back to the conversation with her daughter in time to understand Lupita was frustrated with her new boss, who seemed to regard her as just a pretty face and to underestimate her skill as a paralegal. Lupita had worked hard to earn that certificate, completing it just two years after the birth of her twin daughters. Linda had been so proud of her, and had readily offered herself as babysitter a few hours each day so her daughter could pursue her education.

As soon as the girls had been old enough for preschool, Lupita had landed a job at a small firm specializing in immigration cases and had been working there for two years. She knew she had been hired for her Spanish language skills as much as for her certificate, but her old boss had recognized her potential and encouraged her to pursue further education. Lupita wanted to be a lawyer in her own right, and Linda knew she could do it. She had her father's work ethic and her mother's determination.

But Mr. Gobert had retired and been replaced by a much younger person. The new boss seemed to regard Lupita as little more than a secretary. Linda knew how frustrating it was to be underestimated. She remembered getting talked down to a lot when she worked as a teacher's aide. Several of the teachers had assumed she was a volunteer and not an employee. Others thought she didn't speak English or hadn't completed high school. She had. She had even started college, though she'd had to drop out to see to her mother when her health began to fail. She tried to comfort her daughter.

"He will learn to see your worth. Give him time."

"Him? See? You weren't listening! My new boss is a woman, Mami."

Linda blushed. "I'm sorry, Lupita."

But Lupita was already standing and reached out to gather her purse and sweater. "You know what? Papi is right. Your new job is taking all your focus. You don't have time for us anymore!" She turned and flounced out of the restaurant, floral skirt spinning around her knees.

The other customers in the coffee shop turned to stare. Several of the women at surrounding tables glared at her, and Linda knew they were misreading the situation, but she had no idea what to do about it.

"He's a little old for her, isn't he?" an older woman whispered, not very quietly, to her friend.

Linda sighed, stood, and pulled her wallet out of her back pocket to take out some cash to pay for the unfinished pastries and coffee. She still thought a back pocket was a ridiculous and uncomfortable place to carry your wallet, but it was what men did. She missed the pretty pocketbooks she used to carry. She left the café without a backward glance, but still felt as if the disapproval of the entire establishment was being lasered into her back as she walked away. Her cheeks burned with humiliation.

Lupita was right, in a way, but Linda still felt more than a little resentful about the demands being placed on her. True, she wasn't paying as much attention to those she loved as she once had, but her days were fuller now, and her daughters were capable, young women who didn't need her interfering in their lives. Now that her family didn't need her as much, she relished the freedom, the chance to do something with her life. Her work with the Department filled a hole she hadn't even known she had, and no one in her family seemed to understand that. She fumed as she walked the few blocks back toward the building. She still had nearly an hour before her afternoon session was scheduled to begin, so she decided to take the long way around and walk off the dark cloud hanging around her if she could.

It was embarrassing to realize David had talked to their daughter about how he felt more than he had talked to his own wife. He and Lupita had always been close, and Linda had always been pleased by that, but some things should stay between a husband and wife. Or at least shouldn't be taken up with the children. Even though the children were now grown, there was no need to put them in the middle of any squabbles their parents might be having. She didn't like hearing about his unhappiness secondhand, or the idea that he was afraid to talk to her about it directly.

She and David had been through conflict before. David had once taken a job that kept him away from their home and family for four months without even the opportunity for a visit. She hadn't liked it, but she had gotten through. They'd always been there for each other, or, at least, she'd always been there for him. He'd never had to be the one to make the sacrifices, up till now. It was hard to believe that, with all they had been through—raising their daughters together, job stress, making a home, burying their parents, even an unexpected change in gender—her career would be the one they had the most trouble overcoming.

She wasn't sure what to do about it. The fact was, she loved her work at the Department. She had already learned so much and felt so full of hope about how she'd be able to help others. She felt important, appreciated, needed. The Director shared her enthusiasm, pushing her to consider taking on leadership roles, praising her strategic planning.

Just the day before, Mike, her trainer, had said they were thinking of sending her out on a mission soon, in a supporting role, to get her feet wet. Even without knowing the details, that was exciting. Linda certainly didn't want to pass up these opportunities. She also didn't want to be made to feel guilty about putting herself first for the first time in her life. She had never asked for much, and, now that she wanted something for herself, she resented the resistance she was meeting. She didn't like the way these bitter thoughts tasted. They mixed poorly with the argument with her daughter and the coffee shop's offerings.

Linda rubbed her stomach as she walked. She was so distracted that she didn't notice the small woman dressed all in brown until they had nearly run into each other. The woman jumped and almost fell, and Linda instinctively reached out a hand to catch her by the elbow and help keep her on her feet.

"I'm so sorry," she stammered. "Are you all right?"

The woman nodded and Linda let go of her elbow, realizing she was holding it up at an awkward angle. They stood there for a moment, looking at each other. The woman's eyes were bloodshot and her cheeks ruddy as if she had been crying, and Linda wished she could think of a way to offer her solace. But they were strangers. The most polite thing to do would be to pretend she hadn't noticed. Smiling and shrugging in the way of an additional apology, Linda turned and continued her walk down the street.

A few steps along her path, she turned and looked back. The woman was still standing there, watching her. Her entire body had gone rigid and her fists were clenched at her sides. Linda wondered what she could possibly have done that was so offensive to this woman. She was sure she had controlled her strength and had not hurt her. She hesitated, half turning, trying to decide if she should go back and speak with her again.

The woman seemed to realize what was happening. She put her hands up on her cheeks, covering most of her face, and turned and briskly walked away. Linda was sure she was crying again. The whole encounter left her feeling disconcerted in ways she couldn't explain. Linda barely noticed the rest of her walk back to the offices under the bank. In fact, she carded herself in and made it to the security desk in a complete fog; the agent on duty had to call her back to get her to submit to security protocols.

She apologized to the agent, more profusely than was probably necessary. The agent nodded her head curtly and waved Linda on her way. Luckily, the next part of Linda's day was combat training. She hoped it would be more physical than theoretical today and would let her shake her feeling of vague unease and dissatisfaction.

"Alvarez! Focus!" Mike Lester yelled at her again, as she failed for the third time to pass through the obstacle course quietly enough for him. Linda gritted her teeth and moved back to the starting point. The other agents had been sent to the showers ten minutes ago. But Mike wasn't satisfied with her performance yet. Honestly, neither was she. She knew she could do better.

Lester walked to her side. "Here," he said, handing her the device he used to track the progress of trainees through the obstacle course. "Watch me."

Lester ducked into the tunnel. Linda moved up onto the observation platform, which afforded her a top-down view of the course. It was amazing, seeing it like that. The room was a mass of obstacles—pipes, boxes. As Linda knew from trying to traverse it, the room was a changing landscape, too, with shifts in light and surface texture. Mike crouched at the entrance, waiting for the starting cue. Linda tapped the light on the pad that provided it.

To her surprise, Mike didn't immediately move. Instead, he sat still for several seconds. His head swiveled, indicating he was scoping out the entire scene. When he began to move, though, he did so quickly and surely. He edged through the rooms, sticking to the shadows or moving high or low, where he was less likely to be spotted by anyone watching. Sure enough, Mike avoided setting off a single sensor. He exited the other end and bounded over to Linda, a smile of triumph on his face.

"That was amazing, Mike!" Linda didn't have to feign enthusiasm. She really had been impressed.

"That's what I want to see you do," he said, clasping her shoulder.

Linda shook her head. "I don't know if I can."

"Of course you can," he said. "Tell me what you saw, watching me. What do I do that you don't?"

Linda didn't have to think long. She knew the slow observation at the beginning was key. "I was worried about running out of time, and my speed made me clumsy. I didn't spot things I should have and set off all the alarms. You moved more slowly." She gestured at the time indicated on the observation screen. "Nearly double my time, but you made it past every sensor."

Mike shook his head vigorously. "That's it exactly." He took the pad from Linda and tapped a few controls, changing the arrangement of the room and the sensors. "Now, get in there and show me what you learned."

Linda trotted back to the entrance and took up her starting position. She wasn't going to let anything get in her way.

THE DIRECTOR WILL SEE YOU
NOW, MARY

Mary awoke, still in the chair, some time later. She didn't think much time had passed. The quality of light was the same. She turned to look out the window; when she turned back she came face-to-face with a hard-faced woman with iron-gray, perfectly coiffed hair and an amazing sleek suit. The woman smiled.

"The Director would like to see you," she said, standing. She stood, pulling down her black skirt, and crossed to the door of the room. "I'll be back to get you in fifteen minutes. Please don't keep him waiting."

Then the woman was gone and Mary was staring at the door. She had no idea who the Director might be, but she knew she wouldn't learn anything sitting here in her room. She stood, happy to note that she no longer felt dizzy or fuzzy-headed. The drugs must have finally moved through her system. She also noticed that she urgently needed to urinate. She hurried to the bathroom on the other side of the bed.

Having taken care of those needs, she went to the sink and washed her face. The soap provided on the small stand beside the sink was a nice one that smelled of lilacs. She was pleasantly surprised, as hospitals weren't known for having small niceties like that. The towel also was of higher quality than she expected. It was fluffy and looked brand new.

Moving quickly, she retrieved her clothes from the hook and exchanged the borrowed scrubs for her own outfit. She'd come straight from work to Dr. Liu's house, so she'd been wearing black pants and a plain black T-shirt as was required of all the staff. She pulled on the rainbow colored hoodie jacket and zipped it up. The jacket had been a gift from an ex-boyfriend who had bought it for her in Nepal, or so he said. She had her doubts about the jacket's origin, but she loved it all the same. Putting it on made her feel more like herself.

She was tying her boots when the woman returned. She seemed pleased that Mary was ready.

"Excellent," she said, smiling again. The smile didn't feel genuine, but Mary still recognized the friendly gesture. The woman didn't have to make that effort to set her at ease, but she did. Mary tried to see it as a hopeful sign of what was to come.

"Where are we going?" she asked, standing and pulling her messenger bag across her shoulder.

The woman shook her head and indicated that Mary should leave her bag on the hook. She didn't like it, but she obeyed.

When the bag was in place, the woman answered. "The Atrium. The Director thought you might like a proper lunch."

Lunch? That meant it was at least a full day since she'd been taken. Her stomach rumbled at the thought, and she realized she must have missed at least two meals.

"Thank you," she said and followed the woman into the hall.

There was a very narrow golf cart in the hallway, just one driver's seat with a passenger seat behind. The woman gestured to the white upholstered chair, and Mary climbed in. As soon as she was seated, a belt automatically slid across her lap and secured her in position. The woman stepped into the driver's seat and pushed a button on the dashboard. The cart began to move. It was completely silent. Mary thought it was pretty amazing and wondered again about where she was. If a bubble had only slid over their heads before they started moving, she'd have thought she was in Disney's Tomorrowland.

She tried to watch for hints as to their location as they moved through the halls, but the vehicle was moving quickly, and most of what she saw was simply a blur of movement. At least this time the movement didn't make her nauseated. In what felt like very little time, the vehicle came to a stop. The belt automatically slid back into its holster above Mary's shoulder, and Mary stepped out.

They were standing in front of what looked like a tavern restaurant. Mary's guide or warden or whatever she was indicated she should enter, and she did. She stopped a step or two into the room and stood looking around. The place was decorated in golds and deep reds. She'd been in a few taverns during her semester in Oxford that looked like this place. There were tall, plush booths, a dart board on one wall, and a fountain in the corner. She liked the place instantly.

But there was no one in it.

Mary turned around to ask if there was a back room or something and found she was alone. When she turned around again, there was a handsome young man seated at table just in front of her. It was like he had simply appeared in the few seconds she had spent looking the other direction.

She jumped, and yelled, "Fuck."

The man spoke. "I'm sorry I startled you."

Mary doubted that. She got the distinct impression he had actually enjoyed startling her. It was something in the corners of his mouth. She was sure there was suppressed amusement there. Mary bristled. She didn't like to be the butt of anyone's joke.

"Please, have a seat." He laid a menu on the table in the place opposite his. "They make a very nice fish and chips here that reminds me of my semester at Oxford."

Mary took the seat, eyeballing the man suspiciously. She'd been thinking of Oxford herself not five minutes earlier. It was like he was spying on her thought process somehow. She decided to try being friendly, though. She heard her mother's voice echoing in her head. *More flies with honey, babe.* It wasn't like her semester in Oxford was any kind of secret.

"I had a semester in Oxford as well. What did you study?" She picked up the pint glass full of ice water and downed half of it.

The man refilled her glass from the pitcher that had been left on the table. "Philosophy," he answered.

Mary laughed. "Even less useful than my Victorian literature," she said.

"Perhaps the value of our studies remains to be seen."

"Well, I did enjoy British men," she said, raising her glass. "To Oxford."

The man clicked glasses with her, took a sip, and sat the glass down. "Do you know what you'd like to eat?"

"Do they do Yorkshire pudding with roast beef?"

"For me, they will." He shuffled the menus off to the side, as if the matter were settled, though no one had appeared to take their order.

"Can we get a pint as well?" she asked.

"Of course." He stood and stepped behind the bar. She followed and watched, leaning against the bar, while he grabbed a glass, held it at a perfect forty-five degree angle close to the spigot, and drew the stout. He let the beer settle into the glass before topping it off. She was impressed. He repeated the procedure, then picked up the two glasses and gestured to the table. "Looks like our food is here."

Mary turned and saw that he was correct. "Now, that's getting creepy. Invisible servants? What is this? *La Belle et la Bête?*"

The man smiled broadly, which had the effect of making him look about twelve years old. "I love that movie."

Mary didn't know what she had expected this meeting to be like, but this certainly wasn't it. She began to think the man was toying with her, and the thought annoyed her. "So, who are you? Why did your people kidnap me? Surely you could have just invited me to lunch if that was what you wanted."

"They call me the Director," he said solemnly, ignoring her other questions.

Mary considered. "The Director? Like, what, Cecil B. DeMille?"

"I'll have to get a chair and a megaphone," he said, smiling again. He picked up his knife and fork and gestured that she should do the same. Mary complied. The food smelled wonderful, and she was way beyond hungry. She groaned after the first bite, then blushed that she'd let her pleasure be so obvious.

"Don't be embarrassed," he said. "It has been more than a day since you've had anything to eat. And this is especially wonderful. They've outdone themselves today."

For a few moments, the only sounds were of the silverware working and the two of them eating. Mary didn't know what to make of the Director. She tried to watch him as he ate, without being completely obvious. He looked all of twenty-five years old. She doubted he even had to shave daily. His cheeks were so smooth and ruddy, like a little boy in a Dickens story. There was no particular feature that called her attention. His hair was brown; his eyes were light brown; his nose was nicely shaped; his jawline strong without going over into chiseled. The overall effect was quite nice.

He didn't seem to be returning her scrutiny. His attention was on his food. Mary knew that trick. It was all about timing your glances for when the other person was looking away. You could see a lot in those moments. The Director, for instance, had calculating eyes. His smile seemed open, but it also seemed practiced. When his face went slack, you could see the hardness beneath. Mary felt certain he saw her and everyone else in terms of usefulness. The question was what he thought she might be useful for. That and what, exactly, he was the "director" of.

Her plate clean, Mary made a show of wiping her mouth on the fine white napkin. She downed the remainder of her pint and then leaned back in her chair, letting her arms slip over the back to stretch her torso long and push her breasts out prominently. She cocked her head at the man, then leaned forward like they might arm wrestle. "I appreciate the lunch, but what I really want is to know what you've done with my mother."

He pushed his own plate back, the meal only partially eaten. "I thought you might."

He stood and moved toward the door. The woman was there again, a tablet in her hand. She held the computer out to the Director, who flicked a few things on the screen, then rested a hand on the woman's shoulder companionably. He missed the hero worship on his assistant's face when she looked up at him, but Mary saw it.

"I'll have to take a quick meeting," he said, crossing to her side. He took her elbow as if escorting her into a dance and walked with her to the door. "It was a pleasure to meet you. My assistant will take you to your mother's chamber. I'll meet you there as soon as I can. We have a lot to talk about."

SALLY ANN AND HOW WAR CHANGES A MAN

"**M**s. Lee?"

The woman who answered the door probably wasn't all that tall, but she had to be a good six inches taller than Sally Ann. She moved stiffly in a way that suggested a lower back injury, but was in good shape for a woman approaching seventy years. Her hair was completely white, except for a streak of iron gray that ran along one side of her head, and was pulled back with a beaded barrette that looked child-made. She was still an attractive woman, and Sally Ann was willing to bet she had been quite stunning in a Doris Day sort of way when she was young.

"You must be Ms. Rogers."

The woman's handshake was strong and her gaze forthright. Sally Ann found she liked her already, not least for her accent with shades of home in it.

"Yes, ma'am."

"Please come in. I've got some ice tea made. We can talk on the patio."

Sally Ann readily accepted the tea. It was a hot day. She was pleasantly surprised to find that it was sweet tea. You just didn't often encounter sweet tea this far north. This could end up being a good afternoon even if she didn't learn anything useful.

"So, I must say, I was surprised to hear from you—in more ways than one. What's got the government interested in my ex-boyfriend? And why now?"

"I really can't tell you much about the case, ma'am. I'm just here to fill in the biography for the files."

Ms. Lee nodded. "Ask away. He's gone now. I don't think there's any reason to keep anything I know from you, dear. Claude's been gone these past thirty years. We can hardly hurt him anymore."

"So, you and Mr. Rathbone were high school sweethearts?"

"We were *the* high school sweethearts. Prom king and queen, homecoming. We started dating when I was only fourteen, you know. Claude was just so darn handsome."

Sally Ann smiled. "But you didn't marry?"

Ms. Lee's face darkened. "No. We were engaged, but I broke it off."

"I see. Can I ask why?"

"When Claude came back from the war," she began, then stopped. A struggle of some kind was going on behind the woman's eyes. She began again. "Well, I guess all our boys came back different, didn't they?"

"War changes people," Sally Ann agreed. She had a feeling Claude Rathbone's changes had nothing to do with war.

Ms. Lee sighed. "I did love him once." Sally Ann could hear the truth of the emotion in the woman's wobbly voice. "They said it was his leg that took the damage, but when he came home his head was shaved and scarred. I never understood that. I was studying nursing at the time, and I read all the records he brought home with him, and there was nothing about a head injury or brain surgery.

"Claude was really changed, though. He talked differently. All the Carolina was gone from his accent. The rhythms were different. His vocabulary seemed to have changed; it had become somehow more scientific. Before he'd gone, he'd been a poet." Ms. Lee took a swig of her tea, then went on, the words coming faster.

"He moved differently. Something about the way he held himself.

The first time I kissed him, it felt wrong. I couldn't explain it. I'd heard about other men having trouble when they got back, adjusting to regular life. But Claude did fine at work. He didn't seem stressed or sick. He just seemed different." Sally Ann waited for her to go on, keeping her face a mask of polite interest. Inside her mind was racing, making connections. She was sure she was about to get confirmation that her wild theory that Claude Rathbone, Victor Chaney, and Daniel Price were somehow all the same man was maybe not that outlandish.

Leaning forward, Ms. Lee spoke in hushed tones, like someone might hear her speaking ill of her erstwhile lover and judge her for it. "There was something wrong with his memory, too. Whenever I tried to reminisce with him about old friends or things we'd done, it was like he was just humoring me, playing along, but the memories had lost all meaning for him. He couldn't remember little things about me he used to know, like what kind of soda to get me at the movies or what kinds of books I like to read. He'd get angry if I suggested he see a doctor."

She looked Sally Ann in the face, a defiant set to her jaw that dared the younger woman to question the story she was telling. "That anger was new, too. The Claude I sent to Vietnam was gentle and kind, with never a harsh word for anyone, especially not me. The Claude I got back seemed like a completely different man. Sometimes, I thought..." Ms. Lee let the words die on her lips.

She smiled at Sally Ann, a quick, nervous smile that didn't reach her eyes. Sally Ann tried to look sympathetic and nonjudgmental. She really wanted to hear the rest of that thought. She got her wish. "It sounds crazy, but I wondered if a different man actually had come back. Like a pod person or something."

Sally Ann nodded. She didn't find the idea all that crazy. In fact, it was seeming more and more likely something like that was exactly what happened.

Ms. Lee laughed. "I'm sorry. I've never told anyone that before. You must think I'm senile or something."

"Do you still have the records?" Sally Ann asked, a little breathlessly. For the first time in her life, she was actually eager to put her hands on the papers and see what she could learn from them.

Ms. Lee looked surprised and started to shake her head. Sally Ann's shoulders drooped. She felt in her gut that the next lead was in those records.

"Wait."

Sally Ann waited.

"You know what, sugar? I might actually have those. I'm such a pack-rat. Come on." She led the way out into a finished garage and turned on a light.

The two women stood in the center of the room, looking up at the walls. They were lined in stacks of neatly labeled archival quality photo boxes on shelves. When Sally Ann's eyes went wide, the woman blushed. "I had a bad case of empty nest when the youngest went to college. I organized. Everything." She pointed at the boxes on a high shelf. "It would've been 1967 when he came back home, so if it's anywhere, it'll be there."

Sally Ann sat her bag down on the floor and put her hands on her hips, glad she'd worn slacks for this interview instead of another skirt. "Do you have a ladder?"

A few minutes later the women were back in the living room. Ms. Lee had quickly cleared away the tea things, waving off Sally Ann's offers to help. Sally Ann brushed the fine layer of dust off the top of the box, but waited for Ms. Lee to come back to open it. The woman was being more than accommodating. It wouldn't do to overstep the bounds of politeness. These boxes weren't just papers and old photos to Ms. Carole Lee. They were her life.

Luckily Ms. Lee was quick. She seemed nearly as eager to look inside as Sally Ann was.

"Let's see what kinds of ghosts are in this box, shall we?" She pulled off the lid, making a cardboard squeak, and set it aside. She began lifting things out of the box and laying them out on the table. She flipped through some photographs, neatly ordered with dividers in the front of the box, and pulled out a picture of a man in a formal army uniform holding the arm of a young woman with a flower in her hair. "That's Claude and me, right before he left for Vietnam. They had a kind of reception for us at the church."

Sally Ann picked up the photo and examined it. The boy in the photo was smiling broadly at the camera, his arm tightly wrapped around the tiny woman with a bubble of blonde hair.

"You look very happy."

In fact, happy was all she could glean from holding the photo. It was a giddy feeling, and Sally Ann felt like a voyeur intruding on it. She gave the photo back to Carole Lee.

Ms. Lee held the photo and smiled down at it. "We were. I thought he might ask me to marry him that night. Lots of young people were marrying when the boys got called up. But he didn't. I wonder if things would have been different if he had."

Sally Ann was sure things would have been different. Either Claude Rathbone would have remained the same man he'd been born as, or Carole Lee would have had a tragic end of her own. If Carole Lee was crazy to think a different man came back in Claude Rathbone's body, then her psychosis was contagious: Sally Ann was starting to think so, too. She thought again about the pictures on the bulletin board in her office: different men, standing the same way, leaning on the same cane.

Ms. Lee flipped through the other photographs quickly, not stopping to linger over them. Beyond the photographs were papers of various sorts, folded and placed in carefully labeled plastic envelopes.

"Here!" She pulled one out that said "Discharge Papers."

Sally Ann itched to grab the document from the older woman's hands, but she waited patiently while her hostess pulled the papers from the envelope and flattened them on the table so they could read them together.

There was his honorable discharge with the usual line about "honest and faithful service." He had not earned any particular honors, but then he had also not faced any disciplinary action. Ms. Lee continued to sift through the papers until she found the medical information. She handed the paper to Sally Ann, who managed not to snatch it. A quick scan was disappointing. There was little more than the man's vital statistics and a list of mundane treatments for minor complaints. The only emotion she picked up was irritation, probably from the paper pusher who had to type the things in triplicate and file them.

She asked permission to photograph the papers, and Ms. Lee agreed. When she spread them out on the table, trying to angle the camera to avoid glare that would make the digital images unreadable, a small card slipped out onto the floor. Sally Ann picked it up. She instantly had a feeling it was important. There'd been a lurching feeling when she touched it, like she'd been dropped from a dizzy height.

The paper was torn and had a water stain that obscured some of the words, but she thought it was a piece of stationery from a doctor's desk. On it was scrawled the word "Project Osiris," which had been underlined twice. Beneath that was the name Carradine.

"Do you know anything about this?" Sally Ann passed the card to Ms. Lee.

Ms. Lee shook her head. "No, I don't think I've noticed it before. It was in with these?"

Sally Ann nodded. "Is Carradine someone's name?" Her gut still told her this scrap of paper was significant, but she wanted more than a feeling to go on.

Ms. Lee looked thoughtful. "It rings a bell, but after all these years, it's more of a wind chime than a church bell, if you know what I mean. Let's see if there's anything else in here."

Most of the other papers were uninteresting. Movie ticket stubs. A dried flower. The stuff of a sentimental journey, but nothing that connected the dots with something more substantial than suspicions and half-formed impossible-sounding theories. Sally Ann was ready to call it a day and hope she could find more about the Project Osiris and Carradine through other channels when Ms. Lee gasped.

"Oh my."

Sally Ann looked up sharply and found the woman holding a packet of letters tied with ribbon. "I haven't read these in years. But if there's anything to be found, it'll be in here. Claude used to write the loveliest letters." Ms. Lee wiped back a tear, and Sally Ann felt like a monster for forcing this kind woman to revisit her heartbreak like this. She didn't know if she should ask to see the letters, or leave the poor woman in peace. "I don't think I want to read them again. I think it will be too painful," she said, toying with the ribbon between her finger and thumb. "Here. You do it."

When Sally Ann touched the packet, so many emotions washed through her at the same time that she nearly dropped the packet. She knew that might happen. This wasn't her first rodeo. But, even having braced for it, she was still overwhelmed. She took a deep breath and started to untie the ribbon, but the woman stopped her.

"No. Take them with you."

Sally Ann hadn't expected that. "Are you sure?"

"I trust you. I'll just ask one thing in return."

Sally Ann raised a skeptical eyebrow. "What?"

"When you figure it out, when you know what happened to my Claude, come tell me. No matter how weird or unlikely the story seems, even if you don't think I'll believe you. I just want to know."

PATRICIA AIN'T GOT THAT SWING

Patricia awoke in a small room very much like a jail cell, but nicer —maybe it was a jail cell for holding debutantes who had been arrested at political protests. Her head hurt and her brain felt fuzzy. When Patricia sat up to try and look around, her stomach lurched. She felt hung over, but she knew she hadn't had too much fun the night before. Quite the opposite. She remembered all too well her attempted escape and how easily she'd been taken down.

Patricia checked herself out, looking for injuries or signs of invasion. She was still wearing the lounging pants and tank top she had been wearing when she was taken from her home. The shirt was stretched out and holey now from her transformation while wearing it, and smelled gamey, but it would do. She stretched her arms and legs. She didn't seem to have come to any physical harm. Her limbs were unscathed, and she didn't find any tender or sore places suggesting any trauma.

Only her head hurt, and she knew that had to be from that damn pink sand. How had she not considered that the man would have more of that stuff on hand? She was probably dehydrated as well. Her throat felt dry and scratchy and her tongue seemed large and poofy in her mouth.

Looking around the small room, she saw a sink and toilet in one corner. There was a cup on the sink, along with a plastic wrapped toothbrush and a small bar of soap. She crossed to the sink, her bare feet padding on the tile floor. It was cool under her toes. She filled the cup at the tap and rinsed out her mouth, then opened the plastic wrapper and used the toothbrush. She didn't see toothpaste, but the water and brushing motion still took some of the sourness out of her mouth. She refilled the cup four times at the tap and drank the contents. Then she filled the basin with water and dunked her head, hoping that would finish clearing the foggy feeling.

She sputtered coming back up. The water had been colder than she expected, but it had the effect she wanted. She wiped her head with the hand towel and replaced it on the plastic hook hanging next to the sink. Now that she was awake, she took a better assessment of her surroundings.

She had to still be at the college. The walls were the same institutional egg-white cinder-block she'd seen all over the building. The lighting was the same long fluorescent bulbs that buzzed faintly in the background. Was she in one of the rooms she had peeked into as she tried to find her way out? Or somewhere else on the campus altogether? The room was odd. There were niceties like a toothbrush, but the toilet was just sitting in the main room. Just for form's sake, she tried the door handle. It was locked. As she looked around, she realized there was no place in the room where a person could enclose herself or hide.

That pricked something in her mind and, when Patricia looked up, sure enough, she found a video camera in a high corner, where the wall met the ceiling. It was tracking her movements around the room. Maybe the cell had been intended as some kind of observation room. That's what Dr. Price was using it for, anyway. If she was the mouse in this experiment, there should be some cheese. What did he want from her? How did he hope to get it?

She didn't like being watched. In fact, she thought she'd do something about that. Closing her eyes, Patricia focused her energy and concentrated. Some seconds later, her eyes flew open again, alarmed.

Nothing at all had happened. Her scales didn't slip across her skin, her spikes didn't come out. Just nothing. She sat down on the floor, dropping her head into her hands to increase her focus. She flexed the right muscles, but again nothing happened. It was like the connections were just broken. She could feel the will pulling, but there was simply no response.

What had that bastard done to her? A few months ago, she might have felt like a curse had been lifted, but now she felt handicapped, as limited as if she had suddenly lost one of her senses or a limb. It gave her a sick feeling in the pit of her stomach. She had severely underestimated this man as an adversary. Obviously, he could have done this to her at any time, but he had chosen not to. So that begged the question of what he wanted from her. Had she handed it to him already by transforming in his view, letting him see what she could do? She had performed on cue, just like a circus freak. She felt stupid.

She'd been so naïve. She'd opened the door, picked up the envelope, and opened it. Then, waking in captivity, she'd let the enemy see her strength, handed him the opportunity to study her weaknesses, to assess her abilities. She'd pushed her way through the facility in an unplanned and un-researched attempt to escape, without even a rudimentary knowledge of where she was or what she might find between the door and the road. She'd done this on the advice of a woman who had betrayed her trust over and over again.

She'd just trusted to her invulnerable flesh to protect her. It was useful against bullets, but less so against manipulation and against pink sand. Her overconfidence had cost her dearly. Now he had her captive again, and she was that much more vulnerable and still knew almost nothing about her captor or her kidnapping.

She needed to reassess and see if she could rescue this situation. What did she know? Her captor called himself Daniel Price and claimed to be Cindy's father. He said he was in his fifth body. The strangeness of his movement supported that story. He moved strangely, he smelled odd, and he just generally wigged Patricia out.

Cindy seemed to be a prisoner here, as well, though she had cooperated with this man at some point. That had been her handwriting on the envelope. Patricia knew her friend's script too well to have been fooled, even if Cindy said she didn't send any letter. Daniel knew her name and enough details about her life to make her think Cindy had discussed her with him. The memory of Cindy's tearful face behind the glass haunted Patricia. What had she been trying to say?

She had to find a way to communicate with Cindy. Despite the lies and manipulations of the past, Patricia still felt Cindy was more to be trusted than Daniel Price. The question was how she could arrange to communicate with her old friend. Right now, she was trapped in this room, her every move available to observation, her lizard-self constrained. She suspected it was some kind of muscle relaxer rendering her unable to transform. The helplessness was infuriating.

Patricia took a deep breath and pushed it out through her nose. Letting the frustration build was not going to make her thinking any clearer, and she needed to think clearly. She lay down on the floor in the small room. With her legs and arms stretched out, she could nearly touch the two opposing walls at the same time. The dorm room she had once shared with Cindy Liu had not been much bigger.

The tile felt cool against her back. The floor seemed to hum. Maybe it was the heating and cooling system. In a lot of these old buildings, the chillers vibrated. The one at her alma mater had been similar. Turning her head, Patricia looked for the vents. Sure enough, there was one in the ceiling and one in the floor. The ceiling one was visibly full of dust, so Patricia surmised that it must be the intake. That meant the one in the floor was the blower.

Sitting up, Patricia stretched down over her own legs, turning so she could look at the floor vent. Once she would have been able to reach a few inches past the bottoms of her own feet. Now she could just graze her ankle bones. Keeping in mind that she was likely being observed, she examined the area under the guise of more stretching. The vent was small. Even Jessica would not be able to fit through it, so it was definitely not an avenue for escape.

She had a thought then. It was either really clever or useless and stupid, but it was better than having no idea what to try. If these vents interconnected with other rooms, like they had in her old college dorm, she might be able to overhear something through them. She remembered all too clearly hearing the girl in the room next to her and Cindy's room through the vents. They learned a lot more than they wanted to know about her taste in music and her sexual proclivities.

Trying to make it look like she simply needed a wall to exercise against, Patricia moved into the space at the end of the bed. She lay down on the floor next to the vent, putting her feet against the wall and doing a few crunches, then laying down and just listening, hoping any observer would assume she was resting. At first, she heard only the blowing of the air-conditioning, but when the cycle ended, she could hear distant crying. Maybe it was someone else being held in a similar room.

She wished she knew if the video camera was image only or if the observer was also able to hear her. She didn't want to give away her small advantage through foolishness again. She needed to know more about her situation before she took action. She needed to take it slow and make a plan. Patience had never been one of Patricia's virtues, but now looked like a very good time to learn to wait.

JESSICA CAN'T COOK

Jessica knew Walter was still sitting at the table with her boys, valiantly sawing at the so-called meatloaf she had burned for them, despite excellent directions from Leonel. She was in the backyard, scraping burnt sugar into the bushes and hoping the opened backdoor would air things out enough that the smoke detector wouldn't go off.

She just wasn't very good at this. Walter had been so pleased when she'd invited him to her home, to have dinner with her and the boys. He knew it was significant, her letting him meet her children. It was a big step, suggesting this relationship was not just casual. She had so wanted it to go well. Instead, they were lucky she hadn't burned down the house. She should have ordered Chinese food.

During the meal, Max and Frankie had sat staring at Walter with all the implacable silence of children who aren't sure what to make of a guest. She had told them Walter was her special friend, and that she wanted them to be nice to him. Max had tried, but Frankie had scowled at him and that was that. Big brothers had such power. Frankie, more than Max, understood what had happened with their father. She'd talked to both of them about divorce and about only seeing their father sometimes now. Max didn't seem to find his life that much altered from the way it had been before, but Frankie understood things like calendars and clocks. He also understood that his mother's special friend could usurp his father's place.

At least Nathan had been reasonable so far, sticking to the boys' routines when they were in his care and refraining from saying anything that would upset them. Not that there was much he could have said. She hadn't done anything to him, and he hadn't done anything to her. They just stopped loving one another. That was all. It was completely separate from Jessica's unusual ability. Nathan was ignoring that altogether.

Max had announced, after an early visit to their father, "Daddy doesn't believe you can fly, Mommy."

Frankie told her they just didn't talk about it when their father was around. "It makes him weird."

Jessica peeked through the window from her vantage point in the backyard and could see them all sitting at the table looking at one another. Walter put down his knife and listened to something her youngest said. He smiled and whatever he said back was funny because she heard Max's piercing laugh around the corner and out the door. Frankie said something, too, and Walter's face grew serious. He stood, wiping his mouth on his napkin, then laid it next to his plate and raised a finger in that "wait right here" gesture she'd already become accustomed to seeing him use.

He stepped out onto the deck and called down, "Hey, Fly Girl, want to go get a pizza with us boys?"

Jessica looked up at him, shielding her eyes from the last harsh rays of afternoon sunlight, feeling a complicated blend of emotions from embarrassment to relief. "That bad, huh?"

"I've had worse."

She laughed. "That's nice of you, but I doubt it."

"I'm not kidding. You notice I did not offer to cook dinner for you and the boys. I figured poisoning your children would not endear me to you."

She laughed again, and a queer expression crossed his face, something Jessica recognized as attraction, and fondness, maybe even love. She wondered if he could read the same things in her own face.

"Come on, my treat. Besides, it'll get me in good with Frankie if you agree. He said you wouldn't go for it."

Jessica pulled her cell phone out of her jeans pocket and looked at the time. "It is nearly six o'clock," she said.

"But it's not a school night," he countered.

Jessica bit her lip, thinking. She believed structure was important for her boys, especially when they had just gone through the turmoil of divorce and were adjusting to their mother having a job that made her less available for them. But she also wanted this first family dinner to be memorable, in a good way, not in an acrid smell of burned sugar kind of way. So she caved.

"You're right. There's no school or lessons in the morning. We should get some pizza."

The boys were ready in record time, wearing socks, shoes, and jackets and buckled in by the time Jessica had returned from a trip to her bedroom to pick up her emergency bag. These days, she didn't wear her weights all the time, but she liked to have them with her, just in case. Walter smiled when he saw she was also carrying one of the prototype models of her air jet pack. She hadn't tried it outside of the gym yet, but she was getting quite good at controlling her movements with its assistance.

She wished Walter could have seen her fly when she had access to the Chinese emeralds. Though the science guys had tested a variety of minerals, they hadn't yet found the same stones. Jessica had described them as well as she could, but there were a range of stones that could match the description. None of the near-misses had worked the same way, though she had felt something with a few of them. Walter found the whole concept fascinating: that a gemstone could resonant with some frequency of her body and bring control to what was otherwise helpless floating. He had a team working on figuring out what else in Liu's lab might have had an influence.

As Jessica pulled the mini-van out of the driveway, Walter looked back at the house, a thoughtful expression on his face. To look at the house now, you'd never know there had been burned patches in the roof a few months earlier, but she could picture it easily. There was still a handprint burned into the decking in back. She left it there as a reminder to be vigilant. Watching the house grow smaller in the rear view mirror, Jessica remembered the fight with Helen and the way she'd thrown herself into the fray to save her mother. She'd surprised herself then. She glanced at Walter, and something in his face showed how much he wanted her. Maybe it was time to leap without thinking again.

Anna Maria's wasn't very busy, despite the fact that it was Friday night. Maybe they were lucky in their timing, between early diners and late diners. When they got inside, they got a table within a matter of minutes, and the boys were happily doing the puzzles on the kids' menus while the waiter fetched their drinks. When the waiter complimented Walter on his well-behaved children, he didn't correct the man.

The pizza was just as good as promised. Max swore they had invented some new special kind of cheese.

"This can't be mozzarella!" he insisted. "It doesn't taste like those cheese sticks in the fridge at all."

Jessica let her head drop into her hands at that, but peeked between her fingers at Walter and saw his eyes twinkling with stifled laughter. This was a very good night indeed.

"Your turn, Mom." Frankie handed her the stub of the blue crayon he'd already broken so she could take her turn in their game of Dots.

When Jessica looked up to take a sip of her drink, Walter was watching her. He crossed his eyes at her, and she almost spit out her soda. Max saw the interaction, and his laughter pealed out like the tones of a bell.

You know what would be fun? Walter wrote on a napkin he passed her way. She raised an eyebrow, questioningly. He quickly wrote down his idea. Jessica covered the napkin with her hand to read it without letting Frankie see. *We should show the boys your air pack.*

"Is that allowed?" Jessica asked.

Now both boys were watching the grown-ups with interest. A

look passed between them, a kind of silent communication between brothers.

"I know a place."

"What do you think, boys?" she said, turning to her sons. "Would you like to see Mommy fly?"

It wasn't far to the shopping center. Jessica laughed when she saw the name of the facility they had parked in front of: Defy Gravity. Jessica had been to one of these places before. It was sort of a kids' party place—rooms lined with trampolines and mats and foam. It had been fun. This one was new. There was an "opening soon!" banner stretched across the front windows. She looked at Walter questioningly, and he pulled a key ring out of the inner pocket of his jacket and shook it at her and the boys.

"I know a guy," he said.

While Jessica was getting her gym bag out of the back of the van, Walter went to help the boys with their seat belts, but Frankie had already unbuckled them both. Jessica hadn't been kidding when she said her son was like a miniature adult in many ways.

"He's more responsible than me, I think," she'd said the first time she showed Walter pictures of the boys. She thought of that again now, watching the three of them interact.

Max was jumping up and down next to the van. He seemed like he was half made of rubber and half made of iron, that one. Jessica had been thinking of getting him into some martial arts. At the same age, Walter said he had taken taekwondo lessons and it had made all the difference for him. Or maybe he should try gymnastics. It was obviously in his gene pool.

It was going to be fun, showing the boys what she could do.

The children didn't disappoint them. As soon as they walked through the double doors, both boys let loose with exclamations of impressed joy. "Wow! We get the whole place to ourselves!" They both had their shoes off and were running around before Jessica had even finished walking through the door. Walter smiled and locked the door behind them, then took her hand and led her to the main floor.

"Suit up, Fly Girl. Let's show the new recruits your toys!" Walter handed the gym bag to Jessica, who disappeared into the locker room.

She could hear him helping Max and Frankie explore the lower level of the climbing wall while they waited. It wasn't long, though, until Jessica returned.

She wore a pair of gray spandex pants and a white top. The top was probably made of some kind of amazing material that was light and warm and breathed, but she had not chosen it for any of those features. She had chosen it to get Walter to make the face he was making now, an expression of almost animal attraction. Jessica already had the apparatus strapped to her back, but she spun for Walter so he could check all the straps to make sure they were properly in place. She didn't miss it when he checked out the fit of her pants at the same time.

Max admired the "cool backpack" while Frankie wanted to know how it worked.

"How about I show you?" she said. "Go sit over there with Walter, and I'll show you what this helps me do."

Once the boys were seated, Jessica knelt on the floor, almost in an attitude of prayer. It wasn't that different from preparing to begin a floor routine at a gymnastics competition. She just wouldn't be staying on the floor this time. She moved up into a sort of crouch, like a racer might wait in until the starting gun goes off. She sat silently for some seconds, building her concentration or maybe her nerve. Then, without warning, she popped back her head and burst into the air.

She flew straight up about ten or fifteen feet, then arched her back and spun into a kind of back flip. Then she just hung there, suspended. Frankie leaped to his feet, pulling at Walter.

"We've got to help get her down," he yelled, tugging at Walter's shirt. There was a note of panic in his voice.

"Just watch, Frankie. She's got this." Walter's voice was quiet and gentle, and Frankie sat back down, though he stayed poised on the edge of his seat.

Jessica brought her hands up to her waist and held her arms bent.

From that angle, Walter and the boys couldn't see the joy stick controllers hooked to her gloves, so she was hoping her boys just saw her floating like Superman, holding a heroic pose. Then she moved. Using the compressed air to give her a push whenever she needed it, Jessica went through the ceiling obstacles, hoops and punching bags that were intended for the children to throw balls at and through. She dove through hoops and swung around poles until she threw herself back to the ground, belching into the back of her hand to ensure she stayed on the ground. She grinned broadly as all three of them cheered.

Max slid his warm, chubby fingers into Walter's hand, then tugged. Walter knelt beside the boy to hear his question, but there was no need. Max didn't understand whispering.

"Did you make that for Mama?" he asked, loudly enough for his words to reverberate in the ceiling.

Walter nodded. "Me and some other guys."

"Thanks!" he said brightly, then suddenly hugged Walter around one arm.

Just as quickly, he let go and ran to admire his mother's air tanks, but Jessica didn't miss the softness in his face when Walter touched the place where her son had hugged him. Even if she'd never drunk Cindy Liu's tea, Jessica felt like she could have taken flight now, powered by hope alone.

HOLY MOTHER OF MARY

The assistant didn't say anything on the journey. She simply directed the golf cart through the halls. It gave Mary plenty of time to think. Too much time. She fought down her impatience. It wouldn't do any good to give over her energy to what ifs. Besides, she wanted to believe this woman was taking her to see her mother. In spite of herself, she wanted to trust the man who called himself the Director. She pondered that for a moment, but couldn't make anything of it.

Then they arrived, and the woman showed her into a small room with three chairs and a large window. Mary immediately crossed to the window and looked through into a hospital room. Her mother was there. She looked very small, lying in a bed that looked more like an astronaut's chair in the center of a tiled room. Everything was medical white, making it look like a set from *2001: A Space Odyssey*. Mary felt a sob rise in her throat, and she put her hand over her mouth to hold the sound in. It was such a relief just to know her mother was alive, to see her again, to know where she was. Well, at least to be where she was, even if she didn't know where that was. The sobs tried to turn into giddy laughter, but Mary did her best to stay silent.

She stared. It was definitely Helen Braeburn. She wasn't wearing makeup, and her hair had several inches of gray roots that would really piss her off when she awoke, but her color was pretty good. Other than being unconscious, she looked pretty healthy. Most of her body was hidden under a sheet or in restraints of some kind, but Mary could see she was breathing deeply, like she was in a sound sleep. There was no kind of breathing apparatus on her, and somehow that relieved her greatly.

"Oh, Mama," she said to the glass. "What have you gotten us into?"

She turned and found the assistant had disappeared again. The way that kept happening was really annoying. She crossed and tried the door handle, but she already knew she would find it locked. At least the chairs looked comfortable. She pulled one nearer to the glass and sat down to watch her mother breathe. She noticed the room wasn't really all white, as it had first appeared. There were scorch marks on several places on the floor. Against one wall were the remnants of what appeared to be a plastic hospital tray, melted into the wallpaper. Mary could see her mother had not been a docile or patient prisoner. She was glad. She didn't like the idea of her mother passively accepting capture.

As she watched, a light went off on one of the monitors. Then there were balls of flame in her mother's hands. Mary stood, trying to decide if she should somehow alert someone, wondering if the glass between her and the hospital room was fireproof. Her mother thrashed about in the bed, growing agitated, though her eyes remained closed. She looked like she was having a nightmare.

A pale white mist fell from the ceiling, extinguishing the flames on contact. Her mother's body convulsed for a moment, then fell back into that deep, rhythmic sleep. The red warning light went out and the scene was just as it had been before.

She hadn't heard the Director enter the room, but she felt his presence beside her now, in one of the other chairs.

"She's going to be all right, isn't she?" Mary let a tremor come into her voice. It was often effective with men to let them think you need protecting. She didn't think it would hurt to bring out this man's inner knight.

"We have every reason to think so. Her brain activity is strong. Her bones have knitted well. In fact, for a woman of her age, she's in rather amazing health."

"Why didn't someone just tell me where she was? I've been so worried!" Mary didn't have to fake the shaky tone this time. Her agitation was real. She was angry at the whole situation. All her stress and worry could have been alleviated by a simple phone call. But no one made that call. Who were these people?

"It's complicated," he began, stopping when she cut him off by laughing.

"I'm sorry," she said. "Men always start with that when they don't have a good excuse for their bad behavior."

A strange smile flitted across the man's face. Mary got the feeling he liked her. She hoped so, because she wanted answers. For the next hour or so, she peppered him relentlessly with questions, which he gave vague half-answers to or deflected entirely.

"Where are we?"

"Who are you?"

"How did my mother end up here?"

"Is she all right?"

"Where's Cindy Liu?"

When her questions finally ran dry, she stopped. They sat in silence for a few beats. Mary's mind was spinning. She felt very confused and conflicted about the pieces of the story she was learning. Had her mother really attacked someone with her fire power like this man claimed? It was so unlike her to act out so violently, and Mary couldn't wrap her mind around the idea.

Somehow, she trusted what this man told her. She couldn't explain the feeling. It wasn't like her to be so automatically trusting, and that made her mistrust her own judgment. She didn't think it could still be drugs active in her system messing with her perceptions, unless her delicious lunch had been laced with something that lowered inhibitions and made her more impressionable. They always said you had to be wary of eating or drinking anything when you were in faerie. Maybe it was the same in secretive, quasi-governmental agencies.

Mary laid a hand on the glass of the observation window. She wished she could go in and hold her mother's hand. She knew it was a bad idea, though. In the twenty minutes or so the two of them had stood watching, Helen's hands had caught fire twice more. The Director had already explained that everything in the room was fire-proofed, and that sensors were used to monitor her heat spikes and automatically dispense a nontoxic mist that stilled the flames and acted as a mild sedative.

Mary had her doubts about the mildness of the sedative, given the way her mother's back had arched. She didn't wake up, but Mary thought it had hurt her all the same. She wondered if they were keeping her sedated because of her injuries or because they were afraid she was dangerous. Her gaze darted to the signs of fire damage in the room again. She wondered if her mother actually was danger-ous. She felt sick from the stress of it.

She turned to the Director and tried again to get him to explain himself. "I still don't understand why someone didn't just tell me."

The Director spread his hands. There. She had it. He looked like Jimmy Stewart, young Jimmy Stewart, with his ears a little too large for his head and his clumsy charm. She and her mother had watched *It's a Wonderful Life* every Christmas she could ever remember. She knew the movie backward and forward. This man's wrists even stuck out the bottom of his sleeves in that bony way of boys who are still growing, just like Jimmy's. The impression was complete when he spoke.

"Now, Ms. Braeburn, you've got to remember that, at first, we didn't even know who she was."

Mary didn't buy it. The Director had already practically admitted this hospital was a secret government facility. Did he really expect her to believe the covert organizations within the government couldn't identify her mother in a matter of hours? Without the resources of the big guys, the local police had managed to track down the tape of her mother at the Urgent Care and her abandoned rental car at the college. Surely, people with the resources to keep her mother in a fireproof hospital room could have identified her from her fingerprints or dental records or something. Besides, the doctor she had spoken to first had said, "We didn't expect to bring you in today." They knew who Mary was, and where she was. They had been planning to "bring her in," whatever that was meant to imply.

Looking back at her mother in the hospital bed, unconscious and bruised with a variety of wires and tubes streaming from her body, she could see that her mother had been involved in something violent and serious. Obviously, Helen Braeburn had been the source of the fire on campus that day. And she'd been in a physical fight. It only made sense that the other strange things spotted that day were mixed up in this, too. The official story had been convincing. Mary had even believed it herself. But it wasn't anywhere close to the truth.

Now she was starting to wonder what kind of people she and her mother had gotten mixed up with. A cover-up of that caliber spoke of power and influence. That would be hard to fight. She wanted to shake the man by the shoulders until he stopped pussyfooting around and just told her directly what was going on. But she knew she would learn more by playing along than she would by challenging what she was told.

"But once you found out who she was?"

"We weren't sure what exactly had happened. We still aren't. It was a security matter."

Mary's bullshit detector went off again. "Security" was a handy little word that government people liked to toss around when there was a story they didn't want to get out. She'd heard it used to hide everything from sex scandals to closed-door deals to unlawful imprisonment and torture, things that take years to work out in court with the Freedom of Information Act, by which time it was often too late for the victims. Whenever she heard an official talk about security, her first question was, *Whose security?* She bit it back again. She had to tread carefully. It wouldn't be that hard for this man to make her disappear just like he had done with her mother. Of that, she felt sure.

For all she knew, she had already disappeared, so far as the outside world was concerned.

She ought to be panicked about that. But she wasn't. The feelings of well-being she got when she looked in his eyes just made her that much more suspicious. She didn't understand how he was manipulating her perceptions, but she felt certain he was.

She wanted to have a chance to figure this out.

"Can I talk to her doctors? I'd like to know what the extent of her injuries are and how they're treating her." *And*, she added silently, *who did this to her and why you are covering it up.*

"I think that could be arranged. Let me take you back to your room. Someone has brought some of your things from home. I'm sure you'd like to put on some of your own clothes."

She remembered her messenger bag then, left in the room she'd awakened in. All her research had been collected inside.

"Your bag is waiting for you in your room," he continued.

Mary nodded her thanks, realizing only later, alone in her room, that she hadn't actually asked about her bag out loud.

THE DIRECTOR AND SALLY ANN

"So, what are you going to do with her?" Sally Ann pointed at the picture of Mary Braeburn lying on the desk between them. She knew it had been taken from the girl's apartment, along with the other items in the file box on the work table across the room.

"I haven't decided yet."

Why the hell not? Sally Ann didn't comment aloud, but the Director smiled, anyway. It creeped her out when he did that. She suspected he did it to tease her, that sometimes he couldn't even actually tune in on what she was thinking or feeling, but he let her think he had.

"May I?" She reached to pick up the photo.

He nodded.

Sally Ann closed her eyes and took a calming breath. Maybe nothing at all would happen. Or maybe she'd be bombarded with images and emotions. That was the thing. She never knew what way it was going to be.

This time, it was nothing. So she opened her eyes to see what she could glean through more traditional means. She shrugged at the Director, silently letting him know she hadn't learned anything. His face stayed placid. She was glad he didn't say anything. She never knew whether to be glad or disappointed when her magic touch

147

yielded no information. It was a delicate thing, unpredictable and difficult to channel.

The picture of Mary Braeburn had probably been taken by a lover. There was something in the flirtatiousness of the smile and the tilt of her head. Sally Ann's mother would have sniffed disapprovingly and said the girl had "bedroom eyes." She was an attractive girl, probably about twenty-six years old. Her dreads made it difficult to make a good estimate. They made her look younger and older at the same time. Her face, however, was completely unlined. Average height and weight, but confident in her body. She'd have to be to sport tattoos like those. In the picture, she had her head tilted upwards to look up into the camera. The photographer must have been taller than her.

Sally Ann picked up the photo of Helen Braeburn from the table. She already knew this one held only a feeling of dissatisfaction and a low-grade anger. This time she was more interested in the surface details. Helen was considerably heavier than her daughter. In fact, Sally Ann was sure she could be described as medically obese. It was a posed picture, a studio shot, but it wasn't a bad one. In spite of the stiffness of the hair and the thickness of the makeup, Helen's smile looked genuine, and she knew what angle to tilt her head at for the most flattering view. The picture was probably the headshot she used for her real estate website.

Comparing the pictures, Sally Ann saw little likeness. "Mary must look like her father," she said, handing the pictures back to the Director.

He put them in the folder and closed it, then sat there, drumming his slender fingers on the folder. Sally Ann stared at him and wished she knew what he was thinking.

Sally Ann was enough of a realist to know that good people sometimes had to do bad things for the greater good. She understood the world in all its shades of gray and scoffed at anyone who suggested a simpler view as naïve or idealistic. In a wide, objective sense, inflicting violence on others was wrong. But doing so to prevent harm to others was more than just acceptable, it was the morally right choice. At the same time, Sally Ann also felt there were lines that shouldn't be crossed. The hard part was when her personal lines did not match those of the others around her.

She'd just come off a horrific child abuse case when the Director approached her about leaving the police force ten years ago. The abuser was a wealthy man, and her higher-ups tried to refuse to bring charges against him. Her supervisor had tried to tell her it was a gray area, but she had seen the little girl's fear when her father had come into the room. She hadn't moved, but somehow still seemed to have become smaller, like she'd drawn herself inside and no longer filled her own skin fully. Sally Ann had stuck to her guns. In the court case, her testimony had been praised in the press. That hadn't stopped the police department from punishing her. There had been no reprimands, no official personnel action. She just stopped getting assigned to cases of any interest at all. She'd won her case: the man had gone to jail. But she'd lost, too. They were going to drive her out through sheer boredom. That was when the offer came.

The Director had simply slid into the other side of her lunch booth one day and asked if he could talk with her. Within a week, she had turned in her badge and her gun and signed on with the Department. In her more cynical moments, she wondered if he had mentally manipulated her into joining the organization. Most of the time, she decided she didn't care if he had. It had been a good move.

All the same, she wished the Director would be a little more forthcoming. She'd really like to understand what he was thinking. She understood why he'd want to recruit Jessica Roark and Leonel Alvarez in spite of their lack of experience in anything resembling soldiering or spying. They were both amazingly powerful in ways Sally Ann had never seen. They were also both complete rubes who didn't understand the most basic things about stealth and secrecy. Before they'd been recruited, their antics had the Spinners working full time, trying to control the trajectory of the story through the press and social networks. A lot of people had seen things. Getting them on the inside was good in more than one way.

And the Director had kept Helen Braeburn locked away all these months in the Department's own facilities. In other cases, the criminals who survived capture had been jailed. Did the Director think he could recruit her to their side? Was that why the daughter was here now, too? Sally Ann had serious doubts about a plan like that. And Patricia O'Neill was simply allowed to go about her life, even though she'd let her scalier side be seen on the evening news. Sally Ann wondered at the wisdom of that decision. The man was up to something. It was probably brilliant, and he probably wasn't going to tell her a damn thing until every duck was in a neat little row.

She looked up from her ruminations to find herself looking at an empty chair. The Director had moved to the large window that took up an entire wall of the room. He was standing, hands clasped behind his back, staring out on to the cityscape before them. He looked like the eldest son of a tycoon, poised to take over the world, or at least Daddy's business.

Sally Ann stood and stretched, then loped over to stand beside him. He didn't look at her.

"I know you have your doubts about our current course of action," he said to the window in front of him. Sally Ann waited, and he went on. "Roark and Alvarez are a huge step forward in evolution, Ms. Rogers, as are Ms. Braeburn and Ms. O'Neill. It's an opportunity we can't pass up."

"But they aren't professionals, sir."

He nodded. "That may come with advantages of its own."

"They've already compromised security."

"And they will again. The time for working in shadows may be coming to an end."

Sally Ann was startled. Did the Director mean they might go public? "I trust you, sir," she said. She still meant it. She hoped she wouldn't regret it.

PATRICIA DANGLES LIKE BAIT ON A HOOK

Patricia was surprised when Daniel Price didn't come to talk to her all that day. She expected him at least to want to gloat, to see that his plan had worked and that she was indeed helpless. Not that Patricia had ever been helpless in her life. But she did feel the loss of her armor and spikes.

She hadn't seen another human being all day. Even her meals—two of them, a lunch and a dinner—had been sent in on a kind of robotic tray. Patricia was starting to wonder if the whole compound was staffed by the robots. If she could just get out of the room, she might be able to escape the facility even without her inner dragon lady.

Patricia hadn't realized how little silence she generally allowed in her life. Usually, there was television or music playing when she was alone. But there was nothing like that in her cell. Just the simple, bare furnishings and her own thoughts for company. Her thoughts were not good company, either. They were full of self-recrimination and hopeless spinning of her wheels.

When lunch came, the clatter startled her. She'd been standing on her head against the wall, using exercise to mask her attempt at surveillance through the vents. A flap had opened at the bottom of the door, like a sort of high-tech doggy door, and a small white plastic looking thing had rolled in. It was sort of like a motorized foot stool, or some kind of headless pet. On the flat surface of its back was a small silver tray with a lunch.

Though the lunch looked plenty appetizing, a salad with sugared pecans, cranberries, and chicken, which was one of her favorites, Patricia hesitated to eat. Her captor would need to keep her drugged to keep her from being able to manifest her powers and the food seemed like a logical way to do that.

Then again, his MO thus far had been more bizarre than simple drugs in the food, like the pink sand. She was sure that the initial dose of the muscle relaxers, or whatever the man was using, had been injected into her veins. Patricia had ample time alone in the room to examine her own body thoroughly, and there was a small bruised place inside her left elbow, just where an IV needle would likely have been inserted. She knew from experience that, when she slept, her body reverted to its mushy, vulnerable, merely-human state, except for the permanent chest and back plating. So, if Price wanted to take samples or inject her with anything, he'd had his opportunity when she was out cold.

The waffling about whether or not to eat the lunch took the better part of the afternoon. Eventually, Patricia's stomach won out. She decided to go ahead and eat. So far, her captor didn't seem to want her dead, just contained and constrained. She could worry about how to release her inner dinosaur once she had gathered some information and could formulate a reasonable plan. In the meantime, she'd keep up her strength and not distract her thinking with unnecessary privation.

She spent the long afternoon thinking about the scene in *The Great Escape* where Steve McQueen spent his solitary confinement throwing and catching a baseball over and over, inducing a kind of zen state where he didn't feel the painful slowness of the minutes passing. Patricia wasn't sure she could have done that even if she'd had a baseball. Idleness was torture to her, and she was tired of exercising.

Eventually, she started singing to herself just to hear something. Patricia did not have a good singing voice, but she did have an excellent memory for lyrics and season tickets to two theaters in Springfield. She sang *Evita* from beginning to end, then *Les Misérables*, then *Wicked*. Every show she'd watched in the past few years. She hoped it was driving her captors crazy.

It was disheartening when her dinner arrived on the back of the same robot-dog-footstool thing. How could she get Price to talk if he didn't even come to see her? The waiting was dull and patience had never been Patricia's strong suit. She was a woman of action, and up till now, it had served her well. Often all it took to lead, she found, was a willingness to make a decision and state your opinion with confidence. Even if it didn't work out the first time, people would follow rather than go out on that limb themselves. She had always figured it was better to act now and apologize later, if necessary. She'd rarely had to apologize.

After she consumed the dinner—a nice pasta with a creamy sauce and perfectly cooked pieces of asparagus with a slice of garlic bread and an aromatic cup of tea—Patricia paced the room for a while, restless. *If Price's plan is to drive me mad with boredom, he might just succeed,* she thought. When she made the turn after another pacing circuit of the tiny room, Price was there, sitting on a small stool and looking at her.

She jumped, unable to contain her reaction. She burned inside seeing the amusement in his face at her surprise. "I didn't hear you come in, Daniel," she said, recomposing herself.

"Oh, it's Daniel now, is it?" He chuckled softly, a laugh that devolved into a coughing fit. He tugged a handkerchief from his pocket and wiped his mouth. Patricia watched his movements with interest.

"Well, we're past the formalities, I would think. But maybe I should call you Anton?"

The man stood, balancing himself with a walking stick. Patricia wondered if he really needed it for support, or if it was just another sleight of hand, designed to make her underestimate him. Or maybe he thought he could use it as a weapon against her if she attacked. "Daniel will do. Using his name is the least I can do for his sacrifice to science."

"All right then, Daniel. We're practically family now."

"It's true. Family is the most important thing." He brought his fingertips together above the walking stick, completing his depiction of a sanctimonious patriarch. All that was left was to call her "honey" and pat her hand.

Seeing her opportunity, Patricia pressed. "So, how are you helping your daughter?" She put a heavy emphasis on the word. *Daughter.*

"The tank and the gas mixture inside are keeping her stable for now."

So he had claimed before. But Patricia was hoping to learn more.

"You mean the prison you're keeping her in?" Her face was expressionless, but there was venom in her voice. It wasn't for nothing that Patricia had spent all those years in corporate. She was a master of tone and insinuation.

Price's eyes flashed with anger, and Patricia knew she had found a sore point. Good.

"It's for her own benefit. She's a headstrong girl." His chin jutted out defensively.

Girl? The woman was sixty-eight years old. Patricia bit back her rancorous comment. "Like father, like daughter, I suppose."

Price's mouth twitched, the upper lip taking on an unattractive curl. "Yes. It's a shame we didn't get to know each other sooner. She does have a brilliant scientific mind, for a woman."

Patricia nodded, carefully not reacting to the disparagement of her sex. "She has done some amazing work." *Without the permission of her subjects or the approval of any scientific establishment.* Patricia kept that thought to herself.

Price leaned nearer, and Patricia wanted to cough from the smell of his flesh. It was like mildew or rancid butter. He narrowed his eyes at her. "Yes. You and that other girl—Jessica, I believe?—destroyed a good many of her experiments when you attacked her. It will set her research back months."

Attacked her? That wasn't quite how Patricia remembered it. "I wasn't the one who burned the place down." That had been Helen, Cindy's overzealous new best friend.

Price sat back down, settling his shoulders with visible effort. Patricia wondered how difficult basic movement really was for the man, or if he was performing a dumb show for her benefit. He'd moved quickly enough when that guard had decided to shoot her. He hadn't brought a guard with him this time, she noticed, but one had to be nearby.

"How is your room?" he asked, as if she were an invited guest in his home.

She looked around at the small cell again. "I've had nicer, and worse," she said, shrugging.

"I expect you have," he said. "In the old days, the accommodations were more lush, but my funding isn't what it was during the war."

"Vietnam?"

He curled a lip into a bitter twist that was probably supposed to be a smile. "World War II."

Patricia considered that. If this was some kind of project funded back in the forties, it was likely that most of the people who supported it were actually dead. She filed that thought away to examine more closely later.

"I am curious, though," she said, "how exactly you're suppressing my ability to transform. Is it in the food?"

"Oh, no." He laughed that airy, coughing dry sound again. "You've been agonizing over your meals for no reason at all, I'm afraid. It's a new formula I've developed. I injected it into your veins while you were unconscious. So far, it seems very effective, don't you think?"

Patricia frowned. Getting out of here was going to be tougher without her lizard hide as protection. Patricia was troubled by the idea that her scalier self might be permanently under wraps. She'd come to enjoy having impervious skin and a terrifying aspect. She'd need to find out more about what exactly he'd done to her—after her escape.

Luckily, Daniel Price didn't seem to realize she was far from helpless even in her ordinary flesh. He was probably expecting her to plead with him, or maybe cry. That seemed to be the sort of weakness the man thought came with a second X chromosome. She considered for a moment and decided she couldn't sell that performance. She'd stick with her strengths.

"It's kind of nice, really. It's been difficult, learning to manage the transformations. Tiring." She flopped back on the mattress, dramatically.

Price cocked his head at her. He looked puzzled. That was good. She needed him off balance. She rolled up on one side, leaning into her elbow, and looked at him.

"How did Cindy even find you?" she said, as if the question had just occurred to her.

"She didn't. I found her. I'd been keeping track of her, watching her work. I was just waiting for the right moment for our reunion."

"She told me you were dead." Patricia paused for effect. "She didn't seem that broken up about it."

Price wheezed a hacking laugh. "That would be her mother talking. She said I was a monster and my death was what I deserved. Though, as you can see, reports of my death were greatly exaggerated." He laughed again, amused by his own quote.

Patricia arched an eyebrow. "I suppose it's all in how you define 'alive,'" she said.

That got him. The laughter ceased immediately, and the line of his mouth grew grim. "You don't know the sacrifices I have made for my work; how important it is for mankind. History will name me a hero!" He thumped his chest at that, for emphasis, causing himself to erupt into a coughing fit.

"So, it's not just to keep yourself alive?" Patricia tried to sound interested rather than disbelieving. Either she succeeded, or he was insensitive to her tone in the thrall of his own enthusiasm.

"A great man need not be limited by time anymore. When the body fails, his consciousness, his mind can be transplanted into another. And another. Think what can be accomplished when you are no longer bound by the physical limitations of the flesh!" He gestured broadly in his fervor, the collar of his shirt falling open to reveal a strange scar in the mottled flesh of his neck.

Patricia fought to keep her face from revealing her disgust. Her mind was spinning. She'd heard almost this same speech from Cindy a year earlier, railing against the limits of time, desperate for more time for the work she believed could change the world. Egotistical megalomaniacs, the both of them.

"I don't understand why I'm here, Daniel," she said. "You still haven't said what you want from me, how it is that you think I can help Cindy."

Price smiled, revealing teeth stained slightly red, as if he had coughed up blood in that last fit. "Oh, you've already done your part, Patricia. You'll give me leverage over Cindy when I need it. And now you will also be the bait."

"The bait?" That surprised her.

"I've just heard from my colleague. She's in place to capture our flighty little friend. The investigation to find you has put them just where we want them. Those fools at the Department don't know who they are dealing with."

Patricia wanted to rush to the defense of her friends but held her tongue. If he underestimated them, so much the better. In the meantime, she'd find a way to be a help to them somehow.

"What's Jessica got that you want?" The question burst out of her before she had finished thinking it. So much for controlling herself. Her face burned red from anger at herself.

"It's not what I want. It's what Cindy needs. There's something in her blood, something that could be the key to dealing with my daughter's condition and correcting the flaw in her formula. Cindy was near discovering what it was when her work was… interrupted."

Patricia snorted. Cindy's work had been "interrupted" by the untimely rescue of her kidnapping victim and unwilling guinea pig. At the time, Patricia had not realized why Cindy had taken Jessica. It had seemed a rash and violent act, uncharacteristic for Cindy. Patricia had assumed that her moral compass had become completely skewed, that she no longer saw other people as anything other than lab animals. Patricia's theory was that Cindy believed the key to solving her own age problems was within Jessica.

This was the first real evidence Patricia had seen that she was right. If Jessica really held a key to understanding what was going on with Cindy, the kidnapping made much more sense. It was the desperate act of a woman trying to save herself. Not that it was an excuse, but at least it was a reason. She worried anew about the mental state of her lifelong friend.

Daniel stood. He was getting ready to leave! If she was going to make a move of any sort, now was the time.

"Daniel?" She tried to make her voice honeyed and soft. Instead, her voice cracked—her throat was raw from her afternoon of pushing her voice to Broadway levels. Maybe that was good, though. Maybe he'd take it as a sign of emotion and take pity on her. "Do I have to stay here? In this room? Couldn't I at least get outside and get some air? I'm going stir crazy in here."

Daniel looked her over carefully. He seemed to be considering her words. "We have noticed you've been exercising a lot," he said. "Were you singing this afternoon? One of the techs said it looked like you were doing Andrew Lloyd Webber songs."

Patricia looked down, part of her mind spinning on "looked like" and hoping that meant her room was not monitored for sound. "It's hard, not having anything to do or anyone to talk to." His face remained impassive. "Or even anything to read," she added. She didn't have to fake the emotion of that. Idleness was not Patricia's idea of fun. The only reason she wasn't bouncing off the silent walls was because she'd needed time to think about what to do. But she'd need to get out of the room if she was to find a way to get word to her friends and make sure they didn't become more prisoners for Daniel Price.

"I do understand loneliness," he said, turning and walking toward the door, leaning heavily on the walking stick again.

The panel slid open when he approached. Patricia could only glimpse two armed guards through the opening. She couldn't tell if they were the same men she'd fought outside. The doors closed behind him, leaving Patricia alone with her thoughts once more.

SALLY ANN AND THE STRONGMAN, BRAWN, AND BRAINS

You would like the doctor, buttercup. He's taken good care of my leg and cares for me like a son.

Claude Rathbone's letters to his girlfriend were full of endearments like this. As she read them again, Sally Ann could feel the love he harbored for her, his longing to hold her and kiss her. It was intense enough that she had actually taken the letters home to read, where she could take a cold shower afterward if necessary. She could also feel that he was lying about the doctor.

This letter was the first one that told her anything useful. Sally Ann guessed that young lovers didn't spend their ink on the practical details of life, needing the space for promises and dreams instead. She'd felt like such a voyeur. It was a relief to, at last, begin to pull some practical information from the letters Carole Lee had given her.

Claude Rathbone's doctor in Vietnam was one Max Carradine, born 1916, died 1967. In an investigation full of shady characters, Carradine stood out as the shadiest. In spite of young Claude Rathbone's praise of the doctor in the letters, Sally Ann could feel the patient's trepidation and worry. He had not trusted his doctor. In fact, he was afraid of him. Sally Ann was a little afraid of him herself. He was one strange cookie.

Carradine was old for recruitment to military service in Vietnam, in his fifties at the time, but seemed to have insisted he be given the field hospital to supervise, and, surprisingly, his request was granted. It reeked of political machination.

Under his tenure, there were many irregularities with patient records. Nurses complained that he performed surgeries and gave treatments he refused to explain the purpose of. In fact, paperwork was in progress to remove him from duty, a process that was halted when he was found dead in his quarters. He seemed to have died of a head wound, though no one was ever arrested for the assault. Another surgeon was found with a broken neck, too, either having jumped or been thrown from the roof of the building. Suspicious.

There were far too many dead scientists, doctors, and researchers littering the files on this case. Sally Ann was getting tired of reading about head wounds, too.

In his earlier career, Carradine had been the sole survivor of a super-secret research project that ended in an explosion. Like most super-secret government research projects, it wasn't hard to find information about it. The hard part was figuring out where the truth was in the all the contradictory information she found.

Researching Project Osiris was like reading a comic book. The name suggested an interest in defeating death, in resurrection. The story of Osiris in Egyptian mythology was particularly gruesome, and these researchers liked to show off their reading in their project titles. Like most geeks, they just wanted someone to get it.

Sally Ann got it. It was a story of man who was cut into pieces and sewn back together, missing his dick. A catfish ate it. Plus the story was all incest-y, with Osiris being pieced back together by his wife/sister. Gross. She wondered if the lab guys had thought of that part when they named the project.

The later forties were full of projects that promised longevity, increased strength, or other modifications. It wasn't just the Nazis who thought they could improve on what God had made. In the twenty-first century, everything is about adjustments at the gene level before a child was born and all the moral and ethical fuzziness of that. Back then it was about improving the men that were already men. Always only the men. Patriarchal pigs. Though, at least the men were men, not unborn children—there was some possibility they knew what they were getting into, if the project people were honest. Sally Ann knew that was a big if.

She had been tunneled in for hours, processing information and trying to make all the dots connect into a coherent picture that would tell her something useful, something that would help find Patricia O'Neill wherever her back-from-the-dead kidnapper was holding her. Sally Ann was more than frustrated, so when Leonel Alvarez showed up she welcomed the distraction, even though she didn't have any leads to share.

Leonel, unfailingly polite, stood staring at the bulletin boards while he waited for Sally Ann to finish the thought she was writing down on her notepad. He needn't have waited. It was just her touchstone. "I'm out of time"—the line she'd picked up from the photograph of Daniel Price arm-wrestling Victor Chaney. She was starting to feel like she was the one who was out of time. They were no closer to finding Patricia in spite of all her work.

"Hello, Leonel," she said when she finished. Her voice came out small and weak. She usually hid her discouragement better.

Leonel's face immediately took on an expression of concern. "That doesn't sound good. What's the matter?"

"I'm no closer to figuring this out. I can't find a connection between Daniel Price and Patricia or any hint as to where he might have taken her or why he wanted her. I feel like a dog chasing its own tail, too stupid to know it won't do me any good to catch it."

"Well, show me what you've got. It can help to talk it through."

Sally Ann turned on the light over her bulletin board, illuminating her picture wall. "I warn you. This is going to sound crazy."

Leonel laughed. "There's been a bit of that going around."

"True. I am talking to a super-strong man whose best friend can fly."

"*Ay, m'ija.* If you only knew the whole story."

"Maybe telling me the story can be my reward when I figure this out."

Leonel held out his hand and shook Sally Ann's. "You've got a deal."

So Sally Ann spent the next half hour explaining who the people were in her photo wall and how they related to one another. "Daniel Price, born 1962, 'died' 2004 in a lab accident that left no body."

"And kidnapped Patricia in 2014," Leonel added.

"Exactly. So, he's connected to this guy." Sally Ann pointed to the picture of Victor Chaney and Daniel Price arm wrestling. She didn't mention the impressions she had gotten when she touched the photo. She wasn't ready to talk about the way her particular freak worked yet, not with the new recruit she barely knew.

The label beneath gave the data: Victor Chaney, born 1944, died 2004. Leonel pointed. "He died the same year as Daniel. In the same lab accident?"

"No. Separately. He slipped and fell bashing his head on the bathtub." Leonel nodded but said nothing, so Sally Ann went on. "He left all of his money to Daniel Price's widow and son."

"Were they having an affair?" Leonel whispered, like they were gossiping about someone who might overhear.

Sally Ann had to smile at the conspiratorial tone. As if illicit, adulterous sex was the most shocking thing about this case. "She says not, and, given his health, I think probably not, but not for lack of wanting. There was definitely a connection there." She pointed at the board again, her finger resting on a newspaper photograph. "Now this is Victor Chaney in the early 1980s."

In the newspaper shot, Chaney was standing tall and straight and smiling into the camera. He had ducked his head to one side, causing his hair to fall over his eyes in a rakish effect that Sally Ann felt certain he had cultivated with practice in a mirror.

Leonel examined the two pictures and whistled a low tone. "That's quite a change. Did he have cancer or something?"

"No. But he did have some kind of neurological problem. That's how he and Price became friends. He was hoping Price's research would help him."

Leonel nodded. "So, if they were friends, maybe it's not so weird that he tried to look after his friend's widow and child."

"If that was the only weirdness, I'd agree. But Chaney was totally healthy until he disappeared for a week in 1984."

"Where was he?"

"No one ever found out. He showed up at work a week later, looking thinner and with a head wound, carefully dressed in medical gauze. He claimed complete amnesia about what had happened during the week he was missing."

"Amnesia only happens on *telenovelas*, Ms. Rogers. Not in real life."

Sally Ann punched Leonel on the arm approvingly. "That's what I said! But the authorities at the time seemed to buy his story, even with the Claude Rathbone stuff." Leonel looked at her expectantly, and she pointed at the other newspaper picture on her board. "There he is."

"Another walking *calaca*? He looks a hundred years old."

"In that picture? He's thirty-two."

"What's wrong with him? I'm almost forty-nine, and he looks like he could be my grandfather!"

Sally Ann snorted. "You, Mr. Alvarez, are hardly a typical case." She gestured at his muscular and handsome frame.

Leonel stood a foot and a half taller than her and wore his size well. Jessica said that Leonel was modest, but Sally Ann was still surprised when he blushed at the compliment. She cleared her throat and went on.

"But, yes, he looks terrible for his age. See, here he is when he was eighteen or so, right before he went to Vietnam." She tapped the picture of Rathbone and his sweetheart. Both of them were looking at the camera and smiling broadly, beautiful in that prom king and queen sort of way.

"So, he was hurt in the war? That's why he has the cane?"

"That's one of the weird things. I can't find out. His medical records indicate a leg injury, but Ms. Lee, his girlfriend, says he came home with a shaved head and healing stitches suggesting cranial surgery."

"So, the records are wrong."

"Or missing or changed on purpose."

"Okay, that is weird. Is he still alive?"

"No. And his death is mysterious, too. He was murdered in his home. His head was bashed in. The crime was never solved, and—get this—he left his insurance money to Victor Chaney."

"Now that's a plot for a soap opera. So, Mr. Chaney is missing for a week, unexplained, and his friend dies and leaves him all his money, but no one was arrested for anything?"

"Right. Which says to me that someone is covering something up."

"Which makes you wonder who, what, and why."

"Now you're cooking with gas."

The two stood staring at the photographs together. Sally Ann rearranged the photos by date and looked at them again. Her gaze bounced from one man to another. The faces were different, but the later picture of each was inexplicably similar. It was like some kind of bizarre set of before and after pictures for a program that left men lame.

She tilted her head to the side, studying the photos and trying to figure out what she was seeing. The body language of each man in the later picture was so much alike as to be impossible to explain away with coincidence. Rathbone and Price, especially, since they were caught in a similar pose, standing, leaning on a cane. A cane they each held in exactly the same way. Sally Ann peered at the cane in each picture more closely. It was a plain black cane with a silver head.

Leonel saw it, too. "Would you think I was crazy if I said it looked like we had just changed heads on the same body in these?"

"I told you it was going to sound crazy."

Nodding slowly, Leonel pointed at the photo hanging at the bottom of the board. It showed a group of scientists gathered around a table, posed as if they were deep in consultation with each other. Sally Ann had labeled the names of the scientists, but hadn't gotten much of anywhere connecting any of them to current events.

"Who are these guys?" he asked.

"They are the scientific team for a top secret project from the forties. Project Osiris."

Leonel scanned the faces. "So, how do these guys connect to Claude Rathbone, Victor Chaney, and Daniel Price?"

"That, my friend, is the sixty thousand dollar question." She tapped Max Carradine's head in the photo.

Leonel peered in to look with her at the man. Sally Ann stared, too. The man in the photograph was not particularly photogenic, but neither was he unattractive. He was a thin, lanky man wearing glasses and a lab coat. He was staring across the table at another member of the team, one Anton Lorre.

She tapped the second photo. "This is Max Carradine. I don't know what he has to do with any of this yet, but twenty years after this photo was taken, he operated on Claude Rathbone in Vietnam. Then, he died under mysterious circumstances."

"Another head wound?"

"Bingo."

"May I?" Leonel unclipped the picture from the board and brought it closer to his face. "I didn't bring my glasses," he apologized, then examined the faces in the photo again. He shook his head, seeming to indicate that he didn't see anything of interest and was just about to clip it back on the board, when he grabbed at the photo again. *"Dios te salve, María!* Look at who took this picture."

Sally Ann picked up the photo. It wasn't an original, so she didn't feel anything when she touched it. But she felt something when she saw the notation in the bottom right corner. "Photo by Evangeline Liu, 1947."

"Liu?" Her mind was spinning, trying to figure out how this Liu connected to Dr. Cindy Liu, object of a Department man hunt and wreaker of havoc in the life of Jessica. "Who is Evangeline Liu?"

"She was my neighbor, until she died," Leonel said, his brown eyes growing wide. "She's also Cindy Liu's mother. And Cindy's father was someone Ms. Liu worked with—it's got to be one of these men."

"Shut the fuck up!"

Leonel blanched, and Sally Ann rushed to apologize for swearing. Leonel was such a gentleman, probably the only agent she worked with that she had to watch her language around.

"I'm sorry. But, holy crap! Are you serious?"

He nodded.

"Do you know what this means?" She laid the photo back down on the table, flattening it with her hands to peer at the men around the table again. "This is the proof I've been looking for. Evidence that all of this is connected. Daniel Price. Patricia's kidnapping. Jessica's flight. It all circles around the one woman."

Almost at the same time, they both said it. "Cindy Liu."

To herself, Sally Ann added, "Cindy fucking Liu."

JESSICA IS A WOMAN ON A MISSION

"They think they've found another one of you," Sally Ann said, grabbing her toes and stretching her torso flat against her legs.

"Another one of me?" Jessica let go of her forward stretch to look at her trainer. "What are you talking about? Isn't one enough?"

"Trust me, one of you is plenty of trouble." Sally Ann's teasing smile softened any potential insult with obvious affection. "But I mean we found another Liu-vian."

"Is that what you guys call us?" Jessica turned her face to smile at the other woman, her cheek smooshed against her Lycra pants.

"Usually only when you're not there. Walter started it. I think it's cute."

Jessica frowned. "I don't know if I like being known by her name. It's not as if we were willing participants."

She thought about her kidnapping, the time in the tank in the good doctor's basement. A wave of anger washed over her, still fresh after all this time. It rankled her that Cindy Liu had escaped unpunished, her crimes unanswered for.

Tension shot down her body, and she reflexively rubbed her Franken-arm. It was well past the point of healing where it caused her any pain, so the gesture was about psychological rather than physical soothing. Jessica had a feeling that if she were Patricia, her spikes would be out. Thinking of Patricia made her frown, too. She hoped the woman was okay, wherever she was. It was hard to imagine that anyone could hurt Patricia O'Neill, but if anyone could find a way, it would be Dr. Liu. Jessica was sure Cindy Liu was behind Patricia's weird disappearance. The pink sand alone was enough to convict the woman of the new crimes in her mind. It was just the kind of thing Cindy would have developed.

Sally Ann let her leg drop from where she'd been stretching it on the barre and dropped to the floor for more stretches. Her tone was conciliatory. "Hey, I won't use it if it bothers you. I just thought it was amusing."

Jessica brushed off the apology. "It's really no big deal. I was actually thinking about Patricia. Is there any news?"

"I've been following some leads." Sally Ann hesitated and Jessica turned, her interest clearly piqued. "Daniel Price is not what he seems."

Jessica considered that. "So, he's not a dead scientist mysteriously still moving around and kidnapping people?"

"Actually, he kind of is." Sally Ann snorted against her knee, then looked up, her face thoughtful and serious. "But it's even stranger than that sounds."

Jessica burned with curiosity, but she had already learned that pushing Sally Ann would not make her more forthcoming. She was trained to keep her mouth shut under torture. She certainly wouldn't give in to simple wheedling. She'd try to trust that she would eventually get the full picture. "So, does this bring us any closer to finding Patricia?"

"No."

Jessica's heart sank. It must have shown on her face because Sally Ann looked away.

"That trail is still cold. Though I'm hopeful what I'm learning about the kidnapper will eventually give us his location." Sally Ann seemed to want to say something else, but pressed her lips together and bent back into a stretch.

Jessica bent into a matching stretch and considered what to say. She felt antsy, eager to be of help, but without a lead to follow, she didn't know what help she could be. She was frustrated by everyone's tight-lipped demeanor. Even if they didn't yet have all the answers, they should share what they did know. No one had a more personal stake in this case than she and Leonel did.

Leonel was a basket case. He and Patricia had a complicated friendship, but Jessica knew Leonel really cared about Patricia, and he was obviously anxious over her well-being. In fact, she was worried about how anxious Leonel was. She wished he would talk to her, let her in on what he was feeling, but he had really clammed up lately. This helpless waiting was wearing on them both. Worrying wasn't going to help, though.

Jessica changed the subject. "So, they really think they found someone else like me? Can she fly?"

"No, it's not a flyer. It's some lady the next town over. The story is that she can see incredible distances."

Jessica considered this. It was interesting that Sally Ann threw out "a flyer" like this was a common category of agent. Were there others like her among the rank and file? It didn't seem like the time to ask for a lesson about the organizational structure of her new employer, so she asked about the case instead. "And she has some association with Dr. Liu?"

"That's what they think. She was using some kind of eye drops. A product called ICU." Sally Ann snickered.

Jessica noticed that Sally Ann had the laugh of a middle school boy, and her sense of humor tended toward the bodily function and pratfalls variety.

"The lady has a way with product names," Sally Ann finished.

"Can I go?" Jessica had blurted out the request before she even had time to decide she was going to ask. Once the words were out, she didn't regret them. She really wanted to go. She'd been training for months now, and an actual mission might just be the cure for restlessness she was looking for. If they wouldn't let her work on finding Patricia, at least she could help someone else.

Sally Ann looked confused. "Go where?"

"On the mission. To find this woman and find out if she's like us." Jessica dropped into a back-bend and turned it into a walkover. The movement let her look away from Sally Ann. She didn't want to see it if pity or doubt was what crossed her trainer's face.

When Jessica was back on her feet, Sally Ann stepped up to face her. She peered searchingly into Jessica's eyes. "I think you mean that."

"Of course I do. I didn't join the Department just so I could stretch out with you, you know. Maybe it's time to put some of this training to the test."

Sally looked thoughtful. "You might be right. Show me what you can do."

The training session that followed was the most intense of Jessica's career, including the ones with the ex-Olympic trainer she worked with during her tenth summer. Sally Ann put her through her paces in hand-to-hand combat, stealth, and obstacles avoidance. They worked without the new air-pack for an hour, then for a second hour with it. At the end, Jessica was gloriously sweaty and definitely grateful for the posh shower facilities the gym offered.

Jessica was sitting in the cafeteria with Leonel telling him about her workout to distract him from his strange bad mood when Sally Ann brought her the news. She slipped into the booth next to Jessica and punched her on the arm.

"You're in."

Jessica jumped and hugged the woman, whooping with delight. She only considered the inappropriateness of the reaction when she realized Sally Ann wasn't hugging her back. She dropped her arms and scooted over, blushing a deep shade of red.

"Well," Sally Ann said to Leonel, "no one can fault her enthusiasm, can they?"

Leonel grinned. "Nope. But what is she so enthusiastic about?"

"She didn't tell you?" Sally Ann looked between the two of them carefully. Jessica wasn't sure what her trainer was looking for. But she thought Sally Ann had given Leonel some kind of warning look.

Jessica touched Leonel's arm, a gesture of apology for not sharing what had turned out to be news. "I didn't know if I was allowed to talk about it. Am I?" She turned back to Sally Ann. "Am I allowed?"

"To him? Definitely. He's going, too."

Jessica nearly squealed again, but settled for bouncing in her seat. Sally Ann laughed, placing a folder on the table. "I've got to go. Here's the case information. I'll let you fill Leonel in. We leave at 1400 hours from the motor pool. You'll be briefed on the way."

HOW TO FEED YOUR PET LIZARD

When Patricia's breakfast came the next day, it came with reading material. Her plea for something to occupy her time must have been heard. She pounced on the small stack excitedly, then grimaced. Price either had inane ideas about what a woman might like to read or a petty mean streak. He had sent fashion magazines and a romance novel. He'd also included a note asking for her clothing sizes so he could provide her a change of clothes.

She looked up at the camera when she read that. She would appreciate a change of clothes, certainly, but she didn't relish changing her clothes in front of whoever was watching. It was bad enough when she'd had to use the bathroom. She'd formed a sort of Snuggie out of the blanket from the bed to expose as little flesh as possible while she took care of business. Being asked for her sizes reminded her of the moment in the romance novel when the woman's measurements were worked into the rape fantasy plot. Patricia did not fantasize about rape. Luckily, she didn't think Daniel Price did, either.

Out of desperation, she read the magazines and the book, too. At least the book had made her laugh. She filed away some of the euphemisms for penis to tease Leonel with when she saw him again. Leonel had once confessed that he didn't like all the crass words that men used for their equipment. Patricia had teased him endlessly, making terrible puns that had him blushing like the little housewife he still was on the inside.

Thinking about Leonel made her think of Jessica and about what Price had said about capturing her. She hoped the so-called fools at the Department had trained her friends well, because now they were in real danger and there was nothing she could do to help them, not while she was trapped here reading makeup tips and advertisements for hair products. The only useful thing she'd gleaned from her morning's reading was that she was probably in Indiana, her home state. One of the magazines had still had a partial mailing label attached.

Her mind was spinning uselessly, like a bicycle tire with no gears or ligature to connect it to the machine. That day at lunch, she'd written "better books" on her plate in ketchup before sending it out the sliding panel with the robot-dog-thing. Dinner arrived with another short stack of magazines, science journals this time, and a notepad and a cheap mechanical pencil. Her captor had also included a copy of Mary Shelley's *Frankenstein*. Patricia thought it might have been an attempt at a joke.

She shuddered, trying to imagine how the man had accomplished what he had claimed, moving his consciousness from body to body. How many had he claimed? Five? She imagined the process as something straight out of an old horror movie—something with electricity arcing and a brain in a jar. He'd said he was due for another body now, and Patricia was filled with disgust and worry about whose body he might be planning to overtake.

She wondered, too, who his colleagues might be. He was hardly a lone crazy howling in the wilderness. This facility was well-equipped with technology and even a good kitchen staff. There were security guards, which implied a team. There was organization behind this madman. Organizations came with colleagues that could be sent to hurt her friends.

Patricia picked up the notepad and scrawled her sizes and type of clothing preferences on a piece of paper. She shoved it under the plate and sat watching the small sliding panel, waiting for it to open and take her dirty dishes and her message out to Cindy's father.

She'd spent some time the night before thinking about Cindy's father: Anton Lorre. She'd been pondering it all day, trying to recollect everything she knew about the man. When she had been searching for Cindy, she'd researched the entire family tree, back to Evangeline Liu's parents in California, and back in China before that. Anton she had not looked into deeply. The man was dead, or at least that was what she'd thought. Patricia wished she could look at the files she had gathered back in her apartment. His name had been Anton Lorre, born in Pittsburgh to Hungarian immigrant parents in the early 1900s, maybe 1910 or 1915. He'd met Cindy's mother when she'd come to work as an assistant in his lab, in the early 1940s. They didn't marry.

Patricia wished she knew what his work had been about, but that hadn't seemed important at the time. She had just been looking for family Cindy could have run to. There wasn't any. Anton had been an only child, and his parents were long dead.

Patricia knew Anton had died in a lab accident that burned him horribly. Cindy had been a baby when it happened. She had once told Patricia she didn't have any direct memories of the man, and the portrait her mother painted was sketchy and unflattering. Whatever the man had been working on, Ms. Liu had not approved.

Obviously the man had not died. Though she had doubted it at first, Patricia now felt sure the man calling himself Daniel Price really was Anton Lorre, long lost father of Cindy Liu, just as he claimed. Now the question was what he wanted from Patricia, and from Cindy. He claimed he was working to save his daughter, but Patricia knew a self-serving narcissist when she heard one. She'd worked with plenty of them over the years. Cindy's father might be helping Cindy, but only to the extent that he could also help himself. He wanted her to complete her formula so he could use it himself. And they both thought they could get something from Jessica that would make that possible.

Since Daniel had confessed he was keeping her lizard nature

suppressed with something he had injected her with, Patricia had also been thinking about how to counteract it. She'd been exercising like a madwoman, partly out of boredom and partly hoping to hurry the path of the drugs through her system. She sat down on the floor again now and stretched. Her upper back cracked in a couple places, revealing the tension she was holding in her body. She went back to her dinner tray, which had not yet been picked back up, and downed the remainder of the cranberry juice that had been provided.

Patricia knew medications moved through a body differently, depending on individual variations of metabolism. Over the years, she'd heard from Cindy about the ways different drugs interact poorly with unexpected things like citrus or beets. She picked up the magazines again. One of them had an article about oxidizing enzymes. It reminded Patricia of something she'd heard on a corporate retreat.

Patricia was part of a casual group of businesswomen. They used to get together once a year or so and pick each other's brains about climbing the corporate ladder, balancing work and life, that kind of thing. Patricia valued it for networking. You never knew who you might meet and how knowing them might help you. More than once, the group had arranged a retreat to a spa in Arizona. The whole thing had been a little New-Age-y for Patricia's taste, but even she had to admit she felt better after a week off to detox. One of the gurus had praised grapefruit juice for its power to help the body expedite the processing and removal of toxins. Cindy had used grapefruit juice as the base for the hangover treatment she had hawked to their classmates in college.

She wrote a note to send back out with the tray. *That's better. Would still like fresh air, a conversation with Cindy, and grapefruit juice.*

A late night snack came with a small carafe of grapefruit juice. No mention was made of her other requests, but, if she was right about the juice, maybe she could do the rest herself. She downed the juice in a single gulp.

JESSICA'S FIRST FLIGHT IN THE FIELD

Half an hour before they were due to leave, Jessica and Leonel stood in the motor pool waiting, both of them doing a poor job of hiding their impatience. They'd been over the case file four times together since it had been handed to them. Jessica had the details memorized. Becky White, age sixty-three, of Tall Oaks. Leonel had whistled when they read the address.

"A rich one," he said.

The picture showed a woman with an overlarge smile and an odd tension around the eyes. Jessica wasn't sure if the woman just wasn't photogenic or if she might be a little unstable. Ms. White had come to the attention of the Department through her eye doctor. The research team kept an eye on various medical forums and flagged reports of unusual abilities or situations.

Leonel and Jessica had both blanched at that notation. Neither of them had been to a doctor about their conditions, but it could easily have been one of them that the research team flagged last spring. Jessica tried to imagine what might have happened if she had sought medical attention for her gravity problems. She pictured the chubby nurse that worked for her GP shouting her name and trying to jump into the air to grab at her ankles as she drifted toward the ceiling.

It was even funnier to imagine how it might have gone had Leonel gone to the gynecologist.

"Well, Doc, my hormone problems have gotten worse. Besides the odd facial hair, I seem to have misplaced my vagina and grown a penis. What do you suggest?"

Neither of them had actually seen a doctor about their problems. The only doctors to try and figure out what had caused their changes worked for the Department. In the end, it had been the police and fire rescue teams that brought the Department into their lives after the firefight on campus, the one that had ended with Jessica's arm burned and Dr. Liu's escape with the emeralds. It was weird to be inside the organization that might have been keeping tabs on them only a few months before.

Leonel returned from another circuit of the motor pool. There was an impressive array of vehicles: motorcycles, sedans, jeeps, trucks, limousines, sports cars, SUVs. Even some vehicles that looked combat ready. Armored trucks, small tanks, ATVs. Jessica wasn't particularly into cars, but even she felt excited about the possibilities the extensive collection of transportation options suggested. It was both exhilarating and daunting to imagine the work that might require all this. It was amazing to think this was her life now.

Only a few years ago—even as recently as one year ago—her battles were all internal. She had fought cancer, then depression; she had fought self-doubt and her own ambivalence over her marriage. Then Dr. Liu's tea had changed all that. Her floating problem had brought Leonel and Patricia into her life, and she had fought with them to defeat Helen and Dr. Liu. It had felt good. That was why she had signed so readily when the Department came calling. It would be a relief to fight something she could actually see and touch.

She had just turned to say something to Leonel when the first member of the team arrived. It was a forty-or-so year old man, wearing mirrored sunglasses. Jessica grinned at him, and Leonel held out a hand for a handshake, but the man ignored them both and stalked over to a black van and pulled it around. He stood in front of it with his arms crossed over his chest.

Leonel tried again. "I'm Leonel Alvarez and this is Jessica Roark. Nice to meet you."

The man nodded, but still didn't move to take Leonel's offered hand.

Leonel cleared his throat. "Are you the driver?"

No answer.

"Quite a set of cars they have here, huh?"

Nothing. It was eerie. It was getting to Leonel, too. He gripped the low wall he was resting against and accidentally pulled off a chunk of it. He tried to discreetly set the piece on the ground and wiped the concrete dust off on his pants leg.

Then Sally Ann and Mike arrived, and the group loaded up into van. Both agents were dressed as if they were going to attend a business conference, and Jessica and Leonel looked down at their own much more casual attire doubtfully, but followed their trainers into the van.

The group hadn't even left the parking garage before Jessica felt the nervous tickling in her stomach that she knew meant she was going to take flight. She had much better control now, but it still happened when she was nervous. She shifted in her seat and tried to delicately burp into the elbow of her lavender sweat jacket. She wanted to complete this journey in her seat, not riding on the ceiling of the van.

"So, what's up with the driver?" she asked Sally Ann. "He wouldn't talk to me or Leonel."

Mike Lester laughed. "You should have warned them, Rogers."

"Now where would the fun have been in that?" Sally Ann responded. She grinned mischievously.

"Sorry, man," Lester said to Leonel. "I would have told you if I knew she hadn't. Agent Driver doesn't speak."

"At all?"

"Nope."

"And his name is Driver?"

"Yep."

Jessica could see Leonel thinking back over everything he had said, trying to get a response from the driver. She knew him well enough to know he was trying to figure out if he had said something he would owe an apology for. She pulled a face at Sally Ann, who stuck her tongue out in return.

"I was just having a bit of fun," Sally Ann said.

"Were you watching?" Jessica asked.

Sally Ann winked, her already wide grin widening. "Consider it your hazing, newbie."

Lester tapped her on the shoulder. "The ride isn't that long. Let's get to business."

Business, it turned out, wasn't going to be that exciting. Jessica and Leonel were to stay in the van with the surveillance equipment, which Agent Driver would assist only if called to do so. It promised to be pretty dull. Jessica tried not to let her disappointment show, but she felt it keenly. It made sense that they would go on a few missions in support roles before they would take on any combat or direct dealings with criminals, but that didn't mean she hadn't hoped for a bigger share in the action. Her curiosity was really piqued by the idea that there were others out there who had been affected by Dr. Liu's products. She wished she was going to meet Ms. White.

The rest of the journey the two trainers talked to each other, agreeing on the roles they would take inside. Sally Ann would do most of the talking, unless Ms. White showed a preference for Mike. Jessica would have liked to join in the conversation, but she didn't really have anything to offer. She turned to smile at Leonel. Even if it was going to be dull, this was their first mission. That was something worth celebrating.

Leonel looked very large on the bench seat they shared and seemed really uncomfortable. Jessica guessed there were some advantages to being small—she never had to worry about whether there was sufficient leg room, for one. Leonel crossed his legs, resting one ankle on the opposite knee, then switched, then switched again. His knee brushed against Agent Lester's knee, and he blushed scarlet. After that, he put both feet on the floor and folded his hands in his lap, seeming to try and pull his bulk into the smallest possible space.

Jessica watched incredulously. Did Leonel have a crush on Agent Lester? She tried to catch Leonel's eye, but his eyes were trained on his own shoelaces now. Mike Lester was certainly a handsome man, but she never imagined Leonel being the sort to even look at another man. He and David were so in love.

The van pulled into the loading space at Ms. White's condominium. The two senior agents wasted no time. They did a quick audio check with Driver, and when he gave them a thumbs-up, they exited the van and headed up the walk. Driver circled around and parked on the opposite side of the street under a tree where the three of them would have a good view of the door to the apartment building through the tinted windows of the van.

It was a posh-looking place. There were double glass doors through which the agents had gone. On either side were small well-groomed garden beds, featuring plants that Jessica couldn't name but had seen before in front of office buildings and banks. They were tall and reedy with elaborate blooms that looked artificial in their perfection. Along the street side of the tall complex, there were several business storefronts: a trendy noodle place, a coffee place, an ice cream shop, all of which were included in the same building. They probably all had doors into the main hall and lobby area. A person might never have to the leave the complex at all.

Jessica turned to make a snarky comment to Leonel. Now that it was just them and the silent Driver in the van, she thought it might be okay to make a little conversation. The dialogue upstairs in the apartment was painfully dull. The woman was the chatty sort and kept showing them pictures and going on about her family. They had yet to even broach the reason they were actually there. She tried to make eye contact with Leonel, but he was peering out the window and didn't see her attempt.

Then Sally Ann's voice came over the com. Jessica nearly jumped out of her skin when the device buzzed gently in her ear.

"Driver, check that out, please. Alvarez and Roark, stay put," she said.

Something was happening, but whatever it was, she had missed it in her mental wanderings.

The driver yanked the headset off his head and jumped out of the van without another word, then ran down the street. He had been listening to the conversation upstairs, while Jessica had not, so he must have known what he was supposed to check out. It must've been something serious, too, judging by the size of the gun he had tucked under his arm as he left the vehicle.

The two sat in stunned silence for a few seconds. Then Leonel leaned over the listening array and turned the volume knob up. They could hear a woman's voice, hysterical with fear. It was hard to understand her words, but there was something about a tank coming. Leonel leaned out the van door, peering in the direction the driver had disappeared in.

He came back in, shaking his head. "I don't see anything, but I don't like this."

Then Jessica heard a strange buzzing sound. "Leonel? Do you hear that?" She barely got the question out when a rumbling shook the van.

Gripping a wall for support, Leonel tossed Jessica her gym bag. "Trouble is coming. You'd better gear up. I think we're under attack."

Moving quickly, Jessica pulled off her bulky sweatshirt and strapped the air canisters and rig around her shoulders and rib cage. She didn't know what they would find, but she knew she wanted to be ready for action. The buzzing sound had settled into a pattern, and Jessica tried to stop herself from imagining what awaited them. None of the scenarios her mind was creating were likely to make her feel any calmer, and there was no point in guessing until she had more information.

As she strapped the controls into the holders built into the half gloves Walter had given her, she felt herself become calm. She could see this becoming a ritual like powdering her hands had once been for gymnastics, the movements as important to her confidence as any actual good they do for her performance. She pulled in big gulps of air, triggering the weightless tickle in her stomach.

"Okay. Open the top."

Leonel clicked a button and a panel slid aside in the top of the van, opening a window wide enough for someone as small as Jessica to escape through. "I'm heading for the rooftop of the building across the street so I can see what we're up against. Got your headset?"

Leonel nodded and tapped the earpiece. "Want a boost?" He knelt, holding out his hands to form a stair.

Jessica stepped into his hand, then tapped him on the shoulder to indicate her readiness. With that, Leonel threw her into the air.

SALLY ANN DIDN'T SEE THIS COMING

Crossing to the window, Sally Ann looked out. She didn't see anything at first. A large tree entirely obstructed her view of one end of the street. The part of the street she could see seemed ordinary. Then a flicker of movement in the tree tops caught her attention. It was Roark, flying from one tree to another. *Damn it.* She had told them to stay put. Sally Ann looked back at the van. She could see down into the top from her vantage point. It looked like Alvarez had opened the roof panel to send Roark through. He himself was now crouched down in front of the vehicle, whipping his head around wildly. They would have to work on stealth with this one. He couldn't call more attention to himself if he attached a flashing blue light to his shirt.

Returning her gaze to Roark, she saw her scan the street, then take another leap from the treetops to the top of the opposite building. In spite of her anger at having been disobeyed, Sally Ann was still proud to see her protégée putting her training to such good use. Her movements were fluid and graceful, capitalizing on her gymnastic talent and her unusual abilities. Roark landed in a crouching position and immediately crawled to take shelter behind a decorative outcropping. That was smart. Roark had potential.

"Leonel?" Roark's voice crackled in the ear piece and Sally Ann winced. The newbies always seemed to think you had to shout.

"What do you see?" he answered.

"Nothing yet."

Great, now they were broadcasting only to say they didn't know anything. She'd recommend them both for extra communications training when they got back to base.

Ms. White rose from the sofa and moved toward Sally Ann. Sally Ann placed herself between the increasingly hysterical woman and the window. She tilted her head to the left, signaling Lester to be ready to restrain her if necessary.

"Ms. White, please calm down. We're just here to talk. We're not here to hurt you." She thought about the Paxil she'd seen in the medicine chest alongside the eye drops she had pocketed for testing.

"Can't you see it?" The woman's eyes had gone an eerie pale white that glowed. The watery blue iris beneath was barely visible.

Sally Ann suddenly had no doubt this woman could indeed see something she couldn't.

"What do you see?" She tried to keep her voice calm.

"It's a tank! It's coming this way!"

"From which direction?" Looking back out the window, she saw the van shake.

The windows broke, throwing glass in the area surrounding the vehicle. She still couldn't see the cause, but she was glad Roark and Alvarez had vacated the vehicle. Self-preservation was a good reason to disobey orders. Sally Ann didn't like being trapped on the third floor when something was happening with her agents on the ground.

"Driver? Driver, report in!"

"What's going on here? Who are you talking to?" Ms. White gripped her arm. Her nails bit into Sally Ann's skin.

Sally Ann gently untangled herself and pushed the woman down onto the couch. "Ms. White? I'm going to take care of it. Mr. Lester will stay here and make sure you are safe."

Ms. White clung to Lester's arm when he sat beside her on the couch, drawing him near her side. Sally Ann thought her colleague looked alarmed, but she wasn't there to coddle him. He'd babysit if that's what she needed him to do.

She fled the apartment and flung herself down the stairs in short leaps. "Driver. Report."

Her phone buzzed and a message appeared on the text screen. Driver didn't speak, and no one knew him by any other name than Driver, but he was an amazing field operative. From what he was texting now, it looked like Ms. White wasn't crazy. There was indeed some kind of small armored vehicle working its way across the city. Actually, there had been three, but Driver had already disabled two of them. The remaining vehicle seemed to be heading toward them. Driver indicated it had attacked the van with an electricity-based weapon from quite a distance. Reading that, the hair stood up on the back of Sally Ann's neck. Electricity weapons were not standard for thugs and common criminals. She had to get to her team.

"Lester, call it in! Get us some backup."

She had just gotten to the street when the vehicle in question rolled into view, heading straight for the van. "Take shelter!" Sally Ann yelled to Leonel, who was standing transfixed in the middle of the road. She pulled a small baton from her suit jacket pocket and spun it to expand it. There was an electrical energy crackle as the device spun. She stepped into the street and aimed the weapon at the advancing vehicle.

The tank had the traditional shape, but was very small, not much larger than a Smart Car. Sally Ann could see that it was well-armored and featured an array of weapons. She glanced quickly to the side and saw Leonel on the opposite side of the street. She couldn't see Jessica anywhere. Deciding the best defense was going to be a good offense in this case, she ran toward the tank in a zigzag pattern, poised on her toes so she could dodge if necessary. She covered the remaining distance in only a few seconds, but the tank veered around her and continued toward the van. Sally Ann signaled to Alvarez to stay out of the fray.

Driver came running around the corner on a scooter, which somehow was moving faster than such a vehicle should be able to go.

He made a tight circle around the tank, throwing out a cable that wrapped itself around the treads and brought the vehicle to a shrieking halt. Sally Ann hurried, fully expecting the weapons to turn on Driver. The guns swiveled, but they were aiming high, at the tops of the buildings. That didn't make sense. She and Driver and Alvarez were all down here.

She was analyzing the vehicle for weak points when her headset crackled.

"Rogers?" It was Roark, probably still up on the roof, where the weapons were aimed. She hoped the new recruit had the sense to take cover and let her handle this.

The tank's weapons array spun. There was a roaring sound, and several large tree branches littered the road.

Swearing under her breath, Sally Ann ordered, "Hold your position, Roark. I've got this." She pressed a button on the staff in her hand and felt the device thrum to life. She didn't expect to test the new EMP blast so soon, but she was glad to have it.

Sally Ann aimed for the front panel of the machine, where it seemed most likely all the electronic parts were housed, and loosed the blast. The machine shuddered, then was still. Black smoke curled out of the front of the vehicle and the air smelled of burnt electronics. Her strike had been very effective indeed. She'd have to congratulate the tech team on the first successful use in the field.

Sally Ann approached, letting her staff fall to her side, and scanned the street for additional threats. She didn't see the attack when it came. The next thing she knew she was lying in a heap by the side of the road, Roark hovering three feet off the ground above her. There was a scorch mark in the street where she had been standing.

A crunching sound drew both women's attention back to the small tank. Alvarez had pulled the top half open, rolling it back like it was made of paper, though Sally Ann could see that it was quite solid indeed. They hadn't been exaggerating about this man's strength.

He was reaching inside, pulling at something. There was horrible rending sound. Sally Ann rolled to her feet and held her staff at the ready. She heard a soft tufting sound. When she glanced, she saw

Jessica had floated higher into the nearby tree branches and out of view. That was probably wise given the number of apartment windows overlooking this section of street. The Director was not going to be pleased about the amount of attention this mission had garnered. It was supposed to be a simple interview and assessment with possible retrieval. In and out.

There had been nothing about a tank in the mission parameters. The tank open now, Alvarez reached in. Sally Ann could see his muscles strain as he worked, pulling at something inside. A few seconds later, he had removed the occupant of the mini-tank, still strapped into the seat. He set the seat on the ground and stepped back. He looked toward Sally Ann for instructions.

That was when the cavalry arrived. An ambulance pulled up and three large orderlies jumped from the cab, two of them carrying large handguns. A large truck pulled up and the entire mini tank was pushed inside, next to two other smoking vehicles and the ruined black van. The driver Alvarez had just pulled out was taken into the ambulance, still strapped into the seat. Sally Ann thought she saw a body bag inside and hoped it was one of the attackers and not one of their own.

When the other vehicles had gone, Driver rolled up in a white van labeled with a florist's logo, and Sally Ann got inside. They paused beneath the tree and Roark dropped in from above, landing in the empty space between their feet. They picked up the dazed and rattled-looking Alvarez from where he was still standing in the middle of the road. She let Lester know a car would come for him and Ms. White; then Sally Ann tapped the wall to tell Driver to go, and let her head drop into her hands. This had been a complete disaster. The Director was going to have her ass.

MARY DOESN'T FIND THE PRINCE CHARMING

They said she wasn't a prisoner, but that didn't change the fact that Mary was locked in. She was pretty sure that made her a prisoner, despite the pleasantness of the room.

The room was certainly more suitable than the one she had awakened in on the first day. No bunnies and pink fluff this time. It was a simple room, laid out like a hotel room with a double bed against the wall facing a wall-mounted television and a small desk area. There was also a table with a couple chairs, presumably for eating her meals at, and a decent-sized bathroom. There were bottles of water in the small refrigerator. The walls were painted a warm dusty yellow, one of those tones Mary knew from her class in art appreciation was meant to be calming. The bedding was all white and crisp and reminded Mary of a beachside bed and breakfast.

All in all, it was a lovely cell, but that didn't mean it wasn't still a cell.

And it looked sort of permanent—like they expected to keep her here a while. That worried her.

The Director's assistant—did anyone in this fucking place have an actual name? —had seen her to the room, wished her a pleasant night, and promptly left. Mary had been too stunned to speak up, and wasn't sure what she would have said if she'd had the opportunity.

Mary picked up her sketchpad and examined the sketch she had made of the Director. Her drawing captured his surface details pretty well, but she didn't think it gave a true sense of him. She turned to a blank page and tried again. She tried to capture just his eyes. They were a soft, light brown, kind of small for his face. They were rimmed in lashes that were long and lush for a man, but this had not had a softening effect like she might have expected. When his gaze fell on her, it felt sharp and judging. Mary definitely had the feeling of a mind constantly at work behind those eyes. Analytical was a good word for it. She had felt more like a specimen than a woman in his presence.

Which was not to say he wasn't handsome. He was. And he knew it. It was evident in how he carried himself. His smile was practiced, and he knew how to work an angle. He had not proven susceptible to distraction by a little cleavage or girlish posturing. She suspected he recognized the minor manipulations for what they were and was, for that reason, immune to them. Or maybe he just wasn't attracted to her. That wounded Mary's pride, if she were honest. She was used to positive male attention when she wanted it. It was unusual for her to garner no reaction at all.

She wasn't going to learn anything locked in a room alone, either. She paced the room, following various lines in the patterned carpet as she thought. Eventually, she resorted to watching television from sheer restlessness. Maybe she could distract herself that way. At least they'd given her full access to all the channels. If all else failed, she could maybe find some decent porn and rock herself to sleep. She flipped through all the channels on mute, looking for something worth turning on the sound for. She backed up for the local news when she recognized the street scene that had flashed by.

A guy she'd dated briefly in her stint at college had been from the Tall Oaks area. She'd been invited home for brunch exactly once before he'd started flaking out on her. Mary was sure his "Mummy" had told him she wasn't a suitable choice for a young man of his station, or some silliness like that. He hadn't been worth fighting for, and she'd let him slip away and replaced him with another wannabe rock star. The rock star had at least been fun and hadn't particularly cared what his mother might have to say about his dating choices. She wasn't cut out for a Tall Oaks boy. They took too much coddling.

Tall Oaks wasn't the kind of neighborhood that made the news, though. The quieter sort of rich people lived there, the ones who really didn't want media attention, rather than the kind that said they didn't want the spotlight while grabbing it with both hands. They probably weren't thrilled about finding themselves on the less than reputable Springfield Tonight show. But it looked like something pretty serious had happened there today. When the camera panned the street, Mary could see a large scorch mark and some tree branches lying on top a crushed BMW. There were several people milling about in the street. That was telling, too. People from Tall Oaks did not "mill."

The scrolling bar at the bottom of the screen ran headlines about a tank attack in Tall Oaks earlier that afternoon. Mary turned up the sound.

An older woman, maybe fifty-five or sixty, grabbed the micro-phone when the young Latina reporter held it out to her. The woman turned and looked into the camera, tucking long, white hair behind her ear, and looking awfully red-faced and flustered.

"There was a tank! An actual tank! I saw it coming!" She pointed at the tree branches. "It had lasers or something. Look at Mr. Henry's car!"

A younger woman grabbed the arm of the older one and pulled her away, holding a hand up in a completely failed attempt to hide her face and that of her mother from the intrusive camera.

The program went on to show shaky video clips taken on people's cell phones. It really did look like there was a tank, though it was weirdly small, like a two-seater. A still picture showed a muscle-bound hunk of a man holding a giant piece of metal in his hands. Another clip showed a woman who seemed to be flying around the treetops. The news "story" amounted to showing the clips and basically saying, "Weird, huh?" then asking people to call in if they knew anything. It wasn't exactly chock full of information.

Mary scrambled for her folder of pictures and spread them out on the bed. The flying woman. Mary fumbled with the remote and was happy to find the cable service provided the rewind feature. She froze the screen at the moment in the video that showed the flying woman most clearly. Mary walked up to the television and held up the picture she'd taken from her folder, the one taken on the college campus the day her mother disappeared. It had to be the same woman. The body shape was the same, the hair. And how many flying women could there be in Springfield?

She was still standing there, holding the picture up for comparison to the frozen frame on the screen, when there was a knock at the door.

"Come in," she called, though she found it funny that someone would knock on the door when she was incapable of opening it from the inside. The door swung open, and there was the Director, holding a pizza box and a six pack of Hoppy Toad. Mary smiled at the sight of him, then frowned, mistrusting the feeling of happiness that had risen in her when she saw the man.

"Can you stop that?"

He looked confused. "Stop what?"

"I don't know, exactly. But you're messing with my head."

He set the pizza on the small table near the window and handed Mary one of the beers.

"And this—" She held out the beer, after taking a long swig, and pointed out the label. "You just happen to show up with one of my favorite beers? Even though it's a microbrew and hard to get?"

"We have an excellent research department."

"I'm sure you do. I'm sure they gave you a thorough report on all my comings and goings during the months you left me hanging and worried to death about where my mother was when she was here in your own freak-show hospital all the time."

The Director opened his mouth to speak. Mary could already see the aw-shucks-ma'am forming on his face and cut him off.

"Who are you people? And what do you want with me and my mother?"

The Director stood for long seconds, watching her carefully. He took a pull from his beer, looked at it in surprise, and took another. Then, he set it on the table and sat down in one of the chairs, gesturing for Mary to take the other one.

"We're the Department," he said.

Mary took the empty chair. "Department of what?"

"That would be the question, wouldn't it?" He grinned at her, a self-satisfied smirk that made her want to smack it off his face, even as part of her brain tried to tell her she should trust this man.

"See! There! Again!"

Just for a moment, the smooth facade dropped, and Mary could see the calculating coldness of the man's brown eyes. She knew he was assessing her; she just didn't understand what for yet.

"We're a covert operations group. We handle the weird cases—the things the world doesn't want to deal with."

"You mean like my mother."

"Exactly like your mother."

"Okay, so you handled her. Why is she still here? If she's a criminal, she should be in jail. If she's not, she should be back at home with me."

"It's complicated," he began, stopping when Mary snorted aloud. She wondered if he remembered what he told her about men who claim things are complicated. He started again. "It's not always that black and white."

"I don't know. This seems pretty black and white to me. You've imprisoned my mother here for months, suppressed the investigation into her disappearance, and now kidnapped and imprisoned me when I got too close to the truth. But you want me to believe you're the good guys?"

"We've also given your mother the best medical care, even designing a special facility that could keep her safe while she healed."

"What do you want? A prize? A prison is still a prison, even when it comes with pizza and beer."

"You forgot the lavender soap and plush towels."

"You're trying it again."

The Director folded his hands on the table and seemed to be lost in thought. Mary took a piece of pizza and bit into it savagely. It was good pizza, too. She was happy to have it and the beer, but angry at the feeling of being manipulated. Luckily, suspicion didn't change the taste of the pizza.

"You're right," he eventually said.

Mary nodded. "And?"

"I'll try to stop. It's not that easy. It's kind of automatic."

Mary held back her thoughts about the kinds of people who got want they wanted through sneaky and underhanded means like psychic manipulation. "So, just tell me. Plainly and simply. What do you want from me?"

"We want your help with your mother."

"And you think I can get her to do what you want?"

"If anyone can, yes."

"What is it you want her to do?" Mary crossed her arms over her chest.

"Just submit to some tests. Show us what she can do in controlled circumstances."

"Why?"

"We want to understand what's happening with her."

"Why?"

"Didn't you just ask that?" A flirtatious lilt was back in his voice.

"Stop playing Prince Charming and answer the question."

"What was the question?"

"Why? Why do you want to understand what's happening with her?"

The Director looked dumbfounded. "I would think it would be obvious. We've never seen anything like her before."

Mary waved her hand dismissively. "Yeah. I get that. But what are you after? What's your angle? What do you plan to do with the information if I help you get it?"

His gaze changed from vaguely interested to assessing again. She thought he looked pleased, too. "That's a very astute question."

"Does it rate me an astute answer?"

"I can't tell you. At least not fully. I can tell you that understanding what is happening with your mother will help us help others."

Mary raised an eyebrow at the man. Did he really think this vague reassurance was enough to make her roll over and cooperate? "Let me see her, talk to her. Then, we'll talk."

The smile that spread across his handsome face looked genuine enough that Mary almost doubted her own doubt.

He picked up another beer and passed it to her, then raised his own in her direction. "To working together."

Mary took a deep swig and set the bottle down hard. This was a dangerous game she was trying to play. She hoped she could keep up.

LINDA AND JESSICA PAY THE PIPER

Linda and Jessica were seated on the hard bench just outside the Director's office, waiting while the Director talked to their trainers. Linda wondered if it were uncomfortable on purpose, rather like the stiff chairs in a principal's office. Just one more way to say, "You're in trouble, mister." Sally Ann had hardly spoken on the journey back to the main office. Linda didn't know if that meant she was angry with them, or she was just processing all that happened.

Jessica looked miserable. Linda put a hand on her shoulder and tried to smile reassuringly. "It was my fault we disobeyed orders, Jessica. I'll tell the Director that."

Jessica put her brave face on. Linda recognized it from all their bedside conversations while Jessica was in the hospital healing from her burns. "I stand by my actions, Leonel. I wouldn't do it differently."

The two friends sat in silence for a moment, Jessica swinging her legs to release her nervous energy. Linda remembered what it had been like, being small. Sometimes she missed it, especially when she felt crowded or like the furniture was too delicate. In the months since her initial transformation, she'd gotten very good at controlling her strength. Other than the wall during training, she hadn't broken anything by accident in quite some time, well, not counting the wall in the car pool. Not like in the beginning when it seemed like she broke everything she touched. Now it was only relationships she seemed to be breaking. She checked her phone, which still didn't have any message from David. He never used to leave her hanging like that. Linda couldn't help but feel he was trying to punish her.

Linda listened hard, but she couldn't hear anything. The walls of the Director's office must be very thick, perhaps even sound-proofed. Given that a good portion of the work of the Department was in secret, that made sense, but it was frustrating to have no idea what was going on in there. Not even the tone of the meeting. Linda was growing impatient. Whatever was going to happen just needed to happen already.

She patted Jessica's knee. "You were amazing out there. You're really getting good at controlling your flight. You were just a streak when you knocked Sally Ann out of the way of that tank-blast."

Jessica grinned. "It does feel good. Not quite as amazing as flying with the emeralds, but still. Walter's team did an incredible job on the tank."

"Walter, huh?"

Jessica blushed, and Linda knew her hunch had been correct. "He seems like a good guy, Jessica. You deserve happiness."

"You don't think it's too soon? My divorce only just became final a month ago."

"Time isn't the only thing that makes a person ready. You shouldn't pass up a good thing just because you think you haven't been unhappy long enough yet."

"We're supposed to go to dinner tonight." Jessica's voice reflected a range of mixed emotions.

Linda heard nervousness, sadness, worry, joy, hope, and fear all wrapped up in that one little sentence. She knew the combination. She felt it every day. Today it was more the worry and fear side, but she reminded herself that she and David had already been through a lot.

"Love is terrifyingly wonderful," she said. "Do you need a sitter? David and I don't have plans tonight."

Babysitting with David could be wonderful. Children always brought out his brightest humor.

"Mom's got them."

Linda had just opened her mouth to ask about Jessica's mother, Eva, and how she was doing when the office door opened behind them. Sally Ann was standing there, arms crossed over her chest, Lester waiting behind her, his face unreadable.

"Your turn, newbies. Good luck."

Linda squeezed Jessica's hand one more time, then led the way into the Director's office. Linda had only been inside one other time. She'd done a pre-interview there before she signed her recruitment papers. The room had not changed.

One wall was lined in windows overlooking the city. The view was beautiful and gave a sense of openness, but Linda was sure the glass was not ordinary. The Director's office would be able to withstand a variety of attacks if anyone were to try and break in. The area in front of the windows was empty. Linda wondered if the Director stood there looking out at the city as he strategized.

"It's a nice view, isn't it?"

The voice came from behind them, back toward the door Linda and Jessica had entered through. Linda jumped, and she heard the Director chuckle softly. He was infamous for moving silently, and Linda suspected he enjoyed startling people.

"Ms. Roark," he said, walking toward them and extending a hand. "So nice to meet you in person at last. I trust Sally Ann has been making you feel welcomed."

Jessica took the Director's hand, giving Linda a sideways look. Linda realized she had neglected to warn Jessica that the leader of the Department looked all of twenty-five years old. Jessica assured the man that Sally Ann was training her well. She seemed especially concerned that he knew her trainer was not to blame for their actions on the mission.

"I do understand, Ms. Roark. Training and work in the field are quite different animals. Sometimes an agent has to think on her feet and make a decision. Don't you agree, Ms. Alvarez?"

Linda smiled warmly at the Director and jerked her chin in agreement. Other than her husband, he was the only person who ever addressed her as a woman. At least when they were alone. If they were to talk in front of those who didn't know, Linda knew she could rely on his discretion. His Spanish pronunciation wasn't bad, either. He put the accent on the right syllable of her last name.

Jessica interrupted the moment. "I'm sorry, sir, if our actions made the work of the Department more difficult. We just couldn't stay in the van and not take action when we could make a difference."

The Director brought his hands together in front of his mouth in an attitude almost of prayer. "Let's talk about what happened. Please, come sit."

Linda and Jessica moved to the small seating area the Director had indicated. The furniture was very rich and formal, upholstered in dark leather that crinkled when sat upon. Linda pulled at her clothes self-consciously as she seated herself on the sofa next to Jessica. She felt positively grubby in her jeans and soft gray T-shirt. She wished she had at least put on a shirt with buttons. But she hadn't come to the Department that day expecting a meeting with the Director. She had come for her strategy training session, then ended up on the mission. Linda could see that Jessica was feeling equally self-conscious.

"Please don't worry about your appearance," the Director said, and Linda had, not for the first time, the feeling he could read her thoughts. "The office may be very formal, but I assure you that formality is unimportant to me. We need to talk about your work today."

Linda felt tears prick at the corners of her eyes. She'd always had a tendency to cry when under stress. It wasn't perceived the same way in a man, though, and she worked to control the reaction. She held the tears back by force of will and looked the Director in the face. She didn't find the anger and disapproval she expected there. His eyes were clear and bright, and curious. Seeing his expression, she relaxed a little, waiting for him to ask a question.

The Director turned to Jessica, who was twisting the sleeve of her jacket in her hands. "That was some impressive flying you did today, Ms. Roark."

Jessica blushed. "Thank you, sir."

Linda added, "She was amazing. Sally Ann Rogers would be a smear on the pavement now if not for our Jessica."

The Director nodded. "Agent Rogers indicated as much. She wasn't happy to have to admit it, but she's fair and believes in giving credit where it is due. She praised you for"—he read from a report on the computer he had balanced on the arm of his chair—"'quick thinking and action that probably saved her life.'"

Jessica didn't say anything, but she did stop twisting her sleeve and smile at Linda.

The Director continued. "I've seen some of the footage. It doesn't show me everything, but I saw some of the main bits. Linda, you were also quite effective. It was a good move, getting the attacker out of her tank and away from her weapons." Linda startled—their attacker had been female? The Director went on. "Our investigative team has already found an array of other weapons she would assuredly have used against you when she got over the initial stun."

"Did the agents get anything out of the attackers?" Linda hadn't been part of the questioning. As soon as they arrived back at headquarters, she and Jessica were sent to file their reports, then called to this meeting. All she knew was Driver had taken out two other tanks when he'd run off, leaving Linda and Jessica in the van. When there was time, she intended to learn more about the silent agent. He was obviously no one to be trifled with.

"We think that they were after Ms. Roark, actually."

"Me? What would anyone want with me?"

"We're still looking into that. It looks like this attack came from Daniel Price."

"The man who took Patricia!" Linda leaped from her seat. "Do they know where she is?"

The Director stood and Linda was surprised to realize he was actually taller than her. He gave the impression of being small and physically delicate, but he was actually quite tall and broad. *It must be something in the way he carries himself,* Linda decided. He laid a hand on Linda's shoulder and she felt instantly calmer.

"We're doing all we can, but it will take time, Linda."

Linda fell back into the sofa, causing Jessica to bounce from the impact. "I'm sorry, sir. It's just so good to hear that there's a lead. What do we know about the woman who was in the tank?"

"She's a scientist, a transplant specialist. Her name is Meredith Cushing." There was a rapping at the door. "Ah. That'll be Dr. Peeples."

Linda saw Jessica's reaction. That girl had it bad for this professor. Linda looked forward to checking him out more closely. In the couple of more personal interactions she'd had with him, Linda thought this Walter seemed like a good guy, but he needed to be better than just good to deserve Jessica. Linda sat up straighter, emphasizing the breadth of her shoulders and the girth of her arms. She'd been a parent long enough to know how the father-protector role was played. She'd watch David intimidate the boys who had come calling on their daughters.

Dr. Peeples came in huffing and puffing. He had obviously run at full speed to arrive at the meeting. "Is it true?"

The Director raised an eyebrow questioningly.

"It's Meredith? Meredith Cushing?"

Still not speaking, the Director dipped his chin in the smallest of nods.

"Oh God!" Walter flopped onto the arm of the couch with an easy familiarity Linda couldn't imagine feeling in the Director's office. The doctor had worked here for a long time. He'd told Linda he'd been there at the very beginning.

Jessica reached up and rubbed Walter's arm soothingly. The Director and Linda exchanged a look when Walter grabbed Jessica's fingers. The gesture had been unselfconscious for both of them, but had revealed more than either probably realized.

Walter turned to Linda and explained, "Meredith and I used to work together, back when I was in corporate. They're saying she's involved with the man who kidnapped Patricia." Disbelief resonated in his tone.

"She's not talking yet, but, yes, she was inside one of the tanks that attacked our team on the ICU case."

"So, she knew about the farsighted woman?"

The Director shrugged, which made him look even more like a college student. "Maybe. But she didn't make a move toward Ms. White. It looks like it was Ms. Roark they were after."

Walter gasped. Before he could voice his fears, Jessica spoke up.

"You said that before, but I don't understand. Why would she be after me?"

Linda stood up and paced to the window. Some of the pieces were coming together in her mind, and she didn't like the picture they formed. She remembered her conversation with Sally Ann, and the photograph that was tagged as having been taken by Evangeline Liu. Linda leaned her head against the glass.

"Leonel?" It was Jessica calling out. "Are you all right?"

"I think I understand what's happening here, *m'ija*. And it's not a pretty story. You're in danger."

"I still don't understand."

"It's Dr. Liu."

Linda turned to face the other three. All of them were watching her gravely. The Director, in particular, seemed focused on her every word.

"She must have gone to this Daniel Price for help—it must all go back to Project Osiris, the one Sally Ann is investigating." She gripped Jessica's arm, to let her know she'd fill her in on all the details later. That wasn't what mattered now. She went on. "Dr. Liu must have told this man about you. He came and took Patricia, and now he's after you. Whatever she wanted when she kidnapped you last spring—she still wants it."

"And now she has allies," the Director added, the matter-of-factness of his tone chilling.

"But so does Jessica," said Walter.

JESSICA SEES A FAMILIAR FACE

The woman on the other side of the observation glass was short and pudgy. She was also oddly familiar, though Jessica couldn't place where she might know her from. Moving to another position to look at her from another angle, Jessica guessed the woman was forty or so years old. She had long brown hair that had been braided and was now messy from the helmet she had been wearing when Leonel pulled her from the mini tank. She sat quietly in the chair, her elbows resting on the table and her cuffed hands cradling her head, which hung low, facing the table. She was clothed in what looked like motorcycle gear: a padded jacket and stiff pants that were probably reinforced. They didn't fit her well, and it was obvious that she felt uncomfortable in them. She was the picture of misery.

Watching her through the glass, Jessica felt a wash of sympathy. This woman may have just attacked them, but there was more to the story than there seemed to be on the surface. Walter had worked with her. He said something like this was completely out of character with the woman he had known. Jessica pushed down the wave of petty jealousy that tried to rise. Walter had made no commitment to her, so she had no right to proprietary feelings about him, and besides, there was no reason to assume he and this woman had been lovers and not just colleagues.

Walter was looking at the woman intently. "It's definitely her: Meredith Cushing," he announced. "When I knew her, she was working on experimental transplant surgery techniques. It's hard to imagine what could make a woman so focused on helping people do something like this."

Leonel stood up from the chair he had been resting in and joined them at the window. "Does she look familiar to you?" He pulled a pair of glasses from his pocket and put them on, leaning nearer to the glass to peer at their attacker more carefully.

Jessica looked at him in surprise. "You, too? I was just thinking I have seen her somewhere before." She almost had it. She didn't think she had ever met the woman or spoken to her, but she definitely found something about her face familiar. Maybe she just looked like someone she knew. Her brain was spinning overtime over the all the weird things she had learned in the past few hours.

She desperately wanted this woman to give them a solid lead. She was still confused by the story Leonel and Sally Ann had told her the night before. If they were right, and Jessica was sure they were, then Patricia had been kidnapped by Cindy Liu's father, who had body-hopped his way through most of the past century, leaving a trail of corpses behind him. He was a dangerous man, and everyone seemed convinced this woman was working for him.

Jessica had known in her heart all this was going to lead back to Dr. Liu. Ever since the appearance of the pink sand on Patricia's dining room table, she'd been waiting for the proof to come to the surface. And here it was, sitting in front of them, if they could get this woman to help them.

The tablet in the Director's hands lit up with updates, and he shifted his attention. His eyebrows raised, he tipped the device so the three of them could look together at the article. A Baltimore news-paper reported that Dr. Meredith Cushing, a leading researcher in Johns Hopkins University's experimental transplant program, had been reported missing, along with her younger sister. The article was dated a month ago.

"There have been almost no leads. Meredith had taken a few days off to spend with her teenage sister over spring break. No one knew anything was wrong until she didn't show back up to work when she was expected." The Director pulled the pad back into his hands and pulled up another file, some kind of summary report from the Baltimore Police Department. He quickly scanned through some pictures. "There were no signs of a break-in or struggle. A pizza box with half a pie in it was on the coffee table and the television was still running."

Leonel gasped. "Just like Patricia."

The Director nodded. "It does sound ominously familiar."

They all turned and looked at Meredith Cushing again. She was leaning back now, her gaze turned to the ceiling and her hands folded on the table. Tears were visible on her cheeks.

"Let me go talk to her," Walter said. "She knows me. Maybe she'll talk to me."

"It can't hurt. I don't really want to resort to harsher measures unless we must."

The Director's tone made Jessica shiver. She suspected the "harsher measures" were things she'd rather not know about. Leonel put a hand on Jessica's shoulder and squeezed it reassuringly.

The Director flicked a few things on the screen, then said, "You're cleared."

A resolute set to his face and shoulders, Walter walked from the room. Moments later, they saw him enter the room where Meredith Cushing sat at the table. Surprise was immediately obvious in the woman. She stood and drew her hands to her mouth, then reached out one hand to the doctor.

"Walter Peeples?"

He crossed to Meredith and drew a chair near hers, then sat. She sat back down.

"What's going on, Meredith?"

"I can't tell you." The catch in her voice made it clear she wanted to tell him, and she was afraid to do so.

Jessica, watching, felt a mix of sympathy and impatience that had her floating six inches off the floor. Leonel tugged her gently downward, and Jessica burped quietly a few times.

"I'm here to help," Walter began. "My colleagues have amazing resources. We can get you out of this. But you have to give us something to go on."

"You don't understand. He has my sister."

"Who? Daniel Price?"

Meredith's face crumpled. She dropped her head onto her arms and sobbed aloud. Walter sat there for some moments, obviously unsure of what to do. He dropped a hand on Meredith's upper back and patted at her awkwardly, looking beseechingly at the others he knew were watching through the wall. Jessica wished she could help, but Walter was on his own for now.

After some minutes, Meredith seemed to run out of tears. She sat up, her face red and nose dripping. Walter stood up and pulled a packet of tissues from his pants pocket and offered it to her.

She accepted them gratefully. "I'm sorry. I've been under so much pressure. I'm so afraid. He'll hurt her if I tell you anything."

"What if I tell you a few things? Just see what you think." Meredith looked wary, but she was listening. "Let's start with Daniel Price. Daniel Price died in a lab accident, over a decade ago. But somehow, he was seen on surveillance footage just a few days ago and his fingerprints were found at the scene of a kidnapping."

Meredith gasped aloud.

"We're pretty sure we know who he sent you after today. My question is: what does he want from you?"

Meredith stood and paced the few steps her restraints allowed in a tight little circle. She pushed her thumb against her teeth, thinking hard. Suddenly she threw herself back in the chair. Everyone watching from the observation area pressed closer to the wall, anticipating.

"Surgery. He wants me to transplant his brain into another body."

Jessica stifled a squeak of surprise, but Walter just nodded. "I thought it might be something like that. So, he can't do it himself. It requires someone to complete the procedure."

Meredith picked up her glasses from the table and put them on. "I think he's done this several times now. I was just there to take samples if the woman was killed when we tried to take her, but when the soldiers in the other tanks were taken out, he said I had to step up or he'd kill Maggie." She sobbed again, and Walter paced the room while he waited for her to calm down.

Jessica lost the thread of the conversation after that. It got very technical and what she did understand grossed her out. The Director, on the other hand, seemed to grow more avid as he listened, excited by what he was hearing. Now that the woman had her glasses on, Jessica knew where she had seen her. It was the woman who had followed her a few days back, the one she'd convinced herself wasn't actually following her. Maybe they weren't just crazy to suggest she had been the target. She felt sick.

Moving to the back of the small observation room, Jessica sat in one of the chairs and tried to think. After a few more minutes, Leonel joined her. He tossed an arm around her shoulder and gave her a gentle squeeze.

"It's all very creepy, isn't it?" he whispered.

Jessica nodded her agreement.

"I guess in a way, it's not that different than what Dr. Liu was doing. He's just looking for a way to extend his life." Leonel shuddered.

Suddenly Walter burst back into the room. Jessica jumped. She hadn't realized he had finished talking with Meredith. She felt guilty for having stopped listening, but Walter ignored both Jessica and Leonel and, instead, rushed straight over to the Director.

"Are you thinking what I'm thinking?" he asked, excitement and urgency letting his mild Yooper accent bleed into his usually modulated speaking voice.

"Do you think she can pull it off?" The Director sounded merely curious. Jessica could see the decision had been made, and the

Director would support whatever plan Walter had in mind. This was just the formalities now.

"Yes, sir. I think she can."

More tapping on the device. Jessica and Leonel looked at each other. Jessica could see Leonel was no clearer about what was going on than she was.

After a few moments, the Director looked up. "Strategy session in two hours, Conference Room Alpha."

Walter sort of bowed, then hurried from the room with a quick apologetic smile for Jessica.

"Well, ladies," said the Director, turning to Jessica and Leonel. "If this goes how I hope, we might get Patricia back and get the nefarious Dr. Price in custody all in one fell swoop. Looks like you're getting right back on the horse. We'll need to get you up to speed."

PATRICIA BY NIGHT

At some point, the lights dimmed. Patricia accepted the cue and went to lie down on the small, narrow bed. It was a perfectly good mattress, even if the bed itself made her feel cramped. She had always liked a large bed she could really sprawl in. The one in her condo was a king-size, even though she usually slept alone. When she didn't have house guests, she'd leave her stacks of books and electronics stacked along the far edge. Only rarely did she move enough to disturb the items or knock them to the floor.

In the darkness, with the blanket pulled up to hide her body, she reached to her inner beast and flexed, trying to bring her out. She pushed, gritting her teeth, until her muscles began to shake, then let go. A few scales had erupted on her upper arms, but that was all. It wasn't enough to get her out of this mess.

She lay there waiting for sleep to come, but it didn't. She thought she was doing a fair imitation of a sleeping person, leaving her eyes closed and regulating her breathing, but inside, her mind was spinning, trying to figure out something useful. After a while, she heard the soft sobbing again through the vent.

She rolled over so she was lying on her stomach and hung her head over the edge of the bed. She hoped that, in the darkened room, it would appear to any observer that she was simply sleeping in an awkward position. "Hello?" she called out softly. "Can you hear me?"

The sobbing paused, replaced with sounds of movement.

"I heard you crying."

"What's it to you?"

The voice that called back was young. Teenager young. Female and angry.

"Are you being held here, too?"

Another sob. This was going to be hard. Patricia hated tears, especially from women. She had often thought tears and the inability to control them were responsible for the lower status of women in the world. Men saw tears as a sign of weakness. Truth be told, so did Patricia. But this weepy girl was the only person she could make contact with. So, swallowing her disapproval and trying to put on a friendly, inviting tone, she tried again.

"I'm being held here against my will."

"What does he want from you?"

"I don't know. He said he wants me to help, but I don't think I can. What does he want from you?"

"Nothing. It's my sister he wants." There was a banging sound.

Patricia thought the girl had punched something in frustration. She knew the feeling.

"Your sister?"

"Dr. Price is making her do things for him. And I'm why she has to do it. I'm so stupid."

"He tricked you?"

More crying.

"He tricked me, too. And I'm old enough to know better."

"Shh! Someone's at the door." There were more sounds of movement. Patricia held her breath, listening intently.

"Hello, Maggie." It was Dr. Price. Patricia strained to hear.

"Is she back?" the girl sounded worried.

"No. They've taken her."

"Taken her? Who? Where's my sister?" The girl's voice was

panicky. Patricia didn't think she was playing a part, either. The girl was frightened.

"The Department has her. These damn fool agents they've sent me were worse than useless. Incompetent rubes! Back in my day, they sent me men. Now, less than boys—imbeciles!"

Patricia's heart started beating faster. Jessica and Leonel were at the Department. Did this mean the doctor had made his move on them?

"They've got my sister?" The girl sounded disbelieving. "What are you going to do?"

Patricia feared the worst. If this child was really just being held to motivate this other woman, what would the monster who called himself Cindy's father do when she was no longer needed?

"Nothing changes for you, child. I still need you here, to make sure your sister remembers there will be penalties if she tells anyone about me or my work. I'll get her back. I need her to complete my transfer. This body is done. It's time for another."

The girl started crying again.

"There, there, girl. As long as your sister stays smart, no harm will come to you."

The girl didn't speak again, only cried quietly. The sound was muffled and Patricia thought the girl had probably buried her face in the pillow. She couldn't imagine that Dr. Price would hug the child, nor that she would allow that monster to touch her. A few seconds passed. Then there was a click and a beep. Patricia recognized the sound of the door closing and the security system resetting.

Patricia didn't say anything for a few more minutes. Neither did the girl.

When the girl did speak again, her voice was cold. "I hate that man."

"It sounds like you have good reason."

"Who are you?"

Patricia took a deep breath. She had no idea who she was talking to, really. For all she knew, this person who claimed to be a teenager held captive here was really one of his employees, the scene staged for her benefit. It didn't feel like that, though. Before the business with Cindy last spring, Patricia had always trusted her gut. It had served her well. Her gut said this was an angry child who needed help, not a spy. She hoped she was right. She took a deep breath and started her story.

"My name is Patricia," she said.

LINDA GETS THE SILENT
TREATMENT

Linda hated it when David was angry with her. Worse yet was when he wouldn't admit he was angry. The silent treatment. That's where they were now. David ate his dinner mutely, offering no comment on the food or thoughts about his day. Linda was not crying, even though she wanted to. David had always hated it when she cried, and it was worse now that she wore a man's face. She hadn't felt this sick inside since she had first transformed into a man, when she'd been sure she was going to lose him. She thanked God every day that David was still hers.

She knew what was wrong. After twenty-plus years of marriage, she knew her husband well, and it was clear what was bothering him. She hadn't been there when David got home today. By itself, that was no big deal, but it was happening a lot, and they both knew what it meant. Her work was changing their home life.

David had doubts from the beginning, when the Director had first approached Linda about working for the Department. In all their years of marriage, Linda had never worked more than a part-time job. While David's work had often made him miss a soccer match or a piano recital, Linda's never had. She had always been there. She was grease that oiled the family wheel and kept it spinning. She'd signed the contract anyway, without fully obtaining David's approval. When she told him, he'd lost his temper. "This would never have happened when you were a woman!" Maybe he was right. But she didn't think it was the testicles that made her stand up for what she wanted; it was the opportunity.

Now it was happening more and more that she had to back out of small commitments. Linda felt as if she were being pulled on in too many directions. She loved her family and wanted to be there for them. That hadn't changed. But for the first time in her life, she had something that was just hers. She was important and needed, doing valuable work that could help the world. She didn't want to let that go, the feeling that she mattered.

The weekend before, Linda had gone shopping with her youngest daughter, Viviana. Shopping had always been a bonding time for the two of them. "Retail therapy," she called it. They had always talked through their heart's desires and sufferings as they shopped for what their families needed or just looked at things they might buy if they were wealthy.

Linda was happy to be able to talk with her daughter like this again. Viviana had taken a long time to accept that the new shell housed the person she knew as "Mother." But now, *gracias a Díos*, they were back to meeting for lunch and shopping for special dinners together. Viviana was even able to joke when one of her nosy colleagues had run into them at the mall and spent the entirety of the short conversation examining Linda.

"You know she's running to text everyone at the office now and tell them I'm having an affair. Wouldn't she be embarrassed to know the truth!"

In the same outing, as they sipped fancy coffee drinks together in the food court, Linda told Viviana about the difficulty she was having with doing well at work and keeping the home as she always had. Viviana had laughed so hard she snorted coffee foam. "Welcome to the twenty-first century, Mami. This is what it's like for all of us. You find your balance, or you fall down."

Taking life and marriage advice from her child was strange, but

Viviana was right—the young ones had been doing this for years. She was the one who didn't know how to balance it all yet. She needed to find some sure footing soon, though. It was crazy to think she and David could make it through her transformation into a man but falter over the seemingly smaller matter of her work hours.

Patricia had talked about this. She said that it was the heart of the reason why she had never married. She just wasn't willing to give anyone that kind of sway over her life. While Linda had often thought Patricia's life dull and lonely, she could see where it could be nice to just be able to make decisions that worked for yourself and not always have so many people tugging you this way and that.

She wished she could call Patricia now. For all her protesting that she didn't do girl talk, Patricia was an excellent listener. She didn't exactly tell Linda what to do, but she would help Linda tell herself. "What do you really want, Leonel? What do you intend to do about it, besides whine?"

Right now, Linda intended to go on the mission to rescue her friend. They were sending Cushing back in, making it look as though she had escaped them. Once in, she would help their team get in and rescue Cushing's sister, Patricia, and anyone else who might be imprisoned there. The mission was important, and Linda was proud to have been invited to join the team. It also meant she'd be away from home for several days at the very least.

There wasn't going to be an easy way to break it to David. He was already angry and feeling neglected. She fetched the avocado-lime cheesecake she had made the day before. It would be obvious she was buttering him up, but it still might help. Setting the plate in front of her still silent husband, Linda put on a bright smile.

"We've got a lead on finding Patricia," she said.

David eyed her suspiciously, lowering a fork to the slice of cheesecake.

"I've been asked to go on the retrieval mission," she said, still keeping the tone light, trying to sound as if she were not aware of the depth of David's displeasure.

David dropped his fork on the plate and pushed back from the table.

Linda stretched out an arm to rest a hand on David's forearm. He shook off her touch. Linda bit her lip. It was bad indeed if he wouldn't even let her touch him. Even when things were at their darkest, they'd always at least had a physical connection.

"This isn't what I signed up for, Linda." David spoke to the empty space at the edge of the table.

His voice was quiet, but Linda knew her husband well. Just because he wasn't yelling didn't mean he wasn't quaking inside with rage. She breathed hard through her nose, angry at him all over again for his resistance.

She moved to kneel at his feet, trying to force her face into his view. *"Devolver bien por mal."*

"We always have, Linda. Life has brought us plenty of bad times, and we have always made them good again. But we were in it together."

Linda's temper flared, but she tried to keep it in check. "And now?"

"No sé, mi amor."

"What do you mean you don't know?"

David was looking at her now, shock visible on his face. Linda noticed he looked tired, older than he had only a few months earlier.

"Everything has changed, David." She stood, calling attention to her height to emphasize her point. "I'm not the woman you married anymore. Just as you are not the same man I married. Life shapes us and remakes us all the time. We adjust. What makes this time so different?"

"I liked the way it was." David's voice was small and sad, but Linda wasn't going to cave this time.

"As did I, David. I wouldn't change anything about our life up to now. But I have the chance to make a difference—to save lives. This curse I was handed is also a blessing, but only if I go out into the world and use it."

David's face was dark with emotion. He didn't speak or move.

"I will always come back to you, David. Just as you always came back to me when you went out into the world and I was the one who waited." She stopped, her throat beginning to constrict with tears held back. "Please," she said, begging, "please tell me you will be here when I return."

PATRICIA GIVES VENT TO HER FEELINGS

Her name was Maggie, she said. She was thirteen years old. Patricia shuddered with anger at the thought of this child being terrorized. She would find a way out of this and Daniel Price would pay for it.

Maggie had been visiting her sister for spring break in Baltimore, she said. Her sister was some kind of big deal researcher in transplant surgery at Johns Hopkins. She was always inviting Maggie to visit and their mother had finally agreed, probably so she could get some alone time with the man she was priming to be the next stepdad.

Maggie's voice had brightened a little, talking about her sister. She obviously admired her older sister a great deal. It had darkened talking of the potential stepdad. Patricia understood. Her mother had been a serial wife, too. It meant a lot of upheaval in the name of stability.

When she'd been young, Patricia would have preferred if she and her mother had just holed up together and left men out of it. She suspected Maggie felt the same way. Patricia's mother, like many women of her generation, couldn't accept the idea that they would be okay without a man in their lives. Patricia wondered what Maggie's mother's excuse was. It was the twenty-first century. Well beyond the "fish needs a bicycle" realization. But then, not every woman had weaned herself off dependence as well as she had.

Maggie said the two sisters had been eating pizza and watching TV when the doorbell rang. Meredith, the big sister, had gone to answer it. When she took a long time to come back, Maggie went to check. A man was holding Meredith by her elbow and waving a gun around. Another man stood in the background, his arms crossed over a trench coat. It was the trench coat guy who spotted Maggie.

"Grab the child," he had said.

Patricia could imagine the coldness of that voice. She'd heard it herself. It echoed in her mind now, the words he'd spoken when he'd stopped her escape. *I'm afraid I can't just let you leave, Patricia.* Daniel Price.

Patricia wasn't a hugger, but she wished she could have hugged that girl when she heard the story. The best she could do was make sympathetic noises. After a while, she was pretty sure the child fell asleep. But not Patricia. Her mind was reeling.

So, Mr. Price had kidnapped a scientist known for transplants. He'd said this wasn't his original body. He said the bodies wore out. Something about the electricity. So that begged the question… Actually, that begged a lot of questions.

Where was he getting new bodies to inhabit? How was his consciousness being transferred from body to body? Regardless of how, the time must be imminent. Maybe that was why he moved so oddly, that jerkiness to his step and twitchiness to his smile. Maybe the connections were breaking down, the signals between the brain and the body becoming slowed, sluggish.

Obviously, he needed assistance for this procedure, whatever it entailed. That's where this Meredith came in. And the little sister was her reason to cooperate. Effective. Ugly, but definitely effective. Price had already shown he was not ruled by the same sense of morality as others. A believer in the ends justifying the means. The same could be said of Cindy Liu. Like father like daughter. Apples and trees.

Cindy didn't come to him for help. She hadn't even known he was alive. He said he'd had her brought to him. The phrase gave her a chill.

Brought? Like that little girl downstairs? By men with guns? That also meant he had known where she was. He had to be keeping pretty darn close tabs on his long-neglected daughter to know she was running around in the body of a teenager these days, and to find her on her route. Though, if he had picked her up early in her journey, it would explain why every trail Patricia tried to follow ran cold so quickly. She'd never been able to find a trace of her after the bus station. Until now.

She'd finally found Cindy, for all the good it had done her. Now she was just as trapped as they were. She needed a plan to get out of here. The little girl was depending on her. So was Cindy.

According to Maggie, Meredith had been sent out with two armed guards to get someone. The scientist had gone along so she could take samples if they weren't able to bring the person back alive. Maggie didn't know who they were after, but Patricia had a horrible feeling she did. Her stomach roiled with stress and worry. She got back up and paced the room. She was too agitated to lie still.

Clearly the mission had failed and the woman had been captured by the Department. That might mean help was already on the way. Patricia wasn't sure how long she'd been at this compound, but she knew it had been several days. Leonel never went more than two without calling. Surely by now, they knew she was missing. Surely they were looking for her. Price had intimated as much. And, with the resources of the Department, surely they could and would find her. The question was just whether they could do it in time.

Hope fluttered strong in her chest, but just as strong was doubt in her mind, squashing the hope before it could color her thinking. She couldn't rely on help coming from outside. She just needed an opportunity. She wouldn't squander it this time in overconfidence.

She climbed back into bed and pulled the blankets up over her shoulders again, flexing and relaxing, forcing the few scales she could raise to form and decline on her forearms. Patricia listened to all the small night sounds as she pondered her situation, waiting for inspiration. There was the gentle, mechanical whirring of the camera scanning the room. There was a whooshing sound that was probably the heating and air-conditioning system. Patricia let her eyes fall closed, hoping the sounds would lull her to sleep. There was a tapping in the pipes, rhythmic and insistent. Patricia sat straight up in bed when the realization hit her. Tapping! That was how Cindy had been trying to communicate. It hadn't been Morse code. Cindy would know she didn't know it.

It was, however, a code. It was a system they had worked out in college, a quick way to communicate without letting others know what they were saying. Mostly, they used it to talk about young men. Three quick taps on the side of a beer mug indicated an intention to take a young man back to their room and a request for the other to make herself scarce. A drumming of all four fingers in succession meant, "Don't wait up for me."

Closing her eyes and thinking, Patricia tapped her fingers against her abdomen, trying to remember the rhythm Cindy had sent. It went short-long, short-long, a swing beat. So, that settled what Cindy had been asking for. That was the code for help.

"I'm coming, my friend," she promised aloud. "And when I do, there will be hell to pay."

The nails of one hand sprouted into talons. Patricia smiled. There was hope yet.

MARY IS THE CHEESE

"Miss Braeburn?"

Mary rolled over, shoving her head under the pillow.

"Miss Braeburn?" The voice was more exasperated this time. It sounded like one of Mary's teachers from middle school, the one who always said Mary wasn't living up to her full potential. Mary shoved the pillow aside and glared at the room.

At first she didn't see anyone. She rolled over again and spotted the Director's assistant standing by the door. She sat up, holding the comforter up around her armpits with one hand, while shoving back her hair with the other.

"Morning," she mumbled.

"I'm supposed to take you to see your mother," said the woman, her tone icy.

Mary nodded, wondering what she'd done to earn her ire. "I can be ready in ten minutes." The woman didn't move. Mary looked at her meaningfully and the woman still didn't move. Shrugging, she got out of bed and stalked into the bathroom, naked. *Serves her right,* she thought.

Five minutes later when she came out of the bathroom, clean and more discreetly wrapped in a large towel, the woman was gone. Mary turned on the coffeepot and picked up her clothes from where she had left them on the floor. She sniffed them and grimaced. She'd have to see about getting either access to laundry or something else to wear soon. The clothes were getting ripe. She padded back into the bathroom to dress, just in case the assistant returned before she was decent. She'd already made her point.

She was glad to find the bathroom came stocked with a toothbrush and toothpaste and made use of both. When she raised her head, she saw there was a garment bag hanging on the bathroom door. Her favorite blue jeans and a few shirts and other clothes were inside, along with a bag with fresh underclothes. She decided not to resent the intrusion of someone having been dispatched to gather clothes from her apartment and instead to the focus on the joys of fresh clothes to wear.

She was sitting at the table drinking the last of the small pot of coffee when the assistant returned.

"Your mother is in the breakfast room," she said, keeping her gaze focused around Mary's midsection. "Are you ready?"

Mary hopped up, smiling to herself at the woman's obvious discomfort. "I was born ready," she said.

Just as before, the woman took Mary across the complex in a high-tech golf cart. Mary tried harder to learn something about her surroundings as she rode this time, but it was useless. There were no helpful signs or directional arrows, and the place was so universally institutional looking that she couldn't seem to latch on to any landmarks. One hall looked much like another. She wondered if the employees used some kind of walking GPS system.

Then, they were stopped. Mary waited for the lap belt to lift, feeling a sudden giddy, nervous pull in her belly. She was going to see her mother, but she wasn't entirely sure what that was going to mean. Her mother had done some more than surprising things in the month or so before she disappeared, including some illegal and maybe even immoral things. Not that she was much of a judge of either. She was more surprised than indignant to learn that her mother might have used her newfound firepower to exact a vengeful sort of justice on the world. That seemed strange from a woman whose previous reaction to being wronged was just to say something mean and snarky.

Mary took a deep, somewhat shaky breath and stepped out of the vehicle. The assistant drove away without so much as a look back, leaving Mary standing in the hall wondering what she was meant to do. She looked around. No one else was in the hall to direct her. Then she heard her mother talking.

"This coffee is cold!" she said. "You going to take care of that, or you want me to do it for you?"

Following the sound, Mary entered the room just behind where she had been left standing in time to see her mother holding up a flaming finger and pointing it at a very tight-jawed young man who was sticking out his chin at her belligerently. Three other young men dressed in nursing scrubs were standing around, two holding fire extinguishers and one holding what looked like an Epipen. They were all three large, muscular, tough-looking men, and all of them looked wary. Mary's mother looked irritated, verging on angry.

"Mom!" Mary rushed into the room toward her mother. One of the men tried to grab her with one hand as she ran by, but she dodged him and made it, throwing her arms around her mother.

Her mother didn't hug her back at first, and Mary was confused until she pulled back and saw her mother was holding her hands aloft, several fingers still aflame. Stepping back, she tucked her fingers into the opposite palms, extinguishing the flames against her own flesh, then pulled Mary back for a hug.

"What are you doing here?" she whispered into her daughter's hair.

"I came to get you," said Mary.

The young man with the belligerent chin was dispatched to fetch a second breakfast and fresh coffee for them both. He stalked off, his indignation making him bounce as he walked like some kind of rooster wearing green scrubs. When he got to the door, he tried to slam it behind him, but the safety door closed softly with a small whoosh, and Mary and her mother laughed out loud.

"So, is this your entourage?" Mary asked, gesturing at the three grim-faced nurses.

"My keepers, more like. They've learned to keep their distance now."

She grinned at her daughter and gestured with her head toward one of the men, a young blond with a fuzzy mustache that sat on his lip like a caterpillar he'd glued there.

"Some had to learn the hard way."

Mary turned to look and saw the white hospital bandaging on the man's forearm. Her eyes grew wide. She wondered what the man had done to make her mother want to burn him. Then, she thought about the urgent care doctor and the fire damage at the campus. Had this young nurse really antagonized her into attacking or had her mother had just taken her anger out on him? The Department was holding them both here, though, so what empathy she might have felt for the boy was mitigated by the fact that he worked for kidnappers.

She frowned at the men. There were a lot of things she wanted to ask her mother, a lot of things she wanted to say. But she didn't want to say them in front of these men. "I was so worried about you!" she said, taking a sip from her mother's tepid coffee. "I even filed a missing person's report."

Helen's eyes went wet for a moment before she brushed the tears away brusquely with the back of her hand. "I woke up here a couple of months ago. They said I'd been in a coma."

"Had you?"

She shook her head. "I don't really think so. There are things I remember. Snippets. I think they just had me drugged."

Mary shot the nurses an acidic look. *Assholes.* "Can you tell me what happened before that? I tracked you as far as the college. They found the car you rented for your girl's night with Cindy Liu."

"That bitch!"

Mary drew back. Her mother's face was purple with rage, and Mary was sure the table she was grasping had just grown hotter. "Mom? I thought you were friends. I thought you might have gone with her."

"She abandoned me there. Just got on the bus and left after everything I did for her."

Mary grabbed her mother's arm. It was warm, an unnatural kind of warm, and she pulled her fingers back, waving them in the air. Touching her mother had been like grabbing a piece of meat straight from the skillet. One of the nurses stepped closer, holding up his fire extinguisher warningly. Mary had the urge to try and grab it from him and hit him with it, but she knew she couldn't take all three guards.

Helen wrapped a hand around her coffee mug, and the tepid contents within began to steam again. Her face returned to a more normal color. "Don't you worry, Mary. She'll get hers when I get out of here." She looked sharply into Mary's face, then. "Is that why you're here? Are they letting you take me home?"

Mary shook her head. "Not yet. They think I can get you to cooperate with their tests. They say they'll let us go after they get the data they want." It was a nice story, but now that she was away from the Director and his strange influence, Mary found she felt uneasy saying it out loud.

Helen obviously didn't buy it, either. "So, they're using you to blackmail me?"

Mary nodded, realization dawning. She was the perfect bargaining chip. If this were a movie, some thug would be standing over Helen saying, "We have your daughter, Ms. Braeburn. Tell us what we want to know." A chill ran down Mary's spine. The Director was too subtle for that, but the threat was there all the same. The trap had been set. And Mary was the cheese.

SALLY ANN, THE PLAN, AND THE MAN

"Well, that went well." The Director bridged his fingers in front of his nose.

Sally Ann had always found it a particularly pedantic and annoying gesture, but she kept that observation to herself. She hadn't liked how heavily they were relying on Meredith Cushing. She wasn't an agent or even a police officer. Instead, Cushing was a lab scientist, a surgeon, not trained in duplicity and deceit. She'd said as much to the Director, but he had waved her concerns aside.

"I've got a good feeling about this," he said.

Sally Ann had learned that when the Director had a good feeling about something, it carried considerable weight. He had yet to be wrong. But Sally Ann was a rational woman. She wanted more to go on then touchy-feely mish-mush and the recommendation of someone who used to know the woman in charge.

Despite all her doubts about the plan to let Meredith Cushing escape, she had to admit the first steps had gone by the book. Using the least secure of their secure channels, the word was spread that the prisoner was being transferred. They'd sent her with a single guard, who left her in a secured vehicle while he went to the bathroom and returned to find the door hanging from its hinges and his passenger missing. Just for show, the agent was picked up in an official vehicle, and a search team was sent out, but they already knew where Cushing was going. And if she tried to dupe them, the Department would just use the nanotracer they'd inserted into the flesh of her upper thigh.

Her only remaining doubts were about the man who currently called himself Daniel Price and the mysterious group behind him. He had to be wily to survive this long undiscovered. Five different lives by her count, and only this last one lived in secret. The question was whether he was megalomaniacal enough to believe he had gotten what he wanted so easily, or if he would smell a rat. Her gut said he was going to buy it. She hoped she was right.

So, now it was her turn. She would take Roark, Alvarez, and Driver to an abandoned college campus in the middle of Indiana where Price was holding Patricia and Cushing's sister, Maggie. Cushing had cooperated fully once Walter Peeples had convinced her the Department could rescue her sister. They had maps and everything Cushing knew about the structure itself. They would give Cushing twenty-four hours to send a signal that it was time. If she didn't do so, they'd go in, anyway.

Sally Ann thought about her team. She had full confidence in Driver. He was loyal and capable, and his facility with machines had saved them all in the past. Roark had shown good instincts in her training, but she was still raw with almost no field experience. Her personal connection to the case was both a boon and a cross to bear. She knew more about Cindy Liu than anyone on their team, but she also harbored vengeance in her heart, and that could lead her to make some dumb decisions, the kinds of decisions that endangered her teammates. Still, Sally Ann had her own good feeling when it came to Roark. There was steel in that woman's spine.

That left Alvarez. For all his physical strength, there was something fragile about Alvarez sometimes. He confused Sally Ann. She couldn't put her finger on it, but there was something just a little off about him. It wasn't that he was gay. She'd worked with gay men before and knew a person's bedroom life had no bearing on his skill in the field. This was something else. She wished she'd had more time to work with him and know him better before they were thrown into the pressure-cooker of an intense rescue mission. So far as Sally Ann could see, the strongest man was the weakest link in her team.

A plane ride and a van ride later, the team was in place, in a weed-strewn parking lot atop a hill behind the complex. Cushing's signal was strong. She was there.

From the size of the campus, someone had high hopes for this place, once upon a time. Maybe it had been full of college kids and ambition in its heyday, but now it was empty in a way that made her expect cartoon tumbleweeds to blow past.

The place gave Sally Ann the creeps, especially now that it was night. So far, they'd seen almost no movement from the buildings on campus, though the instruments showed a lot of power being drawn to what had once been the medicine and nursing building. The windows remained dark, and all Sally Ann could hear were the quiet night sounds of wind in the wheat fields and distant birds and insects calling.

All of them were dealing with their restlessness as best they could. Jessica and Leonel seemed to be engrossed in a deep conversation about love and marriage. Sally Ann kept her distance, checking and rechecking all the equipment and weapons, even though she knew they were ready. She wasn't much for girl talk, and while she was glad Jessica and Walter Peeples had found one another, she didn't want the details. She'd be more comfortable at the bachelor party than at the wedding shower when the time came.

Driver slept whenever it wasn't his turn to be on watch. It was a good strategy to pass the time, if you could manage it. Sally Ann couldn't. Her mind spun over possibilities and scenarios, trying to strategize her way through every possible outcome. She had enough experience to know it was a futile exercise. In the end, she'd be more reactive than proactive. But if her brain was going to do this anyway, she might as well go with it. Maybe the very act of working through all these imagined scenarios made her able to act quickly when the time came to improvise. She hoped so anyway. She'd hate to think she was some kind of closet masochist, torturing herself for the hell of it.

Eventually, Jessica was asleep, too, which left Sally Ann and Leonel keeping watch.

He passed her back the binoculars. "Still quiet."

She tucked the binoculars into the side pocket of her pants and leaned her seat back to more easily look up at the stars. "It's nice to be able to see the sky. You never see the stars in Springfield."

Leonel looked at her. "Where did you grow up?"

"North Carolina. Durham. There were no stars there, either, but you didn't have to drive that far to get to somewhere where you could watch them."

"I'm a city girl at heart," Leonel said.

Sally Ann snorted. "Don't you mean city boy?"

He looked at her, his expression calm and serious. Her laughter dried up. Had she offended him?

She leaned forward. "I think you owe me a story, Alvarez."

"A story?"

"Oh yes. You told me that if I figured this out, you'd tell me the rest of your story."

Leonel bit his lip and pulled at his hair. "I did say that, didn't I?"

"You did. It's time to pay up. Besides a good story will make the time go faster."

Leonel cleared his throat, but sat quiet a long time. "I don't know where to start," he said.

"Once upon a time?" Sally Ann suggested.

Leonel smiled. "That'll do. Once upon a time, there was a woman named Linda."

LINDA FLEXES HER MUSCLES

Linda awoke early. The surveillance van was cramped, and she had trouble fitting her bulk into the bunk, but she'd managed to rest well enough, anyway. It had helped, getting the truth of her life off her chest. Sally Ann had listened in silence while Linda had poured out the whole tale, including her recent troubles with David.

Afterward, she'd simply barked a short laugh and said, "Well, that explains a lot."

If only telling her own family had been so simple!

Jessica and Sally Ann were both snoring in their bunks, but Linda was full of restless energy after spending an entire day pent up and waiting. When the Director called and put her and Jessica on a plane, she had imagined busting down doors and bringing Patricia home. But immediate action was not in the cards. Instead, they were stuck out on the perimeter watching and waiting for word from their woman on the inside. Word that, so far, was not forthcoming. Linda only hoped Señorita Cushing was brave enough to see the plan through. Her own sister was at risk. They were asking a lot of her.

Linda padded through the van cautiously, trying not to disturb her resting teammates. Driver was sitting at the control panel, listening.

He glanced at Linda when she went to the coffeepot and poured herself a cup. It was pretty awful. Next time, she'd bring the coffee.

Standing outside to watch the sun edge over the hillside and brighten the sky, she thought about what Sally Ann had told her the night before about the different kind of quiet of the countryside. It was too quiet for Linda, so quiet her ears hurt. She needed something to do. She went back in and told Driver she was going for a jog. He gave her a thumbs-up, and she set off down the road.

Her footsteps raised clouds of dust as she ran. It must have been a while since the area had seen any rain. She picked up the pace, hoping to leave behind the dust of her own movement. After going a mile or so down the road, she paused to catch her breath, beginning to wish she'd brought along some water. Her mouth tasted like the dust.

Running had helped a little, but she wished she could do something more active. Some of the other agents really loved running. Her trainer in particular talked about the way his mind seemed to move into a different state of being when he ran. But it didn't work that way for Linda. To her, running was just a slightly faster way to get from point A to point B. It didn't bring her any kind of thrill. Not like really working her muscles.

She looked around. The road she had jogged down was completely deserted, but there was a glint of something metallic and yellow in the woods. Linda jogged down to investigate. Just behind a small rise, she found a large truck parked in a roughed-out logging road. "Hein Bros Logging Co." was hand-lettered on the side of the truck, not quite covering the older logo beneath. One of Linda's brothers had spent a few seasons logging, and had taken the entire family on a tour of his job site, so Linda knew these trees had already been de-limbed and topped and were simply waiting to be loaded into the truck and hauled away for processing.

"Perfect," she said, brushing her hands together.

There was a pair of thick work gloves lying on the seat of the truck, and Linda pulled them on and started picking up trees. Balancing was tricky, but she was able to lift one end and work her way to the middle, then leverage the tree up into her arms. Then, she did a sideways grapevine walk like the kind they did in her old Saturday morning aerobics class and worked her away among the still-standing trees and tossed the trunk into the bed alongside the others already there.

She repeated the process five or six times, laughing to herself about what the men would think when they returned to their work-site and found the trees already loaded and ready for delivery. She liked the vision of herself as some kind of helping spirit, doing the work of a team of men in the course of a morning. It felt good, too, to exert herself. She spent so much of her energy on holding back these days, trying not to break the objects that came into her path with a thoughtless grip or careless gesture. Flinging the trees freed something in her and made her feel alive.

It was funny how cathartic she found physical exertion now. It hadn't been like that for her when she was a woman. She didn't know if it was a matter of gender or a matter of scale. But picking up such heavy objects was thrilling, and it took some seriously heavy objects to even begin to test her limits. After all these months of training with her, Agent Lester still wasn't sure what her upper limit was.

"I'll bet you could throw a tank, if you had a reason to," he'd said, half-admiringly, half-jealously.

Linda was pretty sure he was right. If combat was coming, she was prepared to inflict some serious damage.

This was the kind of work she loved, the joy her new body brought her in physical work. Not the sneaking around, duplicitous spying kind of work. She wondered if that meant there wasn't really a place for her in the Department. She had always been a lousy liar. She couldn't even successfully keep birthday and Christmas gifts secret. At least, that used to be the case. While she didn't lie to David before she left on this mission, she also didn't tell him the full truth about the dangers she was potentially facing. She felt guilty about the omission, even if it was, in part, to protect him.

These days, she realized she might just be growing into a pretty accomplished actress. This was a point of pride and of shame at the same time. The other agents didn't seem to suspect there was anything unusual about her—well, anything *else* unusual. They had easily accepted her as the man she seemed to be. Even Sally Ann had never suspected the rest of Linda's story.

The last two tree trunks were a bit smaller. She could fit one arm around the trunks, so she lifted one in each arm and hurled them into the truck. They landed smoothly atop the rest.

"*Si podemos!*" she shouted, tossing her arms in the air and spinning.

She stopped when a movement on her left flank caught her eye. There was a man standing just beyond the truck, between Linda and the road. She only had time to register that he was aiming a gun at her when the first dart sank into her shoulder. The effects were instantaneous. Linda had to press a hand into the side of the truck to keep from falling over. When she stood again, she saw she had left a hand-shaped impression in the body of the vehicle. She yanked the dart from her shoulder, threw it, and tried to move toward the man who had shot her, but it was too late. Her balance was poor and she moved like a drunken rhinoceros. When the second dart hit her in the thigh, she fell to her knees and then on her face. Then she was out.

SALLY ANN PLAYS MOTHER HEN

After checking in, and affirming that her team had not yet received a signal from Cushing, Sally Ann went in search of Jessica. Whether the signal came or not, they'd be going in within the next few hours. It was time to get her game face on and that meant making sure her team was prepped.

She found her protégé lying on top of the van staring up at the sky. Well, actually she was floating a few inches above the surface of the van, as if resting on a cushion of air. She burped into her elbow when Sally Ann climbed up there and let her body sink back onto the van roof.

"You think she's in there?" Jessica asked, leaning up on an elbow to look at her trainer.

"Patricia?"

Jessica shook her head. "No, Cindy Liu." Jessica's brow furrowed. Her body became rigid.

This reaction was exactly the kind of thing that had Sally Ann worried. Emotion was not a good place to fight from. It made a person make rash decisions. "Are you going to be all right?"

Jessica looked surprised. "All right? What do you mean?"

"Are you going to be able to handle it? Seeing her again? Are you still going to be able to focus and follow orders?"

"Of course I am. I had an excellent trainer, you know."

Sally Ann gave a small smile, acknowledging the compliment. "You've been a good student, too, but we're not in the classroom anymore. The dangers are real. I need to know you're going to follow my lead."

"I will." Jessica stretched her arms out over her head, then bent her body into a pretzel-like pose. "Where's Leonel?"

"Driver says he went for a jog early this morning. Isn't he back yet?" Sally Ann stood and scanned the road as far as she could see. There were no signs of movement. She'd have to ask Driver for more details about which way he went.

"I haven't seen him yet. He probably needed a little head-clearing time." Her tone was flat and casual.

Sally Ann wasn't sure if Jessica really wasn't worried, or if she was trying to cover for Leonel.

Leonel had seemed much calmer after their long talk the night before, and Sally Ann didn't like the idea that he was so restless just a few hours later. Having two overly-emotional and possibly distracted agents on her team was a recipe for disaster.

"What's going on with him?"

Jessica didn't respond right away. Sally Ann could see the internal battle she waged between duty to her supervisor and duty to her friend.

"He's going through some personal stuff," she finally said.

Sally Ann nodded. Leonel had told her a little about his marital issues. That kind of stuff made her glad she didn't have a significant other. "Is that going to be a problem?"

Jessica was quick to shake her head. "Leonel is solid. There's no one I'd rather have at my side."

Sally Ann wondered if Jessica realized how much she sounded like a woman in love when she talked about Leonel. The two definitely shared an unusual bond. She hoped that wasn't going to cause tension between Walter and Jessica. Sally Ann had been indulging in some matchmaking with the two of them, and she liked how it was going so far. She wanted to see the two of them work out. She knew Leonel was gay, or whatever you called it when a woman in a man's body preferred men. But Jessica would hardly be the first woman to give her heart to someone who couldn't love her back. Leonel and Jessica had been through a lot together. That made people close.

Sally Ann hadn't felt like that about anyone for quite some time. She was both jealous of Jessica for having someone she felt that sure of and worried for the new couple's future. Anyone in the save-the-world business for any length of time ended up losing someone eventually. If Jessica lost Leonel, it might break her in spite of all the evidence of her resilience.

"Okay. Let's talk it through one more time."

Jessica dropped into a more upright position, dangling her legs over the edge of the van. "Driver gets us in. I stay high and back you up as needed. Leonel follows for cleanup."

Sally Ann grunted affirmation. "And objectives?"

"Rescue of Patricia O'Neill and Maggie Cushing is top priority. Capture of Cindy Liu and Daniel Price are secondary only."

Sally Ann watched Jessica carefully as the woman parroted her orders. There was nothing to suggest she had any problem with that set of priorities.

"All right," she said. "Check your gear one more time. Signal or no signal, we're going in soon." She stood again, scanning the road. No sign of Leonel. The small uneasy feeling in the pit of her stomach was growing.

She went back in the van. Driver was still at the control panel, listening and checking various sensors. He was also pulling noodles out of a large plastic bowl with a pair of chopsticks and slurping them down. He put down the bowl when she came in and looked at her, one eyebrow raised for a question.

"What time did Alvarez leave on that run?" she asked.

Driver held up a hand.

"Five o'clock?"

He nodded. It was after seven now.

"Which way did he go?"

Driver unrolled a map and spread it across his knees, pointing down the road they'd come in on. It was a short stretch. Leonel should have had time to make the loop twice already.

"Did he take a comm with him?"

Driver shook his head, pointing at the earpiece still sitting in its basket.

"I don't like this. I'm going after him."

Driver shook his head and pointed at himself.

"No. You stay here. You're the best man to make all this work." She gestured at the electronics surrounding them in the driver's area.

Jessica dropped in through the window, then snagged her gym-bag off the rack and wriggled into her apparatus. "I'll go."

Sally Ann started to protest, but Jessica stopped her. "I'll be faster. I'll stick to the tree line. No one will see me."

Driver looked at her expectantly, and Sally Ann could feel his approval of the plan. "All right, then. Go get Leonel. Get back here as quickly as you can."

Jessica leaped out the open doors of the van, rolled into a tumble on the way, and landed gently as a butterfly before bursting into the air, arms spread. She held her body in a tight line and was off in a streak.

"Showoff!" Sally Ann called after her.

PATRICIA FAKES IT

Patricia was awake but still in bed when she heard the sound of the door opening. She rolled over to see what was heading her way. A woman she hadn't seen before was standing in the entryway along with a black-clad guard with an intimidatingly large gun already trained on Patricia. The woman stepped farther into the room and opened the small silver kit she had tucked under her arm. Legs dropped from it, and it became a small table holding an array of medical devices.

"Good morning, Ms. O'Neill."

Patricia sat up and stretched ostentatiously. She yawned, pretending not to notice the man or the weapon. Inside, her heart sped up. If the guard shot her, she wasn't going to be able to pull up her armor. She hadn't felt that kind of vulnerable in a very long time.

"Who are you?" she asked lazily.

"Meredith Cushing," the woman answered in a clipped tone, picking up a syringe and making preparations with it as she spoke.

Patricia froze for a moment in the middle of a neck roll, then covered by rolling her head in the opposite direction. Meredith was the scientist sister Maggie had told her about—the one who had been sent to get Jessica and had been captured. Patricia wasn't sure what to make of her presence here and now. Did that mean she had escaped? Been released? Never actually been captured in the first place?

Meredith dropped the syringe on the floor. A whitish liquid spilled across the tile.

"Shit," she said, grabbing a swab from her kit and wiping up the meds, then fetching additional paper towels from the dispenser on the wall and continuing to mop up the mess. She turned to the guard, looking up at him from her position on the floor. "Evan, was it? I'm going to need another injection. Can you get us one?"

The man shook his head curtly. "The doc said to keep her covered."

"She's been neutralized already, and I don't have a pass card back into that part of the lab."

The man still hesitated, his gaze bouncing between Patricia and Meredith. Meredith sighed. "Look at her. She's sixty years old. What's she going to do to me?" The woman shot Patricia a meaningful look.

Patricia took the cue and hunched her shoulders. She pulled her body in, pushing her chin down in a way that she knew made her cheeks sag.

The ruse must have been successful because the man lowered his gun. "I'll be locking you in."

Meredith waved her hand at the man. "Hurry back."

When the man left, Meredith went back over to her medical kit and grabbed a blood pressure cuff. She walked over and sat down next to Patricia on the bed to apply the device to her upper arm. Patricia leaned her head in and said, "Are you Maggie's sister?"

Meredith looked up. Her expression was sharp. She glanced toward the cameras.

"I'm pretty sure it's image only," Patricia offered. She figured someone would have commented on her singing by now if they could hear it.

"How do you know Maggie?" She spoke with her head leaned forward so her hair fell across her face.

Patricia thought it a clever way to avoid being lip-read, but not something she was capable of with her short hairstyle. So, she smiled.

She talked through her smile, knowing that her tight stretched lips would be harder to read. "We talked through the vents."

Meredith detached the blood pressure cuff and returned it to her case, recording the numbers on a small sheet of paper. Still bent down to her kit, she said, "I'm supposed to inject you with more of the inhibitor. Price sent me because he's in the middle of preparations for the operation. I think he knows your colleagues are here."

Patricia knew there wasn't time to get the full story from this woman, but she knew an offer for help when she saw one. "What do you need me to do?"

"How's your acting?" she asked.

Just then, the guard returned and handed Meredith a small metal case. "The doc said to be careful this time."

Meredith didn't look up from her needle preparations. "I know you don't want this, but it's the only way. Our man here will shoot you if you don't let me inject you."

Patricia drew on her anger. "Why are you doing this? What do you people even want from me?"

Meredith sighed. "I'm not here to answer your questions. We all have to do what we have to do. Do I have to ask him to restrain you?"

Patricia looked at the gunman. He smiled at her. He had an ugly smile, full of malice. It wasn't too hard to pretend to be cowed by his threatening demeanor. She shook her head, not trusting her voice to project the right kind of nervousness.

She followed Meredith's directions and placed her arm on a pillow and made a fist. "First, a sample." The woman quickly and deftly applied the tourniquet and found Patricia's vein. She filled three small vials with Patricia's blood and placed them in her case, labeling them as she did so. "Then, your treatment." She took the syringe from the case.

Patricia drew back. "I don't want that stuff in me."

"Either you let me or I let him make you," said Meredith, her voice cold and convincing.

Meredith, it seemed, was the actress in the room. At least Patricia hoped she was acting. She had told her that the Department was here, which meant Jessica and Leonel. Rescue could be imminent for them both. Patricia turned her head to the side, acquiescing.

"That's better. This will pinch and maybe feel warm going in."

Patricia bit her lip and nodded. She didn't have to pretend to be nervous.

Meredith gripped her arm and aimed the needle. It slid into the pillow just a centimeter or so beside Patricia's elbow. The plushy material grew damp.

"That feels weird," Patricia said.

"It might leave you a little sluggish for a few hours," Meredith answered, as if this had been an ordinary office consult for some treatment Patricia had asked for.

Patricia bent her arm over the gauze as Meredith directed her, though there was no blood. She leaned back against the wall, trying to seem sleepy. She hoped she had picked up the right cues about how quickly the medicine should take effect. When she opened her eyes again, the pair was gone. Groaning, she lay back down and pulled the blanket over her head, pushing the damp pillow off to the side. She tried not to let herself become giddy with hope.

MARY'S HOT MAMA BREAKS OUT

They'd been playing along for a couple of days now. Mary cajoled her mother and Helen performed like a trained seal for the observers, bending her fire into different shapes, melting different materials, and letting the coats scribble notes and take their readings. Her mother was excellent at playing the irascible old lady who could be calmed by her dutiful daughter, good enough that sometimes Mary had a hard time keeping a straight face. The Director had not been back around, and that was probably for the best. He would be able to see straight through their subterfuge. Mary and her mother weren't waiting to be released. They were merely biding their time for escape.

A few days wasn't much time to learn the rhythms and routines of a place, but Helen had been there for months. She knew the shift patterns and guard positions. With stolen moments here and there, the plan was piecing together. In the guise of a bathroom break that afternoon, Mary had entered the camera room and disconnected the camera to her mother's room and the hallway outside it. She was afraid that if she disconnected more than that, it would call attention to the area. There was a decent chance her interference would be read as simple equipment malfunction instead of a sign of attack, so long as she was careful.

Now, she had to get out of her own room. Mary walked to the door. She knew it would be locked, but she tried the handle, anyway. *Kuh-thunk.* The door shifted in the frame and resisted. The noise did get someone to come check on her, at least. That was a good first step.

"Miss? Do you need something?"

There were lots of things Mary needed. Mostly answers. But this guard wouldn't be able to give them to her.

"Can I get a pack of cigarettes?" She'd been granted a pack three days before, so she felt sure she'd be allowed another.

"I'll ask."

She heard the boots moving down the hall. To her surprise, it was only a few minutes later when she heard the boots coming back. There was a knock on the door, followed by a buzzing sound. The door opened. The man standing in the doorframe was cute in a short-hair and clean-scrubbed sort of way. That might be a factor in her favor.

Mary stood up straighter and smiled winningly at him. "My hero!" She held out her hands for the cigarettes.

He smiled back at her and held them out. Mary patted herself down, as if she were looking for something in her pockets. His gaze followed her hands across the curves of her body.

"Damn," she said. "No lighter. You got one?"

The man stepped into the room and set his walkie-talkie down on the table to free his hand. While he was focused on the compartments in his belt, looking for the lighter, she picked up the walkie. Just as he turned to hold the lighter out to her, she hit him over the head with all the force seven years of Taekwondo classes at the Y trained her to muster. His teeth clicked together and he crumpled to the floor. Moving swiftly, Mary gathered all her things into her messenger bag, including the cigarettes. She stooped and picked up the lighter from where it had fallen as she moved to the door.

"Thanks, buddy. You're a lifesaver," she said and stepped out into the hall, closing the door behind her.

The hardest part of this plan had been learning the route to her mother's room. The Director's assistant had taken her a different way each day. But Mary had eventually managed to make note of enough details to be sure she could get there. It was actually pretty close. She'd realized on the second day that the assistant was driving her in a few circles before dropping her off, probably in an attempt to disorient her.

The first stop was an orderly's closet near her own room to steal a set of scrubs and a cart. She wasn't willing to part with the bag unless she absolutely had to, but she knew walking down the hall wearing it screamed that she didn't belong here. A few minutes later, she emerged, dreads hidden under a poofy white cap, and pushed the linens cart she'd hidden her bag and the stolen walkie inside down the hall, remembering to walk with a sense of purpose and direction.

She wasn't stopped. She saw only one other person, and he was preoccupied with a text on his phone and didn't really look at her. A good start.

The next stop was the closed circuit observation room. She walked in, ready to wield the walkie as a weapon again if needed, but found the room empty. The cameras she had disconnected still showed black on the television screens, but Mary checked the surrounding areas, trying to choose a moment when the coast was clear to bolt across the hall to her mother's room.

Inside, she stood for a moment inside the door, letting her eyes adjust to the dark and catching her breath. Her heart was beating in her ears, and they hadn't even gotten to the really hard part yet. Mary knew they had to make it on the first attempt. If they failed, security would tighten, and it would only be that much harder to escape.

She looked at the bed. Her mother was sleeping soundly. Mary watched her breathing. One long breath in, with two hitches in it, then one long breath out. She knew the sound. Surprisingly, Helen wasn't snoring. The first couple of nights she had spent on Mary's futon after the condo fire had cost Mary hours of sleep. Helen's snores were loud and rattling. Mary maybe could have adjusted to that, but they were also irregular and the constant shifting of the noise level had kept her awake and contemplating the ceiling.

Helen looked peaceful now. Mary watched for a few minutes. The tests that afternoon had been especially intense, and Mary knew her mother wasn't faking the exhaustion. But the lighter night shift was definitely the time for an escape, so she stepped up and shook her mother's shoulder.

Helen muttered something about "fucking doctors." That made Mary smile. That sounded like the mother she knew and loved.

She shook Helen again, this time calling her, "Mom? Can you hear me, Mom? Wake up! We've got to get you out of here."

Helen didn't respond, but there was movement behind her eyelids as if she were dreaming. Suddenly, Mary let go and backed away from her mother's bedside. The railing she had been holding had grown uncomfortably warm beneath her hand. Mary examined her palm and found it mildly reddened. As she watched, the entire bed burst into flames. Lying in it, Helen continued to sleep, but she moved her arms up onto her belly. Mary knew better than to approach and stepped as far back as she could without leaving the room.

The heat engaged the automatic system, and the entire area was suddenly filled with a kind of mist or fog. It smelled of metal, reminding Mary of the shower system at summer camp, which always left her feeling like she'd bathed in aluminum. It left a taste in the mouth she could never forget. The flames went out instantly.

The heat must have also set off some kind of alarm because a short man in light blue scrubs and large, thick, white gloves came hurrying into the room. He moved so quickly he didn't even notice Mary standing against the wall. Mary let the door hide her, grabbing the handle so it wouldn't fall closed again and expose her. The man started checking the various devices and monitors on the wall over her mother's head.

"What do we have here?" he said aloud, tracing the various monitors and cables to their sources. He was bent across his patient when Helen suddenly sat up in the bed, clocking him in the head.

The man reeled, grabbing at his head. Mary took advantage of his disorientation to sneak up behind him. She threw herself onto his back and wrapped an arm around his throat to block his oxygen supply. The man fell to his knees, swatting ineffectively at Mary's arm.

She kept her hold and twisted her body to gain better leverage and a tighter grip. A few seconds more and the man slumped to the floor. Mary let him go and stood.

Her mother was sitting up in the bed, pulling at the damp hospital gown that covered her. Her hair was matted around her face and her skin looked reddened, or maybe it was just that she wasn't wearing any makeup and you could see the natural ruddiness of her flesh. Coupled with the thick gray roots showing after several months without a trip to the beauty shop, it was quite a startling effect. For the first time in her life, Mary thought her mother looked old.

"Mom? Are you okay?"

Helen turned and looked at her daughter. Her eyes had an unfocused look to them and for a moment, Mary worried she might be the next hot dog to fry on this barbecue. Then Helen blinked hard a couple times and seemed to see where she was for the first time.

"What the hell?"

"I'll fill you in later. Do you think you can walk?"

Mary watched as Helen moved to hang her legs off the edge of the bed, fighting her own impatience. Her mother had just regained consciousness and was likely still full of sedatives. Mary just hoped it didn't cost them their opportunity to escape.

The man on the floor remained still. Mary was sure he'd have bruises on his neck from the pressure she'd applied, but she felt reasonably secure he wouldn't suffer any lasting harm. She'd hoped to get out of there without having to hurt anyone, but she didn't regret having acted.

Helen was pushing against the mattress with her fists, trying to raise herself to standing. She kept flopping back down. They were going to have to find another solution. Mary bent and hooked her arms around the unconscious man's upper arms, then dragged him against the wall, moving a cart to hide him more effectively.

Then she hurried to the door and opened it a crack, peeking out into the hallway. It was deserted so far as she could see. She pulled the surgical mask she had used to disguise her face up into place and walked toward the orderly station where she had seen some wheelchairs. She nabbed one and pushed it toward her mother's room, trying to look efficiently quick rather than like someone who was trying not to get caught.

She'd just gotten to the doorway when someone called out. "Who are you?"

Mary's shoulders slumped. She'd been so close.

She turned toward the voice, holding a hand out into the room, hoping her mother would see her hand and take the cue to remain quiet and not give them away.

The woman approached. She stood with her hands on her hips, glaring suspiciously at Mary. Mary kept her face mask in place and tried to look thoughtful and attentive. There was still hope she could convince this woman she belonged there. The uniform she had stolen included a name tag that read "Elin Workman."

The woman gestured at the badge. "You're not Elin."

Mary looked down, lifting the badge with one hand. She affected surprise. "Oh! I must have picked up the wrong shirt in the locker room."

The woman crossed her arms, and Mary could see she was one step away from calling security.

"I'm Emily." Mary held out a hand in an offered handshake of meeting.

The woman took her hand, and Mary yanked her into Helen's room. Unlike the young man she had taken out earlier, this woman reacted with training. She reversed the move, and it was Mary who ended up on her back on the floor.

The woman stood over her, her foot poised over Mary's torso. "I said, who are you?"

"She's my daughter, bitch."

The woman had time for a quick look at Helen in the bed before she seemed to simply disappear. Mary didn't understand at first why she was now covered in ash. It wasn't until she was pushing her mother down the hallway in the purloined wheelchair that she understood.

Helen had vaporized her.

~

The emergency exit opened into a parking lot under a shade canopy. The door slammed shut behind the two women as Mary pushed her mother through the door. She stopped, looking out at the cars and wishing she'd thought further ahead than this. She clicked the brake on the wheelchair, parking her mother at the curb, and ran down the nearest row of cars, trying doors until she found one that opened to her tug.

It was a 1990s era Honda civic. Mary couldn't believe her luck. She knew this car.

"I got one!" she called back to her mother.

Helen Braeburn waved at her daughter encouragingly. Mary pushed away the surreal feeling the whole scene was giving her and bent down to pull apart the steering column. The Swiss Army knife kit her father had bought her when she was a teenager was still earning its value over and over again.

A piercing security alarm went off just then, and Mary jumped up, hitting her head on the steering wheel and cursing. She pushed herself to her feet and saw her mother, now standing with one hand on the wheelchair for support. She had one hand held out toward the door they had just exited through. A tight stream of fire, like something you might see from a blowtorch, extended from her fingertips, and the edges of the doorframe began to melt and solder into a mass of metal. *Brilliant! That should slow down their pursuers.*

Mary went back to her work in the car, ignoring the thumping and yelling she was starting to hear. Within another minute or so she had the car running. She backed out of the parking place and pulled to the end of the ramp, then jumped out and ran to roll her mother to the car. A gunshot rang out, and Mary ducked and pushed the chair faster, nearly ramming her mother into the car itself.

She heard men shouting but tried to ignore it as she helped her mother into the passenger seat. Once she was secure in her seat, Mary slammed the door closed and scurried around the perimeter of the car, keeping her head low and her body near the side of the car.

Without looking back, she flung the car in reverse and slammed the accelerator. Her mom lurched backward and forward, bracing herself with her hands on the dashboard. When she pulled her hands away, melted handprints steamed in the plastic.

"Hold on!" Mary yelled.

She picked a direction and started driving. She felt the car slide as she took corners quickly and prayed the tires were new enough to handle it. She kept checking the mirrors but didn't see any sign of pursuit. Not seeing their pursuers didn't make her feel any more relaxed. Neither did the way her mother's hands were smoking.

Eventually, they came to the far edge of the parking area. It was surrounded by a tall fence and separated from the main road by a patch of grass.

"Keep going!" Helen sounded like she was laughing. "I've got this!"

Mary glanced sideways, then gripped the steering wheel tighter, hoping her mother had a plan. She heard the window roll down and saw it from the corner of her eye when her mother leaned out the window, her hands outstretched. Suddenly, there was a flash of fire, and the section of fence directly ahead of them seemed to melt, leaving a car-sized opening.

Mary curled her body over the steering wheel and drove straight for it. They both screamed as the car bounced through, across the grass, and into a tire-squealing turn before fishtailing into the traffic flow. To Mary's surprise, she knew where they were. This was Springfield. Downtown Springfield. She checked the gas gauge. Full. She turned and grinned at her mother.

"Let's go visit Aunt Maureen," she said, turning quickly onto the little traveled old beltway.

Her mother smiled back, patted her daughter's hand, tilted the seat back, and went to sleep.

SALLY ANN TO THE RESCUE

Things went to hell so fast it made Sally Ann's head spin. One minute her biggest concern had been that her team was emotional and stressed. The next minute Leonel was missing, with every sign that he'd been taken.

She'd known before Jessica even landed that something was wrong. She was flying as fast as her trainer had ever seen her move, faster even than the day she had rescued Sally Ann from a canon blast. She must have found quite a point of leverage to get that much forward momentum going. She was a streak of pink against the cloudless blue sky, hurtling toward the surveillance van. Sally Ann scanned the horizon behind her protégé, but she didn't see Leonel anywhere.

"Driver!" Before she could say another word, he was at her side, gun in hand.

"Something's wrong," she said, keeping her gaze trained on Jessica. "Get us ready to move out."

A second or two later, Jessica spun down from the sky, rolling into a hard landing that raised a cloud of dust behind her. Without pausing, she leaped back to her feet and ran the few yards to Sally Ann's side.

"He's gone! I flew in just like you said, but there's no one there. Just a logging truck." She pulled out her phone and showed Sally Ann the photo she had taken on a man's handprint stamped into the side of the truck. "We've got to find him."

The door to the van flew open, and Sally Ann pulled Jessica inside, yelling, "Go!"

Before either woman had found a seat, Driver had spun the vehicle around and was barreling down the road toward the logging site. Sally Ann was thrown against the surveillance equipment. She could hear the telltale ping of the signaling device Dr. Cushing had worn back in Daniel Price's lair. It was time. There would be no chance to track Leonel—they had to go now.

"Driver—we've got to get inside. It's Cushing!" She turned to Jessica. "Hold on—this is going to get rough."

The van turned around astonishingly quickly, as if it had hovered in the air and spun in a perfect three hundred sixty degree turn, then touched down to drive in the opposite direction. Driver had an affinity for cars. He could get vehicles to perform far beyond their factory specifications. For example, there was no way this top-heavy van should be able to move this quickly or maneuver with this dexterity. Someday, she was going to have to find out more about Agent Driver. Right now, though, she had to hold on and try to think.

Price and whoever else he had in there with him had to have Leonel. It was the only thing that made sense. The Department knew from Cushing that Price was planning a brain transplant surgery— and she was going to play surgeon. It was time for yet another body. He'd burned through this one faster than some of the previous ones. What Cushing didn't yet know, she had claimed, was where the donor body was coming from. Sally Ann had been afraid it was Patricia, but the more she learned about the men Daniel Price had been, the less she believed that. He wouldn't want to live as a woman. He thought them inferior, weak. Even an amazing woman like Patricia with extra abilities wouldn't do to house this megalomaniac. Sally Ann was sure she knew who would, but she'd keep that notion to herself for now. It would only panic Jessica.

"What's going on?" Jessica's voice came from above, and Sally Ann looked up to find Jessica plastered to the ceiling, her feet hooked through a support bar and her hands grabbing some of the netting used to contain overhead storage. It was smart really. She wasn't getting as knocked around up there. If Sally Ann weren't bound by gravity, she might get up there with her.

"Cushing just signaled. We're going in. Remember the strategies!"

"Stay high, watch for the right moment, come back safe."

"That's my girl! We're going to kick some ass and save the day." Sally Ann wished she felt as confident as she sounded. Having Leonel snatched right from under her nose had her shaken, but there was no way she'd let Jessica know that.

Suddenly the van came to a stop. Jessica dropped to the floor beside her, and Sally Ann grabbed her equipment bag and strapped it to her back. She could hear Driver assembling the device in the passenger seat in front. She paused just long enough to pray.

She closed her eyes and whispered, "Not today." It was probably just a superstition, but she felt that she and God had an understanding. She would die when it was time, but he would do his part to make sure that didn't happen sooner than it was supposed to. The wave of energy that moved into her body was all the answer she needed. This would not be her day to die.

They had picked this side of the building after examining the schematics. Coming through here should put them within reach of the essential parts of things. This was the part of the complex with the highest energy readings. The amount of electricity going in there was astonishing. Sally Ann was surprised it didn't put out the power grid for the entire area. She remembered the specs for the Project Osiris lab and felt sick again at the thought of her operative in there with that sicko.

She turned to check on her team. Driver was standing ready, watching her for the signal to go. Jessica was poised to leap from the top of the van. She gave Driver a thumbs-up signal. He flipped a visor down over his face and pointed at it to remind his colleagues to don their protective eyewear as well. Then he gripped the two-handled control. Sally Ann thought it resembled nothing so much as a jack-hammer, with two ears pointing out to the sides. Driver gripped them strongly as if he would make the device do its work with force of will. It didn't look like anything was happening, but after a minute or two, Driver hit the red button on top to disable the device. They all counted ten together, and then Driver walked up and kicked at one of the bricks in the center. A large section of the wall simply fell into the composite bricks in a heap at his feet.

Sally Ann kept her weapon trained on the opening, but nothing happened. Crouching low to the ground, she moved through the opening. They were in what looked like a boiler room. Sally Ann ducked out and gestured to the others. In a moment, they were inside with her, Jessica floating above at ceiling level, nearly invisible in the dimly lit room, and Driver crouched beside her. As they had planned, Driver immediately began exploring the room and found the power grid. He shut down breaker after breaker, and the place went quiet. Sally Ann hadn't realized how much machine noise she was hearing until there wasn't any to hear. They listened. One second. Two seconds. Three seconds. There was a faint beeping sound and then the unmistakable sound of backup generators.

Good. That should mean that only the essential services are running. Sally Ann knew someone would be dispatched to investigate this room in a matter of seconds, so she turned to Driver, bowing, then gestured to Jessica. The two took off down the hall in search of Patricia and Leonel.

PATRICIA MAKES A BREAK FOR IT

When the lights blinked and the air-conditioning's steady hum ceased, Patricia knew it was her chance. She leaped from the bed and to the door, pushing hard against it with her shoulder as she tried the handle. It gave so easily she stumbled into the hall. The hall was dark with only pale yellow lights at intervals. Patricia didn't know what had caused the outage—her rescuers or some accident—but she wasn't going to stick around to find out.

She started running. She was pretty sure Maggie's room was on the floor below, so she needed to find the stairs. She ran past them in the darkness, only processing the "emergency exit stairwell" sign afterward. She slid trying to turn around and ended up on the floor. It was a good thing she did. In the wall behind her at what would have been her chest level, a dart went into the wall with a *thunk*. Patricia rolled to the opposite wall and into an alcove that held a drinking fountain. She pulled herself into a crouching position and concentrated.

"Come on," she whispered through clenched teeth.

After the grapefruit experiment and with great exercise of will, she'd been able to bring out some of her lighter armor, but she'd yet to succeed in bringing out the full plating. After Meredith's subterfuge, she'd found she could do a bit more. She had succeeded in working at least some of the inhibitor out of her system. When she got a hold of Daniel Price she was going to hurt him for castrating her like this. She hadn't felt this kind of helpless in months, not since she found out what her condition meant she was able to do.

She could hear the guard who had shot at her or someone else coming down the hall. She tried not to worry about him but to concentrate on getting her body to respond. She could only hope the shooter's vision was as limited as her own. With luck, he believed she was hit and his guard would be down. Trying to ignore the sound of the approaching steps, she took another deep breath and concentrated, flexing her shoulders and neck over and over, waiting for the feeling of the scales moving across her cheeks.

"I can see you there!" A man's voice called out in the darkness. "Get back to your room and I won't have to shoot you."

Patricia looked down at her chest, at the red targeting light centered between her breasts.

"All right!" she called back. She placed her hands on the floor, as if she were going to use them to push herself up to standing—her taloned hands.

When the nails scraped the tile, Patricia smiled. With a rush, her plating slid into place and her spikes sprung from her shoulders. She threw herself at the man with the gun. He gasped but held his ground. He got off two shots before she tackled him. One of the darts went wild; the other bounced off Patricia's upper arm and took out the light above his head, sending a shower of sparks down on them both. Then his head made a dull *thud* against the wall and he was still.

Not stopping to examine her fallen adversary, Patricia stalked back to the stairwell. Though she stepped as lightly as her armored frame allowed, she still heard each step thud in the quiet hall. The door to the stairwell slammed loudly against the wall, and Patricia winced. She didn't really want to have to hurt anyone else, but she also wouldn't let anyone stand in her way. It didn't appear there was anyone else nearby to be attracted by the sound. They'd left her relatively unguarded, but thanks to Meredith, she had not been unarmed.

She remembered what her intern, Suzie, had told her about the value of being underestimated by your enemies, and grinned.

Paused at the landing, she looked down into the gloomy stairwell. The emergency lighting flickered, but she could make out the next landing, some ten or twelve steps below. She hesitated to go down the stairs, but then saw her own claws and laughed. There was nothing in this stairwell that was scarier than her, certainly. She'd never been so happy to see her scaly green skin. It was good to be fully herself again.

Her heavy steps echoed as she hurried down to the next floor. Patricia stopped, listening for signs of life on the other side of the door. She was glad she had because she heard quite a scuffle. It sounded like at least five pairs of booted feet ran by. She heard a man yelling about Quadrant A-4 and something else incoherent crackling through a radio. She counted a beat of three after the boot-steps faded, then opened the door slowly to a quiet and empty hall.

It was lined in doors. Patricia groaned. She didn't want to open all these doors one at a time. Finding Maggie would take too long at that rate. She didn't know how long they had before Price and his crew got the power back up and their opportunity to escape was lost. She didn't have the patience for this.

"Maggie!" Patricia was still, listening. She heard nothing. She called out louder. "Maggie! It's me, Patricia. Where are you?"

There was a sound of a door creaking, and Patricia turned toward it just in time to see the door slam shut again. She smacked herself on the forehead. She should have considered how she looked. Now the girl was scared of her, too.

"Maggie, it's all right." Patricia took a deep breath and pulled in her spikes. She didn't want to retract her armor—they might still need it —so she left her armored plates and scales in place. "I know I look like a monster, but it's me. We've got to take this chance to get out of here. We can find your sister. I can help you get away from him." She crossed the few steps to the door and opened it. "I'm not going to hurt you."

The room seemed to be some kind of locker area. It was dimly lit in the same reddish emergency lighting that had made the stairwell passable, but creepy. The room seemed empty at a glance, but Patricia knew the girl had to be there somewhere.

"How do I know you're her?" The girl's voice echoed, high and thin, wavering just a little beneath the tone of angry belligerence.

Patricia wasn't going to be able to locate her by sound. She considered for a moment, trying to decide what she could say that would help the girl trust her. "Remember when I told you about my mother? She was like your mother—thinking she couldn't get by without a husband. I told you I used to wish she would just give it up and let us live in peace."

"How many stepdads?"

"For me, seven in all."

That must have been good enough for Maggie because suddenly she was standing at the other end of the bench from Patricia. She was small for her age, barely four and half feet tall, pudgy in the middle the way girls are before puberty rearranges their bodies. She was holding a Taser, down at her side. She turned it to make sure Patricia knew she was holding it.

"Did you have to use that?"

The girl looked at her own feet. Anger rose in Patricia again. Keeping her captive was one thing, but Daniel Price was going to pay dearly for putting a child through this. Patricia curled her hands into fists and resisted the urge to growl aloud.

"Do you know where your sister is?"

"The surgery room."

"Do you know where that is?" Patricia hadn't been able to get much of a sense of the layout of the place, having spent most of her time here in captivity, but maybe the girl had been freer.

They weren't that lucky. "I don't know." There was a catch in the girl's voice. Patricia knew she had to get them moving, even if it turned out to be in the wrong direction. Standing here was giving them both too much time to think and become filled with doubt.

"Okay. We know it's not here, and I know it's not upstairs where I was being held. Let's start with the stairwell. Maybe there's another floor."

The girl wiped the tears off her cheeks with the back of her hands. Patricia looked away, studiously ignoring her distress, giving her time to calm herself. She scanned the room for useful items. Along one wall was a tool cabinet. She stalked over and opened the door. She picked up a large, heavy flashlight from one of the shelves. She weighed it in her hand. It could work to replace that now-useless Taser. It was heavy enough to be used as a weapon, if needed, and probably not too heavy for the girl to handle. She turned it on.

The beam fell on a fire extinguisher, and, above it, the escape route map. A map!

"Maggie," she called, snatching the laminated paper from the wall. "I think I know how we'll find it."

Patricia sat on one of the changing benches, ignoring the straining sound the metal supports made. The girl came and leaned over her shoulder, and they examined the map together. The girl pointed out the places she recognized, tears forgotten. The map must have been made with student egress in mind, so it was helpful that all the doors and stairwells were clearly marked. Patricia eliminated sections of the large building from consideration. She wanted to find her way back to the room she had first been kept in, where she could find and free Cindy.

In the end there was only one part of the building it could be in. Back upstairs in another wing. Practically around the corner from where she had started. She stabbed the spot on the map with one taloned finger and grinned at Maggie.

"Ready or not, here we come!"

JESSICA LEAPS IN

Jessica grappled her way across the ceiling of the hallway pushing off from the walls, the pipes, the fixtures. She used anything she could to get forward momentum, saving the air in her tanks for speed and emergencies only. Below her, Sally Ann raced through the hall, her body held in a ready tension. But there was nothing to react to. No enemies appeared. Jessica's heart rate skyrocketed at each corner, anticipating the fight that kept not happening.

Jessica knew Sally Ann wasn't telling her what her theories were about Leonel on purpose. His disappearance from the lot had been a shock to the both of them, a game-changer. Now there were three lives on the line—maybe more. Jessica wondered if Sally Ann had jumped to the same conclusions she had—that Price was after Leonel's body, literally. It made sense, as much of any of this made sense. If each body only lasted fifteen to twenty years, then Price was in need of a new fleshy home.

Jessica was fighting down panic over and over again as it bubbled to the surface. She was sure they were going to find Leonel strapped to a gurney with his head sawed open. She needed to keep focus if she was going to be able to find and save her friend. Lost in her thoughts, she nearly missed it when Sally Ann turned a corner. She somersaulted to change direction and came around the corner to find Sally Ann standing in a fighting stance, one hand held over her head in a signal for silence. Jessica gathered herself into a ball, prepared to throw herself into the fray to help Sally Ann take down a troop of guards or whatever else had her trainer poised for battle.

Without saying a word, she peered down the hall. She almost yelped when she saw the enemy that had Sally Ann's attention: it was Patricia! She dropped beside Sally Ann and touched her shoulder, then shook her head once. She took a two-step running start, then leaped into the air, streaked to the other end of the hall, and landed in a ball at the monster's feet.

"Patricia!" she cried, throwing her arms around the woman and nearly impaling herself on one of the spikes protruding from her upper back.

Patricia jumped back in apparent alarm, raising an arm above her head with obvious painful intent. Jessica let out a breath, realizing how near she'd come to being injured by her friend.

"We've been so worried about you! Leonel has hardly slept since you've been gone."

"Leonel? Is he here?"

"I think so, but we haven't found him yet. Come on!" She tugged Patricia's hand, intending to lead her to Sally Ann and regroup for the rescue of Leonel.

"Wait—we're on our way to the medical theater. I think that's where we'll find Cindy."

"We who?"

Patricia stepped to one side, revealing a girl standing just behind her, holding a large, heavy flashlight with both hands like it was a baseball bat. "This is Maggie. She's been held here, too. I haven't got time to explain. The man who held us... he's—"

"Cindy Liu's father." Jessica hadn't heard Sally Ann approach.

Patricia apparently hadn't, either. Her spikes came out in full force. The effect was still terrifying. Jessica saw Sally Ann's eyes widen. She understood. It was one thing to hear about Patricia. Seeing her was another thing altogether.

"How did you—"

"We'll talk it all through once we've escaped." Command was evident in Sally Ann's voice and Patricia, for once, allowed herself to be cut off without complaint. "For now, though, we've got to find Leonel. Price has him, probably in the operating room."

Jessica gulped. She'd known, of course. But it was different hearing Sally Ann admit it out loud. Leonel was in serious danger. They had to find him, and quickly.

"Where did you say the medical theater is?"

"This way." Patricia pointed off to the left, passing the emergency exit map she'd been holding to Sally Ann.

All three women started toward the room, Patricia, fully armored and shaking the very floor she stalked across, Jessica floating just below the ceiling, and Sally Ann with her baton at the ready. Suddenly, Patricia stopped. She bent down to the girl she had introduced as Maggie. Jessica saw she retracted the scales on her face and pulled in her spikes. Her face again visible, concern for the child softened her expression.

"Maggie, you don't have to go with us. You could wait here. I'll come back for you."

Maggie looked around at the trio. "I'm coming with you." She pulled the flashlight up into a ready position and stalked ahead of the small group, until Patricia put a sharp-clawed hand on her shoulder and pushed her gently to the rear. That girl was fiercer than she looked.

When they rounded the corner, they came face-to-face with a group of ten or twelve armed guards. Jessica let herself drift behind a bit of duct work, reserving the element of surprise. Patricia decided to go for some good old-fashioned shock and awe. She flexed her arms, popping out all her spikes and armored flesh and screamed in a terrifying way, stampeding for the middle of the group. Sally Ann pulled some small darts from a side pocket of her pants and threw them at four of the guards—the ones standing nearest the door. All four of them smacked their necks as if they'd just been bitten by mosquitoes, then slumped to the floor. Jessica thought she'd have to get some of those.

Patricia had thundered into the middle of the group, and most eyes were focused on her. So, while her friend grabbed men and threw them into each other, Jessica flew for the doorway. No one was standing directly in front of it now that Sally Ann had taken out those guards. She slipped through in the chaos, trusting that her friends would handle that situation. She needed to find Leonel. The door slammed shut behind her.

She found herself in a brightly lit room. The bright light was a surprise, given that the power was out all over the building. If this room had extra backup generators or batteries, then she must be in the right place. Jessica hovered just inside the door, letting herself float high as Sally Ann had taught her.

"People never look up," she'd advised. "Stay high until you see your opportunity, then swoop in from above. They'll never know what hit them."

Jessica could still hear the sounds of men shouting in the hallway outside and the thuds of bodies colliding. She didn't give the guards good odds against Sally Ann and Patricia, so she ignored the sounds and focused on the scene before her. There were two bodies on operating tables, both strapped down. From her angle, Jessica couldn't see their heads, but she knew who they were all the same. The large one was Leonel and the smaller Daniel Price. Leonel was still and unresisting. He had to be unconscious. If he were awake, those straps wouldn't have had a prayer of holding him down.

Standing between the two tables was a figure garbed in pale green. Her hair was pulled back, and she wore a surgical mask, but Jessica was sure it was Dr. Cushing. What was she doing? Sally Ann said the woman had signaled. Didn't she know the rescue team was there? Why was she cooperating? Jessica floated to another vantage point, deeper into the room. That's when she saw the other person in the room.

It was a girl of eleven or twelve years, sitting on a stool and holding a gun that looked too large for her hands. The weapon was trained on Dr. Cushing. The girl was none other than Cindy Liu. A rage filled Jessica. In a flash she was overwhelmed by all the emotions of everything Cindy Liu had done to her and the people she loved. She didn't think; she just acted.

She tucked her feet against the wall, aimed her body, and shoved off. At the same time, she clicked the controls on her air pack to achieve maximum velocity. Cindy never saw her coming. In one rush of movement, Jessica plowed into her, knocking her from the stool and into the wall behind. The gun dropped to the floor, skittering to the middle of the room, at the feet of Dr. Cushing. Cindy Liu was surprisingly strong, and Jessica had to work to keep her from slipping out of her grasp. She fought with the strength of desperation. Jessica felt like she was wrestling a sea creature, grabbing at slippery limbs and struggling to hold them bound.

Unable to look at the other women, she yelled to Dr. Cushing, "Stop what you're doing. We're here. You don't have to go through with this."

Jessica couldn't stop her struggle long enough to check on whether Cushing had listened. She pushed the woman-child against the wall, trying to keep her out of reach of all the medical equipment in the room. Jessica had no idea what was needed to keep Leonel alive or what might be used against her as a weapon. She wondered what was taking Sally Ann and Patricia so long to get in there.

"Stop fighting me, Cindy. You've got nowhere to go. You've lost!"

To her surprise, Cindy actually went still. Her eyes were wide with fear and astonishment. It was another second or two before Jessica realized the object of her fear wasn't her, but something behind her. Grasping the other woman's wrists and pulling them into a hold she could maintain, Jessica twisted the two of them around so she could see.

Meredith Cushing was holding the gun that had previously been aimed at her. She had it aimed at Daniel Price's head. The look on her face was pure, cold loathing.

"No!" Cindy Liu screamed. "Don't do it!" When Meredith didn't look in their direction, Cindy sobbed. "Please. I need him. He's my only hope!"

PATRICIA TAKES A FALL

Patricia whipped around ready to take down the next comer, only to find that there weren't any more. She squatted, feeling winded, and pulled in her spikes and some of her armored scales.

"Maggie?" she called quietly, hoping the girl had kept herself safely away from the fray. She'd been too busy during the fighting to keep track of her.

There was a thumping sound toward the hall they had entered from, and Patricia stood, bringing her claws and armor back up reflexively. One of the guards was moving, shifting on the floor. Patricia readied herself for attack. Then the man simply slumped forward onto his face. From underneath him crawled a small black woman with close clipped hair and a controlled rage in her eyes.

"That's going to leave a mark," Sally Ann said. "Next time, watch where you're throwing them."

Patricia shrugged, stepping over a pale blond man who was bleeding from a small wound on his cheek. "Have you seen Maggie?"

"The girl? No, I—"

"Here I am." The girl pushed aside the trashcan she had been hiding behind and stepped into the center of the hall, smiling. "That was awesome!"

Sally Ann was looking up into the rafters, and Patricia realized she must be looking for Jessica. "I think she went inside," she offered, pointing at the door to the medical arena behind her.

"Without backup?" Sally Ann pulled a baton from a holster on her thigh and wielded it in front of her. She rushed toward the door.

"Maggie, take cover," Patricia ordered.

The girl didn't look happy, but she nodded. Patricia saw the girl had already taken another Taser off of one of the unconscious guards. She smiled approvingly, and hoped the girl wouldn't have cause to use the weapon. It was a relief to know she had the gumption to arm herself just in case.

Sally Ann tried the handle. "Locked."

"Here." There was a clatter as a set of keys landed at her feet. Patricia turned to praise the girl, but she was nowhere to be seen. Nice.

There were at least ten keys on the ring, but only one looked large enough for the lock on this particular door. It clicked loudly when Sally Ann turned it.

"You first," she said, then opened the door wide.

Patricia rushed into the room full bore, then stopped short, not knowing where to go or what to do. First, she saw Jessica restraining Cindy, who looked all of eleven years old and was sobbing and flailing in an attempt to get away. Then her gaze was drawn to a woman dressed in green hospital scrubs holding a gun on the prone form of Daniel Price, who seemed to be unconscious and strapped to a table. On another table, Leonel lay still, apparently unconscious as well.

"Put down the gun, Meredith." It was Sally Ann, suddenly standing in the middle of the group, her hands spread in a gesture of peace and soothing. "You don't want to do anything rash."

The woman looked up, wild-eyed, and Patricia saw it was Meredith Cushing, the scientist who had helped her—Maggie's sister. Patricia thought this woman did indeed want to do something rash.

"He has my sister here somewhere." The woman's voice was a hair's breadth from complete hysteria.

Patricia edged forward, trying to put herself in a position to protect Jessica, Cindy, and Leonel if she could. Whatever was coming next, she wanted to be ready to defend them.

She growled back at Meredith Cushing. "Maggie is safe. She's with us."

The woman spun, now aiming the gun squarely at Patricia. "Who are you?"

"I'm a friend." Patricia stepped toward the woman. "It's me: Patricia O'Neill."

"Don't come any closer!" The woman seemed to be trying to watch all of them at the same time, and Patricia was worried she'd shoot someone before she could do anything about it.

Patricia stopped, then brought down the scales from her face, hoping the sight of her human face might alleviate some of the woman's fears. It seemed to do just the opposite.

"It *is* you. He said you were the key, that having you would bring us what we needed."

The gun seemed to be everywhere, bobbing with her hands as she spoke. Patricia knew they had to get it away from her before someone got hurt. Patricia saw Sally Ann slipping behind the woman, moving sideways and keeping low.

Suddenly, everything seemed to happen at once. The door burst open, and Maggie rushed through, yelling, "Meredith!"

Sally Ann moved forward and knocked the gun from Meredith Cushing's hands with a deft twisting of the wrist. As the gun fell, it bounced against the gurney that Daniel Price lay upon, and went off. Patricia, reacting to the gunshot, jumped across the room to put her armored body between Jessica and Cindy and the gun. Cindy pulled free and ran to Price, injecting him with a syringe on the surgery tray. Jessica bounded in one flash of movement to Leonel's side.

Everyone was yelling, and Patricia had no idea what to do.

Then one sound rose above the others—Jessica's scream. Everyone went silent.

"It's Leonel! He's been hit!" Jessica had her hands pressed down on a blossoming red spot on Leonel's rib cage.

Patricia moved quickly now—ripping away the restraints and

hospital gown that had covered Leonel. She was no judge of bullet wounds, but the amount of blood could not be good. Leonel had not moved. Whatever had kept him unconscious up to now was still doing so.

In another instant, the gun woman was there, pushing Patricia aside. "Let me help."

Sally Ann caught Patricia's eye and gave a quick nod. "Let her."

So, Patricia did. She felt as though the world had contracted in around her and become little more than the widening red patch of blood soaking the thin mattress beneath Leonel and the sounds of the three women moving to save his life. She felt helpless and useless and stupid. If only she had moved toward Leonel instead of Jessica, he wouldn't have been injured. It was all her fault again.

She backed up until she was stopped by a cabinet that resisted her movement. For a moment, it knocked her off balance, and in that moment, she saw a slender brown leg disappearing through the door. Cindy! Looking back, she saw that the others were all focused on Leonel—Leonel who now lay on the only gurney in the room. Cindy was escaping with Price! It would be up to her to stop them.

She yanked the door open and rushed into the hall, only to find it empty. She stood still a moment, listening. Silence. Then a small bell chime sounded at the far end of the hall. An elevator. She hurried toward it and arrived just in time to see the door closing. She thrust an arm into the narrow gap. She could hear Cindy's exasperated cursing. She worked to widen the gap, flexing her arm and pushing against the door, which resisted. Soon the opening was wide enough to see into.

Cindy was crouched over the body of Daniel Price, still strapped to the operating gurney. He groaned. Cindy looked more like a feral beast than a girl. Patricia called out to her.

"Cindy! Stop this! He's dangerous. He's a madman."

"He's my father!" Cindy's voice quaked with rage-filled tears.

"I know, but he's also a kidnapper and a killer." Patricia shoved harder at the doors, but they seemed jammed. If Leonel were here, he could yank it open, but the best she could do was use her armored flesh to keep it from closing fully. Thinking of Leonel made her angry again.

"What was going on in there? What did he want with Leonel?"

Cindy didn't answer. She just glared, scrubbing angrily at the tears she'd been unable to hold back. The face she turned to Patricia was terrible with black rage and wild-eyed desperation. Patricia gasped to see it.

"I know there's good in you, Cindy Liu. We can work this out."

"Patricia, I've never been the woman you thought I was."

"Let me help. We can save you. I know we can."

Cindy stabbed Patricia in the palm of the hand with something, sliding the needle in the small gap where her plating allowed her fingers to bend. The effect was swift. Patricia felt herself slumping to the ground. The last thing she heard was Cindy's cold, hard voice.

"I've got to save myself, old friend."

JESSICA UP ON THE ROOF

A few hours later, Jessica stood on the roof of the college, looking down at the field that stretched out between the building and the road, trying to think, but having trouble pinning down any thoughts. She didn't know how she felt. Angry, betrayed, worried, triumphant? The mix was impossible to separate, and she found what she felt was really nothing—she was numb. She felt as though she had been drained through a sieve and the meatier parts of her were somewhere else in a bowl. She was little more than the broth of herself. She stared out at the campus, waiting.

The field was overgrown with tall grasses that, even from above, looked like they'd be knee high or taller on Jessica. They were kind of pretty when the wind moved them, golden in the last light of the day. Night bugs were beginning to sing. Was it really the same day?

Looking over the grounds, she could just barely make out grown-over bricked paths that led across the field in different arcs. The campus had probably once been beautifully manicured and populated by men and women eager to make something of their lives. Now it was like a hidden picture, something you had to already know was there in order to be able to find it. If she weren't standing atop the building, she'd never guess that field was anything more than unused land.

The dust had settled after the departure of the other vans and emergency vehicles. Dr. Cushing and her little sister had been taken into custody. Jessica hoped they would let their mother know her daughters were okay. She pushed away thoughts of her own children. They were safe with her mother. There was no reason for the panic that threatened to rise in her chest. They were safe. They were safe. They were safe.

The ambulance containing Patricia O'Neill had taken off in the opposite direction, sirens blazing. The syringe that had been used on her was found clasped in her hand, and the preliminary testing had already revealed that the concoction was not going to be fatal. Jessica wasn't sure if that was luck or a limit to the evil Dr. Liu would perform to save herself.

Another team had already left in pursuit of Cindy Liu and Daniel Price.

She turned her attention to the sky. She couldn't see the helicopter anymore. She felt guilty for having lost track before it had actually disappeared from view. She looked down at her blood-stained clothing, trying not to think about how stiffly her shirt was drying or whose blood was staining it.

The medics had pulled her away from Leonel's side, and Sally Ann had held her back, saying, "Let them take him, Jessica. It'll be all right."

She had not wanted to let him go. In her head was a very different place than in her heart. Her heart hurt like it had been hollowed out, and she still thought she might lose her best friend. The moment of the gunshot flashed in her brain again, so fast and so slow at the same time. In her mind's eye, the bullet cut across the operating room like a comet, a streak of fire. She could see it, but there was nothing she could do to stop it. And Leonel, for all his strength, was not bullet-proof. The little movie her brain had made to torture her played on an endless loop. It was only exhaustion that kept her from succumbing to the shakes or tears. They were supposed to walk out of here together.

Leonel, Patricia, and her. But it was only Jessica who was leaving under her own power.

Below, Driver pulled the van up. Sally Ann threw open one of the doors, stepped out into the flattened grass area and called up to Jessica. Jessica could see the stress of the past few hours in the way the woman stepped gingerly, testing her footing before committing. Even her seemingly indestructible trainer had not come through unscathed.

"It's time to go!" She stood there watching Jessica expectantly, her hands on her hips and her head thrown back.

Jessica thought, not for the first time, Sally Ann was bigger than her own size, the definition of larger than life.

Jessica put her hand in her pocket, and pulled out the gemstones she had pulled from Dr. Liu's neck as they fought in the lab. They felt warm in her hand, almost alive. She wasn't sure if they were actually glowing or only reflecting or refracting rays of light, but they were beautiful. Looking at them, she felt a kind of strength run through her, a determination. Turning away from her colleagues, Jessica tucked the gems into her sports-bra, promising herself she'd find a secure way to wear them when she got back home.

"Which way is the hospital?" she called down to Sally Ann.

"Southwest." She pointed in the right direction.

Jessica looked at the distant horizon, unaffected by the beauty of the setting sun. She shaded her eyes against the bright flat disk of yellow remaining among the pinks and oranges. She thought she could see some tall buildings in the distance, but she might have imagined them. "How far?"

"About ten minutes."

Jessica tossed her air pack down to her mentor. Sally Ann looked up at her, confusion evident on her exhausted face.

"I'll meet you there," Jessica said. With that, she crouched down and flung herself into the air, waving to Sally Ann as she flew into the darkening sky.

ACKNOWLEDGMENTS

I'm one very lucky girl. This becomes especially clear when I turn my family's lives upside down for my creative endeavors and they not only roll with it, but jump on board and start bailing water right alongside me. Without the support of my husband, daughters, sister, parents, and extended family, my life as a writer is a dream I would have to let go. So, thank you to my lovely family.

I'm lucky in my writing life as well, having had the opportunity to work with a fantastic critique group, insightful beta readers, and supportive fellow authors, editors, proofreaders, and marketing folks. Maybe my real secret superpower is finding good people to work with.

ABOUT THE AUTHOR

Samantha Bryant is a middle school Spanish teacher by day and a mom and novelist by night. That makes her a superhero all the time. Her secret superpower is finding lost things. She writes because it's cheaper than therapy and a lot more fun.

When she's not writing or teaching, Samantha enjoys time with her family, watching old movies, baking, reading, gaming, walking in the woods with her rescue dog, and going places. Her favorite gift is tickets (to just about anything). You can find her on Twitter @mirymom1 or at her blog/website: http://samanthabryant.com